In The
MIDST
OF
TRIBULATION

MARY GRIGGS

Bella
BOOKS
2013

Bella Books, Inc.
P.O. Box 10543
Tallahassee, FL 32302

Printed in the United States of America on acid-free paper
First Bella Books Edition 2013

Editor: Medora MacDougall
Cover Designer: Linda Callaghan

ISBN 13: 978-1-59493-377-6

Other Bella Books by Mary Griggs

Unbroken Circle
Crash Stop

Acknowledgment

To CM who took me to the mountain hideaway that became the setting for this story. I've never forgotten that road trip or the view from the outdoor toilet.

This story was originally hosted on The Athenaeum (http://xenafiction.net/), an archive site that showcases an extensive collection of lesbian fiction. I want to thank the readers who took the time to review and offer constructive criticism, all of which helped me improve the book.

I thank Jennie Brick for her emotional support and Brian Brick and Charlotte Klasson for being my beta readers—I might not have always taken your advice but, when I did, the book was better for it.

I'm very grateful for my editor, Medora MacDougall, whose enthusiasm and encouragement gave me the confidence to address the story's flaws. Her editing suggestions made this a much better book than it might otherwise have been. Of course, any errors that remain are my own, alone.

Everyone at Bella Books has been a pleasure to work with and I really appreciate the marvelous job Linda Callaghan did on the cover design.

Dedication

Dedicated to my Mom and Dad who taught me, each in their own inimitable way, that proper prior planning prevents piss-poor performance.

Semper Paratus

About the Author

After a decade of running bookstores for Borders Books and Music, Mary Griggs turned her attention toward nonprofit management. She co-owns a consulting firm that specializes in non-profits and serves as Board Chair for Forum For Equality Louisiana, a statewide equality organization that protects the rights of lesbian, gay, bisexual, and transgender people. When she is not advocating for social change, she is exploring the food life of New Orleans and finding new things to write about.

http://www.marygriggs.com

Tribulation is the period of immense suffering and sacrifice, greater than anything before in history, that is generally predicted to occur before the Second Coming of Jesus and the end of the world.

For then there will be great tribulation, such as has not been from the beginning of the world until now, no, and never will be.
Matthew 24:21–22

CHAPTER ONE

Martha felt a blister forming. The boots she had taken off the newly dead body that morning were practically perfect, except for where they were rubbing on the bottom of her right heel. At almost six feet tall, Martha had had enough trouble finding shoes that fit her size eleven feet before the violent dissolution of the United States. Like many people following the Christmas Cleansing five years ago, she had been reduced to robbing the dead.

Since she and the six others of her group had passed through a small town a week ago, they hadn't seen another living person for a while. They had been moving northward, hoping to escape the violence that plagued the ruins of the major cities. Coming across the body had been a surprise, both for them and for the gang of teenagers that killed him and had been stripping him when they appeared.

The dead man didn't have much on him that his killers hadn't already ripped away. Martha removed his footwear and her partner, Susan, took his pants for her son to wear when he grew into them. Cody had not wanted anything to do with the clothing, but rather than end up naked when his current growth spurt ended, he stuffed the pants into his pack.

"What are we going to do with him?" Susan asked. She was worried and her pallor made the freckles across her nose and cheeks stand out.

Martha looked over at her best friend and former police partner, Piper. As usual, the two of their minds were in sync and they didn't need to exchange words to agree on what needed doing. Piper grabbed him by the ankles and Martha took his wrists.

"On three," she muttered as they swung him over the gully. When they released their hold, the body went tumbling down the hill.

"At least he won't be a nasty surprise for the next people going this way," Piper said, using a faded blue handkerchief to wipe her brow and hands. She patted it over the short Afro curls on her head before stuffing it back in her pocket. After resettling the sling of her rifle across her chest, she went back to the cart she had been pulling up the road.

Martha nodded as she scanned the woods in the direction the youths had disappeared. "No, but those kids could be one. We need to get moving and put some miles between them and us. Everybody ready?"

She glanced around the group. Her niece and daughter were huddled next to each other but they nodded bravely. Susan gave her a small smile. Her sister was standing apart from the group with her arms wrapped around herself. Martha walked over to her. "You okay?" she asked.

Doris scowled at her. "How can you ask me that? No one can be okay after what we've seen, what we've had to do."

"Get a hold of yourself. We didn't do anything. He was already dead, and those kids were more scared of us than we were of them."

"I'm not talking about now. I'm talking about the whole thing." Doris began rocking in place. "I don't think I can take it anymore."

Martha took her sister into her arms and held her slightly smaller frame against her body. "Shh," she whispered soothingly. "It'll be all right." After counting to three hundred, she let go and gazed into Doris's eyes. The watery brown eyes stared back. Martha smiled and said, "I know it's tough, but we'll be safer if we can keep going a little farther. Can you try?"

Doris sniffed and nodded.

Sighing, Martha waved the rest of the group on and ignored the rolling eyes from Piper and the smirk on Susan's face.

As they journeyed farther from the gruesome scene, the elevation continued to rise. Soon, everyone's entire attention was focused on placing one foot before the other. Birdsong in the forest and the squeaking right wheel of the cart were the only sounds they could hear. The serenity and their exhaustion took the edge off of their fear.

Martha was startled out of her thoughts when her partner appeared at her shoulder. "What's wrong?"

"Are you okay? You're limping," Susan stated bluntly. During the past month of their travel, her hair had lightened enough for the auburn highlights to shine. A small, slightly built woman, she no longer had the veneer of gentility from her youth or any extra weight. The events of the past five years had seen to that.

"It's these boots."

Susan nodded. "You want to stop?"

"Not really. I'll look at them tonight."

"Good. I think we're getting close. Maybe by tomorrow afternoon."

"I hope you're right." Martha peered back over her shoulder at the two other women and three teenagers following them. "The natives are getting restless."

"Part of it is our most recent brush with death."

"We didn't kill him," Martha replied.

"But we took advantage of his death anyway."

"I know it's hard reconciling who we once were to who we are now."

"You've got that right. In my wildest dreams, I never considered that I would be able to steal from the dead."

"He didn't need the clothes anymore."

"I know that, it's just what it represents." Susan kicked a rock out of her path. "I don't know how to explain how bad I feel at how easy it is to justify what we've had to do to survive."

"I think I understand."

"Does it bother you?"

"Not to your extent. I guess it's easier for me since I was trained as a cop."

"Yes, you were taught to have a limited set of responses to threats." Tapping her partner's shoulder holster, Susan mouthed. "Bang, bang."

"You never seemed to mind when it was your life in danger."

"I don't think I'm really complaining about it now. I'm just whining for my lost humanity."

"It's difficult for you to face that we are not only at the top of the food chain but that we're predators that weak people should fear."

"I don't like that violence is our only option."

Martha laughed. "It must be especially hard with you being a bleeding heart liberal."

"I haven't been a liberal since they killed Cheryl."

"I know, honey. I'm sorry I joked about it."

"No, I just spent my entire life trying to believe the best of people. To know that these last five years were not just a bad dream." Susan wiped her eyes. "I can understand self-defense and I can understand protecting others. But I will never understand the rape and murder of…of…"

"Shh, sweetie. You'll make yourself sick." Martha tried to reach a supportive hand out for her lover, but Susan pulled away.

Susan snatched up a fallen branch and used it to beat against a fallen tree beside the roadway. When the piece of wood disintegrated from the fury of her blows, she threw it down the embankment. "When will it stop hurting?"

"I don't think it will ever stop."

"Thanks, just what I needed to hear. I was expecting a platitude like 'time heals all wounds.'"

Martha took hold of Susan's hand. "Darling, time only dulls it. The best that you can hope for is that the joy of her life outweighs the pain from her death."

"I hope you're right."

Looking back, Susan saw the worried looks from her two surviving children. They looked a lot like their father as they stood shoulder to shoulder, identical lines between their eyebrows and pursed lips. She had grown used to that look from him in the months before she finally confessed that she was a lesbian and wanted a divorce. Her kids had been toddlers then, but it still amazed her how many of his traits they had. She gave them a thumbs-up and tight smile. After walking for a while in silence she whispered, "All I've got left is hope."

Martha cocked her head. "Why do I get the feeling that we're not talking about the dead man anymore?"

"You always did know me too well."

"What are you thinking about?"

"I'm a little worried about our reception." Susan sighed. "I don't want to have come all this way for nothing."

"What exactly concerns you?"

Susan pushed her light brown hair away from her face. "I don't even know if she is still there."

"She'll be there."

"You're probably right. She went and made that land a sanctuary. If anyone could survive, she would."

They hiked quietly for almost a mile before Susan asked, "I wonder how bad it got up here."

"We haven't seen much bomb damage since we passed Sacramento. I don't think they had too hard a time of it."

"What about the roaming bands we've seen?"

"We haven't seen that many. And what there is hasn't been a danger to us." When Susan rolled her eyes, Martha said, "Seriously, that group of punks wouldn't have lasted ten minutes in the city."

"They were so young. What do you supposed happened?"

"I'm not sure. I do know that juvenile delinquents have been around since before this mess. It's just that without any official structure anymore, there are few opportunities for anyone to get anything without bloodshed. It's a vicious cycle."

"They're alone up on that mountain."

Martha scoffed, "You don't really think Jay would have made an easy target?"

"Not intentionally, but you know as well as I do that superior numbers can overwhelm a better fortified foe."

"True, but Jay wouldn't have easily given up any advantage. She always struck me as someone who planned for every contingency."

"You've got that right. She can be down right obsessive in considering every possible outcome."

Martha kept her eyes on the road and her voice low, "Do you miss her?"

"Miss her? What kind of question is that?" Susan smiled at her lover. "Do I miss being with her? Sometimes. She was one of the most driven people I had ever met. When my firm was in the process of merging, her advice and support really helped me stay on top of the negotiations. Without her, I wouldn't have gotten that windfall payment nor the corner office." She shook her head. "But afterward, when everything calmed down, I saw how much she thrived on going from crisis to crisis on her white steed. I needed someone to make time for me and that wasn't her. She was like a shark, never sleeping, always in motion toward the next thing. There was no way for me and the kids to fit in the life she made."

"That is what is so weird about her chucking it all and heading into the mountains."

"When her consulting firm was bought out, she had more money than she knew what to do with. I figured she would eventually get bored being out here away from the bright lights of the big city, but the longer she was out here, the more the lifestyle came to fit her."

"I always liked her."

"Sometimes I thought you two had more in common with each other than either of you did with me."

"Nonsense."

"Oh, no? You both are athletic, like the outdoors, listen to jazz and read mysteries."

"Unfortunately, she pushed too many of my buttons."

"I thought that was what made a successful relationship?" Susan squeezed Martha's hand. "Seriously, though, she always did like to challenge people."

"And I never cared to be challenged." Lifting up the clasped hands for a kiss, Martha laughed, "I'm glad you two stayed friends."

"I knew that if I really needed her that she would always have my back. Even you have to admit that she never once gave my kids anything but her best." Sighing, Susan added softly, "I just wasn't important enough on my own."

"You are to me."

"That's why you have me and she doesn't."

"I have you? You said I have you?" Her grin lit up the trail. "You never let me say that before."

"Pig."

The two of them strolled along companionably, listening to the sounds from the surrounding forest. The wind was rustling through the treetops, and there was a faint sound of water flowing over rocks. Finally, Martha asked, "Is she going to have a problem with me?"

"No way."

"You're sure?"

"She'd never begrudge me my happiness and you make me very happy. It also helps that she likes you."

Martha squeaked out, "Likes me?"

"Darling, you always did have more in common with her than I did."

"I still don't see it."

"You just don't want to see how alike you two are. My tough girls."

"Finally, you accept your attraction to butch women."

"You goof, I've never denied what drew me to you."

Martha shrugged. "Sometimes I get the feeling you resent it."

"The whole 'strong, silent type' can be a little wearing at times," Susan said as she bumped hips with her lover. "But I wouldn't trade your strengths for anything. You fill my empty places."

"You just want me for my many skills."

"No, sweetheart, I love you unreservedly."

"Thank you. I love you too."

"Besides, I think Harmony keeps her on a pretty short leash."

"Would Jay play around on her?"

"Not on your life. She is very old-fashioned and has always taken her commitments very seriously. Is anything else bothering you?"

"I don't want her to be jealous or act spiteful."

"Don't worry, love. Even if Harmony hadn't had her pretty well whipped, that ship has sailed."

"Did you know her, too?"

"No, Jay met her after she moved up here and was only working part-time on special projects. She had gone to Sacramento to reorganize a horribly dysfunctional company. Harmony was brought in to help and she used her mind-control powers to weave her web and wrap Jay around her finger."

"Sounds like someone has an issue with the current Mrs."

"Oh, don't call her that. Jay has issues with the institution of marriage." She gusted out a breath. "It just seemed like they had very little in common and that Harmony was more calculating than Jay ever gave her credit for. I've got no reason to worry, after all this time, and neither do you."

"As long as you're not going to make a play for Jay or pull Harmony's hair out, I'll be okay."

Susan glanced behind her at the others and then made eye contact with her lover. "Sounds like someone needs some reassurance."

Martha blushed. "I just want to make sure that we're doing the right thing. I don't want you getting short shrift because of me."

"The best thing we ever did was getting out of that city. Even if, for some insane reason, we can't stay, we're safer out here, away from there."

"You can say that even after what just happened?" The voice interrupted their private conversation.

Susan turned to face Martha's sister, Doris. "Since we left the main highway five days ago, that was the first hint of trouble."

The two sisters both had dark hair and eyes and that is where the similarity ended. Martha was tall and solid where Doris was only Susan's height although much thinner. Their attitudes were different too. Where Martha constantly looked for solutions, Doris only saw more problems.

"That man was dead. They killed him." Doris's voice was high and thin.

"He was stupidly traveling alone. Even you know better than that," Martha told her. "Besides, we must have seen more bodies in a single week in Oakland than we've seen since leaving it."

"I'm worried, okay? Can't I be a little concerned about you dragging us up here when you aren't even sure that your friend is even alive or that we'll be welcomed."

"Jay knew the country was heading to hell when she built out here. I've never met anyone so well prepared for disaster."

"All the preparation in the world couldn't make her ready for a horde to invade."

Susan smiled tightly. "Before we lost all contact, she made several offers for us to come up and join her. I doubt that the offer has been rescinded."

"Even considering that you're bringing more than just you and the kids?"

"One of her greatest traits is her sense of generosity."

"Things have gotten worse all over. You can't expect that she'll be any different."

"Yes, I can."

"How?" Doris demanded. "Everyone wants something."

"You don't know Jay."

"What if she wants us to pay?"

"Then we'll work it out." Susan stopped, forcing the rest of the group to stop. Waving her son and daughter closer, she took their hands. "Look, we knew the risks when we left, but we all agreed that we couldn't stay any longer. After what happened to Cheryl, I wasn't willing to just let the mob take any more of my family."

"It's cool, Mom." Cody shifted the pack on his back and adjusted the sling of his shotgun. Freeing his hand, he patted his mother's back. With a voice that was just starting to crack, he said, "I like it out here."

"I agree with him. With winter coming it may be tough out here, but anything is better than where we were."

Everyone looked in amazement at the speaker. Piper rarely strung more than five words together in a day, and she had more than tripled that in a single statement. The stocky, dark-skinned woman shrugged off the attention and started walking again. "We're burning daylight."

Martha nodded. "Let's try to put in another couple of hours before we stop for the night."

The small band reordered itself with Martha on point and Cody bringing up the rear. The last several weeks had seen him shoot up another couple of inches, bringing him almost to the height of his mother's partner. With his bigger frame came an increased sense of responsibility as the only male of the group. The fact that most of the women of the group were better armed and experienced did nothing to dampen his enthusiasm. Sometimes Susan found it difficult not to laugh at her son's earnest attempt to define his nascent manhood.

The seven refugees continued to follow the cracked blacktop up the mountain, taking turns in pairs to pull the heavily ladened cart. The sounds of their passage didn't disturb the natural sounds from the trees of bickering squirrels and singing birds. Except for the weapons they carried, they could have once been mistaken for a vacationing family out enjoying the late summer in bucolic northern California.

Since the War, however, no one had much time to be outdoors enjoying much of anything. It started with the riots that broke out after the Electoral College voted to send to Washington a president who had failed to win the popular vote by a wide margin.

In a move so bold that it had to have been planned well in advance of the election, the Tea Party and militia movements of the South and the Midwest joined forces with the National Guards of seventeen states. Together, they seized control of the military bases in their territory. Calling themselves the Confederacy of Christ, they imposed martial law in the cities and a revocation of all civil rights not written in the original Constitution and Bill of Rights. They instituted the death penalty for all behavior they defined as deviant and required that their new citizens must be reborn in Jesus Christ and swear, in English, an oath of allegiance.

The federal government never had the chance to use its police powers against the insurgency. Instead, the Department of Homeland Security went rogue and arrested the members of the Senate, the House and the incumbent president under the guise of restoring public order.

That Christmas saw the end of the United States of America. The Confederacy's first offensive used the missiles and ordnance that had been scheduled to go overseas for the never-ending conflicts in the Middle East and turned them instead toward what they termed "the sinful and godless cities of America." Every city with more than a million citizens was targeted by at least one bomb. The largest cities saw carpet-bombing that rivaled Dresden or Tokyo during World War II. Because the military had removed the nuclear warheads from most of the missile stockpile at the end of the Cold War, the weapons were only ballistic, but the damage was still irremediable.

On the East Coast, the once beautiful cities of Boston, New York, Philadelphia and the District of Columbia were in smoldering ruins. Only craters remained of the Capitol Building and White House. The Pentagon, which had survived the terrorists on 9/11, fell under an onslaught of cruise missiles.

Florida lost a third of the state to missile strikes and the resulting fires. Furious over being targeted by those that they thought were allies, the surviving counties allied themselves with the government of Cuba to blockade any shipments to the Confederacy through the Gulf of Mexico.

In California, Los Angeles and San Francisco were the main targets. Over one hundred and fifty short-range ballistic missiles were fired into each city. The City of Angels was left a virtual wasteland and the surrounding farmland burned. The resulting forest fire, blown by the wind, became an inferno that consumed most of Arizona, New Mexico and Nevada before the January rains finally doused the flames.

More than forty-five million lives were lost in the first week from the immediate impact. Many of those who pulled themselves from the rubble faced a painful death from their injuries because few hospitals, medical staff or emergency supplies survived. Collateral damage to major highways and railroads left few routes of escape operational. Poisonous gas leaks and toxic spills closed most airfields and ports and continued to this day.

The bombs triggered natural disasters as well. Massive earthquakes and seismic activity were recorded from Guatemala to Alaska. Registering seven and higher on the Richter scale, the shifting of the tectonic plates toppled any tall buildings that had escaped the missile attacks. The resulting tsunami drowned most of the residents of the Hawaiian Islands and Osaka.

Following the law of unintended consequences, the ones who pulled the trigger found themselves facing disaster. They faced the worst winter in decades without heat or electricity as most of the country's power plants were in the impact zone. Shipments of oil, natural gas and food were disrupted when Mexico and Canada, with the support of the international community, demanded reparations for the fallout to their countries. The Confederacy refused and so the northern and southern borders were sealed.

Now, five years later, a small group of survivors had left Oakland to try and make a new life in the wilderness.

CHAPTER TWO

Martha leaned against one of the weathered mile marker signs and waited for the stragglers to catch up. As the day had wound on, the group stretched out over a couple hundred yards. They had been able to cover six miles since the encounter with the dead man and they were all tired.

Martha held up her hand as they reached her. It had been a while since anyone had the gasoline necessary to drive these roads, much less use the passing pull-offs but the wider expanse of road at this spot offered them a quick and easy campsite. Martha asked Piper, "What do you think? Should we set up camp here?"

Piper nodded. "It looks safe enough for one night," she agreed.

The two of them had taken on the leadership role, falling back into their habits of when they were police officers together. The section of road they were on was fairly straight and they could see several hundred yards in both directions. With the mountain to their back and a fairly steep descent to the river at their front, it was the best they could hope for.

The tired band eagerly shrugged off their packs and sat down on the ground where they stopped. The furious pace was depleting their meager resources.

Martha and Piper stood together to talk. "Is there enough daylight left for you to get anything?"

"Won't know until I go," Piper answered.

"A little meat would go a long way."

"Start a pot of water boiling."

"You're that confident?"

"Don't worry, I'll bring back something."

"No squirrel," Eva and Carol begged in unison before falling into a fit of giggles. The two girls had gravitated toward one another on the journey. After the murder of her older sister, Carol had withdrawn from her family and rarely smiled. Eva had never really recovered from the loss of her father during the first bombardment. Their friendship had returned smiles to their faces. The sound of their girlish laughter was delightful to hear.

Piper stuck out her tongue at the giggling girls. The light pink muscle stood out in stark contrast to the deep mahogany of her skin tone. "I don't like the taste any more than you do, but we'll have to make do with whatever I can get." Starting back the direction they had come, she said, "I'll check our trail too."

Everyone in the group had an assigned task when setting up camp. They had the experience of more than two months on the road to practice, and now they could prepare a meal and shelter quickly and with a minimum of fuss. They knew the sooner the chores were done, the sooner they could rest.

Cody and Carol collected everyone's canteens and a couple of pots and went off to find water. The road they were on followed alongside the Trinity River, and they only had to go about a hundred yards downhill to find a shallow creek. Their biggest challenge was finding a safe trail that they could use to travel both down and up again.

Once at the slowly moving stream, the two teenagers took off their shoes and waded in the shallows. Showing their age and closeness, the two siblings splashed one another with the refreshingly cool water until they were soaked to the skin and their feet were numb. Laughing, they stood dripping as they filled all the canteens and the cook pots. They made two trips and only had to go back once to fill a dropped pot.

Doris and her daughter, Eva, went off to gather wood for their supper fire. They were looking for limbs and branches that had fallen earlier in the year. Dry wood wouldn't smoke as much as green, and they sure didn't want to telegraph their position to anyone in the area who might be watching the skies. They didn't need too much wood, as it was not safe to have a fire after dark.

Collecting enough to cook their meal, the mother and daughter worked silently together. Each trip, Eva brought almost twice as much wood back to the camp as Doris.

Susan and Martha pulled out the three tents and began to set them up. The tents they had were old but still waterproof and protection from the wind.

"It's getting colder," Susan said. "Should we bring out the sleeping bags?"

Martha looked up from hammering a stake into the soft ground on the shoulder. "Yeah. Better to have them and not need them than to not get any rest because we're shivering all night."

"At least I have you to keep me warm."

Rocking back on her heels, Martha leered at her lover. "I could do better than warm you if you could keep quiet."

"Big talker," responded Susan, her arms full of bedrolls. Dropping them close to the entrance, she pulled out a tight roll of plastic. With a deft snap of her wrists, Susan unrolled the ground cover inside the largest tent. She crawled inside to smooth the plastic sheeting down. About to back out of the tent, she found herself being pummeled by soft projectiles.

"Hey," she yelled, as she ducked and covered her head. When the barrage stopped, she saw that she was surrounded by all the sleeping bags. She looked over her shoulder at the all-too-innocent look from Martha.

"Oh, sorry. Didn't see you there."

Susan rolled over on her back and settled her head on one of the sleeping bags. Making sure she had Martha's attention, she braced her heels on the ground and lifted her pelvis. Watching her lover from under lowered brows, she languidly stroked her hand down the length of her body, being sure to draw her fingernails down her inner thighs. "You didn't see me?" she asked. Using both hands now, she hefted her small breasts and circled her nipples with her index fingers.

Clearing her voice, Martha tried to talk. "Uh…oops?"

"Maybe you should come in and show me how sorry you are."

Martha glanced over her shoulder before she crawled into the tent, zipping it closed behind her. She started to undo the buttons of her shirt but stopped when Susan shook her index finger at her.

"If you really wanted to make it better, you would see to my needs first."

Tugging on her bangs, Martha answered, "As you wish, my lady." She crawled over on hands and knees to straddled her partner's prone body and give her a kiss. Walking her lips over her lover's lips and jawbone, she whispered into the delicate ear, "Tell me what you need."

"Oh, baby. I just love the feel of your lips on mine." Susan writhed against her. She twined her fingers through Martha's long, dark hair and directed their lips together again.

"Good 'cause I sure like kissing you."

Their lips met slowly, deliberately. Moving across each other's face, they touched and tasted one another. Martha's tongue teased the corner of Susan's mouth and lightly nipped the full, red lips.

"Mmm," Susan moaned as she opened her mouth inviting Martha's tongue in to play.

Leaving her lips, Martha trailed bites and licks down the length of Susan's neck. She swirled her tongue around the pulse point and had just shifted her weight to free one arm to explore her lover's body when the sound of a crash outside the tent startled them.

Martha barreled out of the tent. "What's wrong?" she demanded, as she only saw her sister standing there.

"You," Doris spat.

"Come again?" she asked in disbelief.

"I can't believe that the two of you would be satisfying your disgusting carnal desires, especially when the rest of us are working."

Out of the tent now, Susan stood beside her lover. "Now, hang on just a minute, Doris. Martha and I will complete our chores as we have every evening. There is no reason why we can't also reconnect intimately on occasion."

"There are children here."

"Where? They weren't in the zipped-tight tent with us."

"I won't have my child exposed to your sinning and you should be ashamed about exposing your own kids."

"I'm not ashamed of who I am, but it sure sounds like you are." Her voice derisive, Susan continued, "My children are exposed to love and I think that is a hell of a lot healthier than your homophobia."

"Enough! Both of you calm down," Martha shouted. "Doris, we have been sensitive of your feelings and have not been anywhere near as affectionate as we would normally be. But you need to deal, sister, because we love each other and that is who we are." She turned her head to her lover. "Susan, let's finish our discussion later tonight."

Susan tossed her hair out of her eyes. "Fine. I'll go finish with the other tents."

"Great," replied Martha. "We'll need a lot more wood than that," she said, pointing at the meager armload that Doris had thrown down upon her return to the camp.

Sullenly, her sister stomped back toward the forest. Martha smiled crookedly at her niece, who had been watching from the edge of the road. The youngster started to raise her hand but aborted the movement at her mother's glare. Shrugging, she followed her mother back into the woods.

She watched Susan struggle with one of the tents before going over to help her. For a while, they worked in tense silence. Unable to take it, Martha asked, "You ever going to talk to me again?"

"I thought we were going to hold our discussion until tonight."

"I didn't mean this discussion," Martha replied, waggling her eyebrows. "I meant our earlier, more physical '*discussion*.'" She made air quotes around the word. "We can totally talk about what happened, if you'd like."

"I'm not sure talking is going to do any good. I'm getting really tired of being the target of Doris's hate."

"Once we get a place to rest up and recover, she won't be so bad."

Susan folded her arms and raised one eyebrow. "Do you even believe the words that are coming out of your mouth?"

"I've got no choice but to try. She might drive me crazy but she's my family. What else am I supposed to do?"

"I don't know, darling." Susan hammered in another tent peg before setting down the hammer and taking Martha into her arms. They swayed gently together in the hug. "I love you and I'm trying not to make this harder than it already is, but we get so few chances to be together. If she ruins another intimate moment, I'll snatch her bald headed."

"I hear you, love." Martha squeezed Susan tightly before letting go and looping the guideline over the peg. "I'll talk to her again."

Once the tents were finally set up, Martha dug out a pit for the fire. The fold-up entrenching tool was very handy, as the hatchet helped break up the tough ground. "We're going to need some rocks, babe," she called out.

"No problem. Part of the hillside has fallen down over here." Susan raised a couple of stones over her head.

"Better from the cliff than river rocks again."

"Yeah," Susan wholeheartedly agreed. Several nights earlier, stones that had been collected from the stream had exploded as they heated. They were lucky that no one had been injured. Susan carried her burden over and set them in the bottom of the pit. It took her several trips to fill the bottom and make a ring around the outside.

As Doris and Eva brought in their next armloads, Martha laid the sticks and branches among the rocks and then filled in the spaces with dry grasses. Susan used the magnesium fire starter to spark the tinder to flame. Patiently, she fed the flames with kindling until several of the larger pieces of wood caught. Satisfied that the fire was burning, she carefully slid the small block of magnesium back into an inner pocket before standing up.

She walked over to Martha, who was looking down the gully at Cody and Carol playing keep-away. Their light brown hair danced in the sunlight with their antics. "Cody needs a haircut."

Martha glanced up. "I do too. Maybe we can play barbershop after eating." Opening her arms, she welcomed the smaller woman into her embrace. "How about you and me go take a bath together while we're waiting to see what Piper brings back for dinner?"

"You're reading my mind, darling," Susan replied, running her hand down Martha's back and cupping her firm buttocks. "I'd like to get my hands on your skin." Giving the butt of her lover a final pat, she turned to go fetch the bathing supplies.

Martha called Cody and Carol over. "Hey, guys. Why don't you watch the fire while your mom and I go down to the stream?"

Carol shivered dramatically. "The water is awful cold," she warned.

"Hmm, that may put a damper on things." Martha ruffled Cody's hair as she walked past him. "Plan on losing some of this later!"

The youngsters plopped down around the campfire. Being off their feet after their long march was almost euphoric.

Mesmerized by the flames, they were nearly asleep when they heard Piper return.

"Yo, the camp," Piper called out. She raised her fist with a grin. Dangling by their ears were two brown rabbits. "We're lucky tonight."

"Man, I'm getting sick of rabbit," Cody complained.

Doris glared at him. "You should be grateful. We've had more meat on this journey than in the past year."

"I know. I just wish we could have a bigger variety."

Eva retorted, "It's better than squirrel."

"You've got that right," Martha agreed as she and Susan returned to the camp, their hair wet and ardor temporarily cooled.

"I saw a doe," Piper offered. She pulled out a sharpening stone and began to hone her knife. "She was about a half mile back. I could probably pick up her trail again."

"No. Right now we would waste too much of it." Taking the rabbits, Martha handed them to Cody. "Since you opened your mouth, you get to clean them."

"Try and keep the fur in one piece this time," Carol joked. "Nobody is going to trade for holey pelts."

"Carol, I'm sure I can find something for you to do if you have nothing better to do than torment your brother," Susan warned. She set their salvaged grill onto the rocks in the fire pit and balanced the pot of water on it. Sifting through their dwindling supplies, she found a few soft potatoes. Quartering them, she added them to the pot with several wild onions they had picked the day before.

When Doris stepped up for a closer look, Susan shook her head. "We don't have much left."

"I hope your friend is feeling generous."

Piper looked up from rinsing her hands. "We could always have stone soup."

"Stone soup?" asked Eva.

"Don't you know the story?" All three of the teenagers shook their heads. Their eyes were big as the usually taciturn woman began to tell them the fable.

"See, this beggar came to a town during a famine. The people said they didn't have anything to give to him to eat. He said no problem, that all he wanted was stone soup and, in fact, he was going to make enough for everyone to share."

Piper put away the knife and sharpening stone. Using her hands, she mimicked stirring the pot.

"He pulled out a big cauldron and filled it with water. He made a pretty big production of pulling out his special magic stone and adding it to the water. For a while he just stirred, occasionally tasting the soup and smacking his lips. Intrigued, the people of the village came closer. He casually mentioned that once he had stone soup with salt, pepper and paprika and it was the best he had ever had. An old woman stepped up and offered him some spices. He thanked her and stirred some more. He warned them that the soup might be a little thin, as he has been using the same stone for a week. Perhaps if someone had a little barley, that would make it all right. And, lo and behold, one of the villagers found that he had a double handful. After more tasting, the beggar began to reminisce about other pots of soup he had made better with just a little potato, diced into the soup to give it a robust flavor. One of the farmers remembered about a couple of potatoes in his basement and those were added. Slowly and surely, as the pot simmered, more and more folks found things they could spare. Someone had a scrap of meat, another had some carrots and someone else brought forth an onion. Soon, everyone had added some small portion to the pot. When he finally served the soup, they all declared it to be the best thing they had ever tasted."

"I heard that it was a lost soldier," Doris said.

Susan sighed. "It doesn't matter whether the main character is a peddler, a vagrant or a soldier. The point is that individually, we might have very little to spare. Once we combine our efforts or our supplies, we find we can work miracles."

"He deceived them into giving up their food. How can that be a good thing?"

"Sometimes you have to fool people into doing what's right." Martha winked at Piper. "Of course, we wouldn't know anything about that."

"So, is Jay the villagers or the beggar?" Cody asked as he handed the quartered rabbit to his mother.

"Jay? She is one of the most open-handed people I've ever met. You remember her, don't you?"

"I sort of remember playing around during the summer." Cody flicked his long bangs out of his eyes. "I don't really let myself think of the time before."

Martha reached over and squeezed his knee. "I know, buddy. It's better not to dwell."

"Anyway, she and Harmony had all of you up several times before the War. I was working all the time once I made partner and needed a place for you three to go when you were out of school for the summer."

"I remember swimming in their pond."

"Good."

"It will probably be dry," said Doris with a sniff.

"I doubt it. The mountain has a spring-fed stream."

"Tell me more about them," asked Piper.

"They've always been very generous to us." Susan set the meat on the grill for a quick sear. Turning the pieces with her knife, she added, "I don't think we are going to need to trick them into taking us in."

"How did you meet them, Mom?" Carol asked.

"Jay and I played soccer together in the women's league in the city." She smiled at the memory. "When we moved out of that apartment in the Mission, I found another team, and we became more than just friends. When my firm merged, she got hired as an organizational development expert. It was good for my career but it put an end to our relationship. Luckily, though, we realized we made much better friends than lovers."

"She's your ex-lover?" Doris gasped. "Did you know about that?" she asked Martha.

"I have no secrets from Martha," Susan replied. "She knew about my past. Besides, Jay and I were over long before I ever asked my self-defense instructor out for a cup of coffee." Susan tossed the browned meat into the simmering water. She stirred the pot and sat down near her partner.

"To think I almost declined." At Piper's look, Martha said, "I didn't want to get involved with a student."

"I was pretty persuasive and you knew a good thing when you saw it." Susan tugged on Martha's right leg. "Let me look at your heel while we still have some light. Why don't you check your boot?"

"Good idea." Reaching down to the other side of the stump, Martha picked up the shoe and loosened the laces. Running her fingers along the insole, she found a raised place on the heel. After struggling to get a grip with her short nails, she pulled out her knife. When she pried the insole up, there was a hollow in the shoe.

"What have you got?" Cody asked.

"I don't know." She worked a folded piece of paper out of the recess and opened it. Reading it carefully, Martha shook her head. "It's a deed to a plot of land."

"Where?" Doris demanded. "Maybe we should go there instead."

"It doesn't belong to us."

"More so to us than to a dead man. How far is it from here?"

Susan stood up. "Enough. We're going to Jay's place. If we find that there is a problem, we can consider other options later."

"She's right. This doesn't change anything." Martha placed the refolded document in the pocket of her Windbreaker. Standing up, she walked to the edge of camp and pulled up some grass to stuff into the hole in her boot. "All it's done is give me a blister."

Piper stretched and asked, "Is dinner ready? I'm starved."

"Yep. Everyone have the bowls out?" Susan asked as she started to ladle out the stew. "After chores tonight, we should turn in. I know it's early, but we're all tired."

"We seem to be walking the same amount," Eva stated. "Why am I so wiped out?"

"We've been hiking uphill. We are quite a ways above sea level now and it's just going to get higher."

"Piper, you take first watch and I'll take second." Martha chewed a piece of rabbit. "Thanks for doing the hunting."

"No problem." Piper slurped the rest of the liquid from her bowl and went down the hill from the creek to wash her dishes. On her way back, she quietly made a full circle about a hundred yards out from the camp. All was quiet, so she took a position on a small rise and stood guard while the rest of the group finished their evening tasks. Even with the impromptu barbering, it did not take long for them all to crash in their tents in exhausted slumber, confident with Piper watching over them.

CHAPTER THREE

The afternoon sun was burning down on her head as Susan studied the roadway before her.

"How's it going, babe?"

Susan growled in frustration, "Do you have any idea how hard it is to translate the difference between driving and walking the same road? Nothing looks the same."

"I don't envy you." Martha took her hand, and they smiled at one another. "Does anything seem familiar?"

"Not really. Everything is so overgrown."

"Why don't you try and remember the things she told you to look for when she gave you directions?"

"You know, that's a good idea. Jay always did pepper her maps with numerous landmarks." Susan grimaced. "Goodness only knows how much things have changed. We might have already missed the turnoff."

"You really think so?"

"I don't know. I'm just so frustrated."

"Don't work yourself into a lather. Just let the memories come to you," advised Martha. "We haven't passed it yet, trust yourself." The taller woman squeezed her hand gently.

Wracking her brain for scenery clues, Susan was just beginning to describe a tiny rest stop at the foot of Jay's mountain retreat to her partner when she spied the remains of a small building just off the road.

"Hey, everyone. Hold up a second." Susan practically bounded across the decrepit bridge that crossed over the culvert between the road and the rest area. The single building was missing its roof but the signs for the men's and women's restrooms were still hanging. She walked around the ruins and saw, beyond the small parking lot, an overgrown driveway leading up the side of a mountain. She came racing back. "I think this might be it."

Doris crossed her arms. "Might or is?"

"Look, it's been a long time. I'm as close to positive as I can be." She took off her cap and ran her fingers through her hair. "Guys, what do you think?"

Cody and Carol looked at one another. "Mom, it was a long time ago," Cody began. He paused and shrugged. "It could be. I don't remember."

"Yeah, we were just here to enjoy the summer, not to think about how to find it again. Sorry."

"What was this place?" asked Doris.

"The last rest stop before you entered Trinity National Park." Susan answered absently as she surveyed the area. "Why don't we bring the cart over here and I'll go up and look? If it isn't the right place, we can still camp here tonight."

Doris looked at the sky. "We could go a little farther."

"No, Susan's right. We're all pretty tired and we haven't seen anybody today. I think it would be safe." Martha hopped over the bridge and left her rifle and backpack against a convenient sapling. "Ready to heave?" she asked the group around the cart.

"On three," Cody said. "One, two…three."

Working in tandem, they maneuvered the two-wheeled cart over the broken bridge and into the shadows at the side of the building. Susan took the rifle from Martha and left her group relaxing in the shade and headed up to see if there was anyone or anything up the road to welcome them.

She stepped over the rusty chain that was stretched across the bottom of the weed-choked gravel road. Walking around the bend, she stopped suddenly in dismay. Blocking the road was a ten-foot section of concrete pipe. It was taller than she was and, to get around it, she was going to have to scramble around the open end that hung off the edge of the cliff.

"Don't look down. Don't look down. Don't look down," she muttered as she made the traverse. She was breathing hard and her hands were sweaty when she reached the other side to continue up the road. The path wound its way under the firs and redwoods. Her footsteps muffled by the rich red dirt, Susan shook her head at a rusty, bullet hole-riddled sign with its warning against trespassing.

Coming to a three-way fork, she chose the middle direction. Following it around the first turn, she was surprised to suddenly be on pavement. Striding along its wandering course up the mountain, she arrived at a brick wall that had collapsed to block the entrance to a driveway. She climbed over the bricks and walked toward to the house she could see ahead of her.

Before she reached it, three large dogs suddenly surrounded her. Disconcertingly, they didn't bark. The small pack just circled around her in malevolent silence. She held out her hands, but they didn't come close enough to sniff.

"May I help you?"

Susan started at the voice. She looked up to see, staring back at her, a woman of medium build with short black hair that was starting to gray at the temples. The woman was holding a crossbow pointed in her general direction.

Despite the threat, she couldn't help the smile that drifted across her face. "Have I changed so much, Jay?"

The woman took several steps closer. "Should I know you?" She studied the smaller woman for a few moments before her eyes widened in recognition. "Susan?"

"Yeah."

"Wow. You're so thin. I mean, you look good."

"Thank you."

Jay pointed the crossbow at the ground. "I'm glad to see you survived."

"You too."

"My god, but you're a sight for sore eyes."

The two of them smiled for several minutes, drinking in the sight of one another. "After coming all this way, do you suppose I could I get a hug?" Susan finally asked, hesitantly.

Jay ordered the dogs to relax, and she shared a laugh with Susan as they all plopped down on the ground with their tongues lolling out. The two women embraced under the dappled shade from the overhanging trees.

"Where's tall, dark and dangerous?" Jay asked as she released her.

"I left her with the others at the bottom of the hill."

"Others?"

"Yeah." Susan didn't know where to start. "Um, well."

"Sounds like there's a story there." Jay stated dryly. At Susan's hesitant nod, she said, "All right. Come into the house. It sounds like we've got a few things to talk about." Jay put her arm around Susan's shoulder and pulled her forward. She made a motion with her other hand and said, "Watch," to the dogs. With doggie smiles, they left their supine positions on the ground to range around the yard.

"Well behaved."

"They're good dogs. It's a little amazing what can be accomplished when you've got the time to devote to training."

Jay led her old friend into the two-story stone house. The coolness was a welcome contrast to the heat of the day. A massive fireplace dominated the open living and dining area. The sofa, armchairs and dining room table with eight chairs seemed to take up very little of the available space.

As they walked through to the kitchen, Susan exclaimed. "This place doesn't seem to have changed much."

"It's true. We didn't see much action up here," Jay responded mildly.

"I don't know what I expected, but it wasn't this." Spreading her arms, Susan indicated the quiet interior.

"Wasn't I always trying to convince you to expect the unexpected and to plan accordingly?"

"I know, but this is exactly like I remember it. If you didn't know it, you'd never realize what's happened to the rest of the world."

Jay pulled on her earlobe. "Things must have been really bad for you to leave."

"It wasn't a picnic." Susan sighed. "We lost so much."

"You look good." Sensitively, Jay changed the subject. "Would you like a glass of water?" she asked as she opened one of the cabinet doors and removed two heavy glasses. She poured them both a glass of water from the spigot next to the sink. The ice-cold, metallic-tasting well water was drunk in silence while the two women appraised one another.

"I'm glad to see you," Jay simply stated. "I thought of y'all often." She stared into the bottom of her glass. "I wondered if you all had come through the aftermath of the bombings."

"It was the end of the world as we knew it." She refilled her glass and drank deeply. Taking a deep breath, Susan said in a rush, "We came to see if we could stay."

"Okay."

"We couldn't live down there anymore. I know it's sudden and all..."

Jay interrupted. "It's all right."

"That's it?"

"Yeah. That's it. You guys are as near to family as I've got."

"But we're more than you could have bargained for."

"I would never turn you away. I'm just glad you finally made the move. From all I've heard it isn't safe out there anymore."

"We haven't felt safe in a long time."

"As you can see, my isolation has protected me."

"This place looks untouched. It's like stepping back in time. I can hardly believe my eyes, I think I'm dreaming."

"Shall I pinch you?"

Susan swatted at her hand. "Goof."

"Goober."

"I really missed you."

Reaching out, Jay pulled her into another hug. "I am so glad that you're alive."

"You might not be so happy once you find out how many people I've brought."

"Oh? What are we looking at? A cast of thousands? Your entire neighborhood?"

Susan laughed. "No, nothing like that. There are seven of us."

"What are you so worried about? That's only two more than the five of your family."

"No." Susan set her glass on the counter. "Cheryl was killed."

"Oh, honey. I'm so sorry."

"I should have made us leave before, and now it's too late for her." She wiped furiously at the tears in her eyes. "It's my fault."

"No, it's not. It's the fault of whoever killed her."

"Whatever."

"Can you tell me what happened?"

"I can't just yet. It hurts too much."

"And it will for a while." Jay turned away from her and looked out the kitchen window. "I'm sorry for your loss."

"Thank you." She cleared her throat. "Well?"

"Well, what? I said you're welcome here. That doesn't change because you picked up three strays. Heck, with your track record, I'm amazed you didn't bring more."

"I need to go back down to tell the others." Susan was nearly dizzy with relief.

"You do trust them, right?"

"I think so."

"You want to try for a more ringing endorsement?"

"Sorry. It's just that I never met Doris and her daughter before the missile strikes. She's Martha's younger sister and, frankly, a tight ass. I should warn you that she disapproves of our 'lifestyle.'"

"It's a life, not a lifestyle."

"Not to hear her on the issue. I hope you and Harmony can overlook her narrow-mindedness."

Jay shrugged and turned her gaze to the window. After a moment, she sighed and said, "You wouldn't think that bigotry would be an issue when you're struggling to survive."

"You'd be wrong. It's not usually too bad, just uncomfortable sometimes. She and Eva moved in with us at the beginning of the year. We've been taking care of them ever since."

"And the other one?"

"Martha's best friend. She's been a rock throughout everything, mostly because of the skills she learned in the military, but also because she's been the voice of reason when Doris goes off on one of her rants."

"She's not the very model of a modern major general, is she?"

"No, nothing like that. She served her twenty and then got out. Piper is at least ten years older than Martha and that made her the oldest in her class at the police academy. She ran circles around them and she still run circles around us."

"Sounds like an interesting group."

"I think we've been cursed to live with interesting people, in interesting times," Susan laughed.

"Good as explanation as any but if you say they're okay, then that's fine enough for me."

Susan rocked on her heels. "They've never given me a reason to think that they'd be a danger to my family and Piper has more than pulled her weight on this trip."

"Good." Jay scratched her chin. "You suppose that they're hungry and thirsty?"

"Definitely."

"Okay. Let's fix a quick picnic and I'll come down with you and see what you've brought me."

Jay opened up the cabinet above the wood stove and pulled down a loaf of bread. She cut several tomatoes and a cucumber. Popping a piece of tomato in her mouth, she rolled an onion across the counter to Susan. "Chop that for me."

Susan shifted from foot to foot. "I really need to get back and tell them I'm okay."

"Better you bring food than go empty-handed." Jay tapped the onion. "The faster you get to chopping, the faster we'll be able to head down."

"All right, all right. Where is a knife?"

"In the block on the other side of the sink." She collected the cut vegetables and tossed them in a bowl. Reaching into a crock by the door she scooped out a handful of olives and shook the brine free from her fingers. From the refrigerator she grabbed a hunk of cheese and crumbled some into the bowl.

Susan set her knife down before stepping around her and reopening the door of the refrigerator. She watched the light come on and then closed the door to watch it go out. In disbelief, she put her hand on several items inside, marveling at the coolness under her touch. "You have electricity?"

"Yep."

"I don't believe this. I haven't see anything like this in years. How?" she demanded.

"Now, now. You knew I was trying to get off the grid well before everything went down."

"I thought off the grid meant no power."

"No, it means that I didn't want to have to rely on the utilities to provide my power. I have solar panels on the roof that provide enough to operate what I need and batteries to store excess for those rainy days."

"What other surprises do you have?"

Jay winked. "You'll have to wait and see. I'll give a thorough tour once we bring the rest of your people up." Jay ground some pepper into the bowl. She pointed to a row of bottles near the stove. "There is olive oil in the green bottle and vinegar in the blue. Pour a couple of turns around the bowl." After that was done, she secured a lid on the bowl and slid it into a backpack. "Shall we?"

Slightly dazed, Susan followed her back out of the house. "Sure."

"So, tell me more about this best friend and the sister."

"Piper met Martha at the police academy and they served together in San Francisco as patrol cops. They were partnered together briefly after they passed the sergeants exam and stayed close even after Piper made Inspector first."

"Cops are useful."

"She's a good hunter."

"That's a valuable skill. Anything else?"

"Back before, she was president of the LGBT officers association."

"Brave."

"Yeah, she even sued the city when a promotion to homicide was denied to her."

"Did she win?"

"You bet."

Jay laughed. "Sounds like she's a real go-getter."

"She's pretty focused when she puts her mind to something. These days she's all about safety and security."

"Neither of which is a bad thing." Jay stepped over the brick wall. "What about the sister?"

"I'm afraid I don't have much positive to say about the sister. She was getting on my last nerve before we set out on this epic road trip."

"You didn't pass any handy ravines? I know that there are plenty places around here to hide a body."

"I wouldn't want to give Martha any other reason to feel guilty or to upset her kid. Her daughter is great and has been a ray of sunshine."

"How are Cody and Carol doing?"

"Cody is quite the man. He's growing tall and his voice is breaking." Susan climbed over the bricks blocking the driveway. "I'm worried about Carol, though. She never was one to make a fuss, and now I don't know what she's thinking or feeling."

"The peril of being the middle child is that nobody understands you."

"For so long she was withdrawn from everyone. Not even Martha has been able to get her to smile."

"In time, she'll find things to smile about again."

"The one positive is that she and Martha's niece, Eva, have become best friends. I think that's been helping a lot."

Jay led the way past the mouth of the pipe. "Did you see many people on the road?" she asked over her shoulder as she swung one-handed to solid ground.

"Yesterday, before we turned off the highway. A gang of five had killed a man." Her voice almost breaking, Susan said, "They were just kids, Jay."

"Kids can be vicious. You're lucky that they didn't take you on."

"There were more of us than them."

"Kids don't usually think about the consequences." She helped Susan around the mouth of the pipe. "Anybody else?"

"We haven't seen anyone since."

"That's good to hear. We don't much care for trouble." As she neared the old rest stop building, she suddenly halted.

Susan nearly stepped on her heels. "What? Why'd you stop?"

"Is that one of your friends?"

"Where?" Susan peered around Jay's back to see Piper standing off to the side with her shotgun leveled at them. "Yes," she said softly. In a louder voice, she called. "Piper, it's okay."

Martha stepped around the other side of the building. Her rifle was also pointed at them. "Step away from her, Susan."

"What the hell is going on?" Susan asked as she looked back and forth.

"There are the remains of at least ten people around this building." Martha said, "I'd like an explanation before we proceed any further."

"Damn right," Doris called from around the safety of the trunk of a large pine tree. "How do we know she isn't some sort of whack job waiting to kill us too?"

"Jay?" Susan asked timidly. "What's this all about?"

The other woman was standing easily, although her right finger tightened on the trigger of the crossbow. "I won't talk at the barrel of a gun."

"Then we've got a bit of a problem."

"Not my problem. You drew on me."

Susan stepped between the three armed women. She held her hands up in the universal sign of surrender. "Everyone calm down. We can talk about this. I'm sure Jay can explain."

"What's to talk about?" Doris asked. "I knew this was a bad idea." She kept popping out from around the trunk before ducking back again.

"If you thought it was such a bad idea, why are you here?" Jay asked.

"My sister believed the stories her lover told her about a perfect sanctuary."

"Not perfect, but it is safe."

"For whom? Certainly, not for the poor saps just left to rot here."

Jay took a deep breath. "I'm willing to tell you what I know, but I'm not going to stand here and be accused without defending myself." Looking around, she pointed at the picnic table. "Why don't we sit down?" She waited for a moment, and then she slowly began walking to the table. Once there, she unslung her crossbow and put it on the ground between her feet before sitting down.

The four women held a quick conference behind her back. As she waited, Jay saw a movement out the corner of her eye. She turned and saw Carol standing in the protection of the shelter. She couldn't help the smile that blossomed on her face to see another familiar face. "Hey, kid. You miss me?"

Suddenly shy, Carol blushed and dropped her head to study the ground. Cody stepped out toward the seated woman. "Hey, Jay." He pointed at a tall and skinny girl who had moved closer to his sister. "This is our cousin, Eva."

"Glad to meet you." She waved them all closer and opened the bag of supplies. "Why don't you come over and have some lunch?"

"We want some answers first," Doris demanded from behind her.

Jay tensed but didn't turn around. "Ask the questions then."

"Who are these people and what happened to them?" asked Martha, stepping around the table.

Jay gazed at her. "I don't really know." She shrugged her shoulders at their disbelieving stares. "That's the truth. We heard the battle. There was a lot of gunfire and we barricaded ourselves in the house. Once things quieted down, Harmony and I came down to investigate. We saw lots of bodies but no answers."

"You expect us to believe that you had nothing to do with this?" Doris was nearly jumping up and down in irritation.

Flicking her fingers dismissively at both the bones and Doris, she said, "I don't really care what you believe."

"Why didn't you do anything for these poor souls?" Doris demanded dramatically. "My sweet Eva stumbled across a corpse."

"I've found that they have a certain *je nais se quoi*. Besides, I'm not sure what you're complaining about. It's been long enough that they no longer stink."

"Seriously, Jay," Susan pleaded.

"They are better than any no trespassing sign." She sighed. "Look, a building, no matter how run-down, attracts squatters. However, not many people are going to stick around a building that is surrounded by the violently dead."

"That's pretty callous."

"What would you have me do? Offer them a proper burial? I don't owe them a damn thing."

Martha spoke up. "When was this?"

"About two years ago."

Piper and Martha exchanged glances. "Based on the state of the bodies, that's the right timeframe," Martha allowed. "I want your word that you weren't involved."

"Not in those deaths," she answered, stressing the word "those."

"Damn it, Jay. Don't split hairs," Susan responded.

"And I suppose you all survived this whole time with your hands clean?"

"Don't try and make a joke of it. This isn't the time."

"I would have to disagree on that. In fact, I remember that you and I rarely agreed on what was funny. It was probably a contributing factor to why we didn't make it."

Pinching the bridge of her nose, Susan muttered, "Not now."

"That, on the other hand, I can agree with. Look, let's introduce ourselves and try and chat like civilized folk." She waggled the covered bowl. "I brought a salad."

"You don't think we're going to be able to able to eat knowing what's right there."

"You people lived in Oakland, right? And had to know about the blast zone from what was once San Francisco?" At the nods of agreement, she continued. "I find it hard to believe you haven't seen dead people before."

"We haven't eaten over them."

"No, you just steal from them." That last was a shot in the dark, but she could tell it was a hit by the guilty glances. Grinning at their discomfort, she asked, "So, it appears that none of us are without sin."

There was a short and uncomfortable silence. Jay finally sighed. "Believe me or not, you don't have to fear me. Now, you want to tell me who's who?"

Susan pointed to Piper, Eva and Doris as she named them. Cody and Carol took a seat at the table on either side of Jay. Susan sat across from her, flanked on either side by Piper and Martha, who kept their weapons at the ready. Doris dithered for a moment before sitting next to Cody and making Eva perch on the small amount of bench left.

Jay uncovered the bread. "Freshly made this morning," she said invitingly. "Susan can attest to the freshness of the rest as she helped make it." Jay tapped the bowl. "Are you really going to let this go to waste?"

The group slowly dug into the bowl, eating faster as the tastes of the dressing and vibrant vegetables hit their tongues. Piper tore off hunks of bread and passed it around. No one spoke as they devoured the salad.

Jay took her time studying the group as they concentrated on the food. "Hungry much?" she asked when she caught Martha's eye.

"We haven't seen too much in the way of fresh food in the last few years. It's been no-label cans and what we could scrounge on the small piece of land in the backyard."

"You grew all this?" Eva asked timidly. She spit an olive pit into her fist and looked at it in wonder.

"The cheese comes from my neighbors on the next mountain over. They keep goats. The olives and oil come from the valley to the west. Everything else came from my garden."

"This is great."

"Thank you. There's more where this came from."

Martha leaned her elbows on the table. "We've come a long way and need a place to settle."

"I know we didn't get off on the right foot, but you won't find a safer space."

"You have enough room for us?"

"Things might be a little tight and may even get a little tough this winter, but I've got stores of food set aside. With a little work and everyone pitching in, we can make it."

"You're willing to have us join you?"

"I must say that I'm a little less willing now that you've drawn a weapon on me, but I'm trying not to take it personally." She bared her teeth at Piper and Martha, who had the grace to look abashed. "Seriously, I stand by the offer I made to Susan all those years ago and I include those she calls family and friends. There are a few ground rules, though."

"What do you want?"

"I want your agreement on some stuff before I take you up." Jay splayed her hands on the scarred surface of the table. "Mine isn't the only place on the mountain. I want your assurance that none of you will do anything to put any of us in danger."

"You mean more danger than we are already in?"

"Who are you again?"

"Doris. Mrs. Doris Matlan," she primly insisted.

"I don't see a husband."

"He died a hero."

"Didn't they all?"

Doris sniffed. "Jesus Christ was his Lord and Savior. He was saved."

"And that's the important thing out of all this." Jay rolled her eyes. "Anyway, we tend to keep a low profile, we don't tell anyone we're up here and we try not to do anything to tip anyone off to our presence. Can everyone agree to that?"

At the nods from around the table, she smiled. "Okay, the next thing is that out here, there is no free ride. I expect everybody to pull their weight."

"And if we do so?"

"Like Engels wrote, 'From each according to their ability, to each according to their needs.'"

Doris spoke up again. "Who decides?"

"Well, me, of course." The smile on Jay's face never made it to her eyes. "It's my house, my rules. I'll share all I have but only to those who work as hard as I do."

"I don't think that's very fair."

"Shut up, Doris." Martha leaned across the table. "We don't expect something for nothing. We're all willing to work and we'll all chip in."

Pointing at the bones bleaching in the sun, Doris spit out, "If we don't, are you going to do us like you did those people?"

"First off, I didn't kill them, although I would have had they endangered me or mine." Her voice cold and remote, Jay made eye contact with everyone around the table. "Secondly, if you don't agree, you go no farther up the mountain and neither do your friends." There was an uncomfortable silence. "Everyone out here has made it this long without the kind of trouble that is common down below, and we're not about to sacrifice it all for folks we don't know."

"You know Susan and her children."

"Yes, I do. I also know Martha. Susan vouched for the rest of you, and I'm willing to risk it but not without your assurance."

"You'll just take our word for it?"

"Well," Jay said, pulling a knife out her sleeve and flicking her thumb against the blade. "It will be more official in blood."

Leaping up, Doris shouted to Martha, "Stop her! She's going to kill us."

"Not funny, Jay. Put it away." Susan rubbed her temples. "That isn't helping," she scolded.

"Sorry." Jay slid it back into the sheath on her forearm.

Doris was still hopping mad. "Sorry isn't good enough."

"Doris, knock it off. She was trying to be funny and the operative word is 'trying.'" Martha was close to losing her temper at her sister's intransigence. She addressed Jay, "All you want is our word?"

"Yes. Tell me that our safety is your safety."

"You have it."

Jay looked around the table and got agreement from all of them. She had to wait the longest before Doris finally threw up her hands and nodded.

"Excellent. Are y'all ready to head up?" Her soft Southern accent still in place after two decades on the West Coast, Jay stood up and started to clear the table.

"Um, Jay?" Susan began. "How are we going to get the cart up the trail?"

"That is the first secret that I will be trusting you with," she replied slyly. "Help me clear away all trace of our meal and I'll show you."

CHAPTER FOUR

With a lazy grin, Jay waved for them to follow her up to the path. "We decided from the beginning that we needed to camouflage our presence. So many people only see what they're expecting to see. Starting with this chain here. We soaked the lock in battery acid so it would rust quickly. Strangers see it and think the road is abandoned." She pulled one of the stakes out of the ground and lowered the chain to the ground.

Jay returned the stake to its upright position once the group had pulled the cart past. Continuing her monologue, she walked past the small group. "There are four homes sharing this mountain, and none of us want unexpected visitors. We set up a way to protect ourselves by making access difficult. Luckily, one of the guys was an engineer before he retired."

At the pipe, she asked which two of them were willing to get damp. Martha and Piper volunteered. She indicated that they should enter the dark pipe after her. "Come in about two feet and feel around on the floor for a metal rod," she called out, her voice echoing in the dark.

They looked dubiously from her to the water covering the bottom of the pipe. "Go on," she encouraged.

Piper reached down and felt around until she found the rod. "What now?"

"Lift it up and turn it enough so that it can't reseat itself in the indentation." After Piper did so, she directed them back out of the pipe to the other side.

She poked her head out and looked at Doris and Susan. "You guys push on the left side." She got out on the other side and told Martha and Piper to push on their left side. With almost comical ease, the pipe rotated, leaving plenty of room for the cart to pass. Once they pulled it past, she had them replace the pipe and the rod in their previous position.

"Can I borrow your canteen?" she asked Martha. Taking it, she said, "Remember to return the water to its previous level," as she poured out the contents to cover the rod.

Cody blurted, "That's so cool!"

"Right you are," Jay replied. "It's remarkably simple but also elegant."

Stepping out, she waved the group on. "Ever forward and choose the middle ground," she intoned.

"What?" Doris asked.

Susan shook her head and smiled at her friend. "Up ahead, there is a fork in the road. We take the center path."

"Where do the other paths go?"

"The lower road eventually hits the far side of my property before leading to one of the neighbors. The upper leads to the house of my, I mean our nearest neighbor and then past him to the folks who live at the top of the hill."

"Tell us about them," Martha asked.

"Carlos and Emily were pot farmers before the War. Josh was an engineer. On the other side, Brandy and John are born-agains who came out to wait for the end time. Old Man Titus has been living on the top of the mountain since before I was born." Jay smiled. "He's quite the curmudgeon and I haven't even seen him in a couple of years. Not after he ordered Harmony and me off his land."

"You see the others?"

"Not regularly. We check in with each other occasionally and will help out in an emergency." She stopped at the barrier to the driveway. "Most everybody out here came here to get away." She patted the bricks. "We've all got walls and they should be respected."

She showed them how removing two bricks allowed the center section to pivot on a metal rod, making it easy to push part of the wall out of the way.

Once the group walked through with the cart, Jay tugged the wall back into place. Carefully, she brushed away the telltale marks of its movement before she replaced the brick stops and continued to lead the group forward.

Approaching the house, she whistled for the dogs. When they bounded up, she made them sit. "Can you come up one at a time and meet my gals?" she asked.

As they did so, she introduced the refugees to the motley pack of mutts as friends. Ginger, Duchess and Georgia seemed to relax once they knew the visitors were friendly. After the animals had sniffed each hand and gotten a scratch behind their ears, she directed everyone the short distance remaining to the house.

Letting go the cart and dropping their bags, they looked around the yard in amazement. They were on a fairly large plateau and could see for miles in all directions except for where the mountain rose at their backs.

Sitting to one side of the two-acre clearing, the house was gray stone with black solar panels covering the roof. To their right was a small pond with a short pier. On it was an upside-down canoe. There were several cords of wood stacked under the nearest trees. Beyond the pond was what looked to be a small greenhouse, almost hidden at the edge of the forest.

Jay watched the group as they took their first looks at their new home. She wanted to laugh at the wonder in their expressions, but the tension was still too high for them to find any humor in the situation.

Instead, she spoke gently. "Welcome, to my, and now, your home. Come inside and let me show you around."

Almost stumbling because their eyes were not on where they were walking, they followed her through the front door. Piper noticed the heavy shutters on the windows and the thickness of the door. At her raised eyebrow, Jay shrugged. "I could tell you the winters are really bad here, but, the truth is, I wasn't just interested in their weather-stopping ability."

She waved everyone in around her. "I designed this place to have the highest R-value possible. The walls are insulated concrete forms that extend from basement to eaves. They have an additional layer of stone on the outside. Not only can they withstand a two-hundred-mile-an-hour wind, they can withstand anything short of an armor-piercing round."

"You get many of those?" Martha asked.

"Nope, but it doesn't hurt to be prepared." Jay continued, "I don't know whether you noticed the solar cells on the roof?" At their nods, she said, "I went for a system of photovoltaic cells that convert sunlight into direct current electricity." She grinned at their blank looks. "I'll explain it when we get to it. Suffice to say we have power."

"You're kidding? Power?"

"I wouldn't kid about something like that. All the appliances were the best of their time, with high efficiency ratings and low power requirements." At their excited looks, she shook her head. "Calm down, you can't run everything at once, but then again, I planned this place to require little but produce a lot.

"During construction, I did everything I could to get off the grid. I didn't want to be at the mercy of the greedy bastards in charge of the utilities. I hadn't considered the greedy bastards of the Confederacy but, since the bombing, we've been entirely self-sustaining."

"Self-sustaining?"

"Yep. Water comes from an artesian well and the septic system I have will last for decades. The real work is to collect food and wood."

Carol stepped forward and hugged her. "I already feel better for being here."

"I am glad you are here and grateful that you made the journey in safety. It gives me hope." She snapped her jaws shut over anything else she might have said. Taking a deep breath, she shrugged off their curious looks. "Anyway, let me give you the five-dollar tour."

"I thought tours only cost a nickel?" Susan asked with a smile.

"For guests who aren't expected to pull their weight, yeah. However, you guys are family, and since I'll be putting you to work tomorrow, I think it best I show you everything."

Pointing behind the group, she indicated the two doors on the same wall as the front entrance. "Right by the front door is a closet that mainly has coats, weapons and ammunition. Next to it is the door leading downstairs."

She opened the door and directed everyone inside. "Let's start with the basement." They walked down a flight of stairs and stopped around a pool table. "Down here is a guest room with bathroom." She opened the door and they peered in at two single beds separated by a nightstand. The room had a line of narrow windows near the ceiling that brought in a surprising amount of light. "We can discuss later where everyone will stay."

She opened up another door that led to the storage area. She flipped on a light and everyone gasped at the flickering bulb. Ignoring that, Jay went on. "As you can see, we are pretty well stocked in staples." Filling the center floor-to-ceiling racks were canning jars filled with vegetables. Other racks along the walls contained sacks of flour, rice, pasta and sugar. There were cans of olive oil on the floor and stacks of things they could hardly identify in the darkness.

"My goodness gracious." Doris held onto the doorframe in disbelief. "It's been five years since the War and you have so much."

"Two people don't use that much and you learn to be frugal." At the doubting glances, she raised her hands in surrender. "Okay, so we stockpiled a few essentials and canned a lot of vegetables." Shooing them back out the door, she added, "There'll be plenty of time to see everything later. Let's get through the rest of the house now."

Flipping off the light, she directed the group to a door to the right of the stairs and entered the laundry room. She walked over to the circuit breakers. "Gather around, gang. Let me go over exactly what powers the house."

Jay waited while the group circled around her. Once they had stopped fidgeting and had fallen silent, she began to lecture. "I've got a 3,400-watt solar array on the roof that consists of six 24-volt direct current sub arrays." She pointed at a dial. "This indicates the power that is currently being consumed. Beside it is a digital readout of what is being generated by the photovoltaic panels on the roof."

Kicking a double line of car-sized batteries along the floor, she continued, "These twenty Delco batteries are attached to an equalizer that keeps the battery banks charged so that all the batteries have the same capacity." At their blank looks, she explained, "Running down the batteries shortens their life.

"With just Harmony and myself, the house used to average about 2000-kilowatt hours a day. At maximum efficiency, the system provides about 3,500-kilowatt hours a day." Jay smiled. "Now that there will be so many of us, I'm glad I oversized the system."

She opened the breaker box. "Each item is labeled with the amount of kilowatt-hours required once that breaker is engaged and all the items plugged into it are running. I've got a list here of what is currently using power." She unhooked a clipboard and calculator from a nail beside the breaker box. Flipping through the pages, she ticked off various items. "The upstairs fridge and the freezer are listed with steady watt use, see? I flip on the hot water heater in the morning and shut it off at night, so those numbers are added in." Jay waited until everyone had seen the figures.

She jerked her thumb at the digital readout. "Right now, the system is delivering 2,128 watts of continuous use, leaving us plenty of watts to play with. On a cloudy day, we might only be getting 1,000 watts. On such a day, using the washer would exceed our capacity."

"What do you do then?"

"Remember, we can subtract 60 once we turn off the light and maybe even turn off the freezers for a bit." She looked around to see if everyone was following her. "Before you turn on anything else, you have to do the numbers. Exceeding the base load is really, really bad. I can't stress that enough. We could lose what is in the cold cases." She hooked the calculator back on the wall. "Worse, we may never get the system back online again."

Piper flipped through the pages on the clipboard. "You can do all this with solar power?" she asked, hardly able to get her mind around what Jay was telling them.

"That and a well-designed house and energy-efficient appliances. Neat, huh?"

Cody asked, "What about during the winter?"

"As the days shorten, we won't be able to run as much. But I built the house so that the panels can be realigned to collect as much sun as possible and we have the benefit of the battery system to supplement our needs. In any event, you'll still be better off than you were." Wagging her finger at everyone, she sternly repeated, "Check the numbers before you turn on anything."

"Got it." Susan spoke for everyone when she added, "We never expected anything like this."

Jay laughed. "Darling, you haven't seen anything yet. I've got loads of tricks up my sleeve." She pointed at the numbers. "As we've still got several hours of daylight, I figure that we have enough power to run at least two loads of laundry through the wash and for everyone to shower. We'll have to hang everything to dry, but at least we don't have to wash by hand."

"Oh my goodness," Doris's voice was hoarse. "Are you sure you're not kidding us?"

"I have a sneaking suspicion that y'all wouldn't respond well to me pulling your leg. The system is everything I've said it is."

"I just can't believe it."

Martha ran her fingers over the dials. "We figured you were just surviving out here. I don't think anyone thought that you'd be living so well."

"You took a big risk coming out here in that case."

"Susan had faith that this was the place for us to come." Martha touched the back of her hand to Susan's cheek. "As usual she was right."

"We sure stepped through the right looking glass," Piper added.

"Nothing that fantastic. It was a simple matter to build around a worst-case scenario."

"I don't think anyone else on the planet planned so well for disaster." Her voice dry, Susan couldn't help but smile at her ex-lover.

"Hey, I tried to get you on board, but you thought I was a cockeyed pessimist."

"More like the boy who cried wolf."

"Just because Y2K was a bust and the Loma Prieta and Northridge quakes didn't shake your particular corner of the state doesn't mean that you were entirely safe," she chided Susan.

"Not the first time I was wrong."

Jay laughed, loudly. "Yeah, but I never tire of getting you to admit it." She put her hand on Martha's shoulder. "You can back me up on how nice that is, right?"

"No comment. You don't think I'm stupid enough to agree with you?"

"Coward." She went on her tiptoes to ruffle the taller woman's hair. "All right, let's go see what's upstairs." Leading the way back to the stairs, Jay stopped at a closet. "Oh, here are pretty extensive medical supplies. Does anyone have training in first aid?"

Martha nodded. "It was a while ago but both Piper and I are certified."

"Good. I've also got the army's *Combat Medic Field Reference* on disc upstairs. In case of a real emergency, anyone can follow directions and become a surgeon."

"I'm not so sure that I want any of you operating on me," Doris threw out.

Jay laughed. "Hey, when it comes down to the wire, I don't think I'll be concerned about checking qualifications."

Nodding, Susan agreed. "I wouldn't care if someone played connect the dots with my entrails as long I was still alive at the end of it."

"Hear, hear, love." Martha kissed her partner and looked over at her sister. "Don't worry, Doris. We'll respect your wishes to die from your injuries instead of receiving any amateur treatment." The two siblings stuck their tongues out at each other.

Leading them back upstairs, Jay opened the door next to the basement entrance. "Here is the first guest room on this level." Inside was a double bed and a desk with an extensive computer setup. "The Mac uses a lot of juice, so it should only be accessed on really sunny days or after you've turned off everything else."

"Why do we need to use it at all?" Martha asked.

"I've got a lot of reference manuals downloaded on it and on disc from before. I also use it to write."

Susan cocked her head. "You still working on the Great American Novel?"

Her cheeks reddened from embarrassment, Jay answered, "Just some journaling and the occasional short story. It feels good to be able to escape into the words sometimes."

Cody stepped into the room. "Is there Internet access?"

"Sorry, you won't be able to check in with any of your Facebook friends. The Internet might still be operating, but without a satellite connection, we're completely cut off out here."

She directed everyone to the next room. There was a queen bed against one wall and a couch along the window. Opening one of the closet doors, she revealed a television. "I've got a pretty good collection of videos and DVDs but, again, they should only be used on the sunniest of days or at night when we've turned everything else off and can expect a sunny day the next day."

In front of the entrance to the main floor bathroom was a circular staircase that led to the upper floor and Jay's attic hideaway. A large bed dominated the floor space there. A number of large windows gave the room plenty of light and all the available wall space was filled with built-in bookshelves. She showed them her small half bathroom and Franklin stove. "This room can be shut off from downstairs to help with the heating. You'd be surprised at how much heat the damn thing puts out."

Susan walked over to the bed. There were books and a half-filled glass of water on one nightstand, but the other one was clear of anything but a candle. Her brow furrowed, she asked, "Jay, where's Harmony?"

For a long moment, it didn't look like she was going to answer. When she did, her voice was hoarse. "She went to find her brother in Los Angeles."

"That's crazy. There's nothing left."

"At first we thought that too. When we went down the mountain to Willow Creek for spring trading there were about twenty refugees from Monrovia. She left to look."

"How long has she been gone?" Carol asked quietly.

"Almost nineteen months."

"You think she's coming back?" Doris's voice was derisive. "She's long dead by now."

Jay had Doris on the floor with her hands around the other woman's throat before anyone in the room could react. She shrugged off the attempts by Martha and Piper to pull her away. As Doris clawed at the fingers around her throat, Jay started to cry. With a final shove, she pushed the choking woman's head hard against the floor before standing up.

"If you want to stay here, you won't ever say anything like that again," Jay snarled. Without looking at anyone else in the room, she stomped down the stairs.

Susan and Eva helped to pick Doris up off the floor and support her while she tried to draw breath. Everyone was shocked by the suddenness of the attack.

"Easy, Mom." Eva led her mother to the bed and helped her to sit.

Cody spoke for all of them. "That was pretty scary."

"I don't know Jay at all, but I can't believe that's typical behavior." Piper crossed her arms and leaned against one of the windows.

"You're right. I've never known her to fly off the handle like that." Rubbing Doris's back, Susan didn't look at the group as she spoke. "What you said was very hurtful."

"That doesn't mean she should be allowed to hurt me!"

"Can you blame her for being upset?" Carol shouted. "Just think how scared she must be for Harmony. It must be driving her out of her mind."

Martha walked over and took Susan into her arms. "I don't think I would be able to stand it if I didn't know what was happening with you."

"She nearly killed me!" Doris was outraged at the lack of overt sympathy.

"You shouldn't have said what you did," Carol spat back, glaring at her. "You don't know anything."

"Oh, get real. You know I spoke the truth."

"No." Piper was adamant. "We don't know that. All of us have seen miracles of survival. None of us can say for sure that Harmony isn't on her way back here right now."

"For damn sure, until we do know, we can keep our mouths shut." There was no room for debate in Susan's voice. "I've put up with your prejudices because you're my partner's blood and I wanted there to be peace. Jay doesn't have any obligation to you and, if you want to stay, you should apologize."

"I will not."

"Then you stay as far from her as you can, and you keep quiet about things that don't concern you." Susan looked around. "I hope we can get past this because I don't want to leave."

Carol was crying. "I want to make a home here."

"I don't feel safe," said Doris.

"Then maybe you ought to leave," Susan snidely responded.

Cody crossed his arms over his chest. "Nobody is keeping you here."

"Everybody, just chill." Martha's voice was commanding. "I don't think we should let one incident drive a wedge between us all. Let us all take a deep breath and continue the tour without verbally or physically attacking one another. Okay?"

The group nodded and went back downstairs. When they rejoined her, Jay was standing staring into the empty fireplace. At the sound of their feet, she turned and wiped a hand roughly over her face. Swallowing, she said, "I apologize for losing my temper."

Susan touched her lightly on the arm. "Honey, no one wishes Harmony ill. We didn't know, and I'm sure Doris didn't mean anything by it."

The woman in question was dramatically rubbing her throat and coughing. She ignored Susan's significant look.

"My sister is a boor. I'm sorry she upset you. Don't hold the rest of us guilty for her foot in mouth disease," Martha added.

"I'll try not to let it happen again."

"Try?" asked Doris, hoarsely.

Jay glared at her. "Maybe there should just be some things that are off limits to discussion."

"We agree," Martha said quickly and then grinned at her sister. "Right?" After she received an answering nod, she asked Jay, "So where were we?"

"Pardon?"

"What else were you going to show us down here?"

Jay cleared her throat. She didn't meet anyone's eyes as she finished the tour. "Out here, we've got a sleeper sofa and two daybeds," she began, waving at the living room. "As you can see, there is plenty to read and a good-sized fireplace to keep the chill away." She indicated the walls of books. "Feel free to borrow anything that interests you. I've got a little bit of everything from general fiction, lesbian romance, politics, history, cookbooks, poetry and classics. There are also a lot of survival manuals in hard cover too."

She walked over to the dining area and leaned against the back of one of the eight chairs around the table there. She looked drained but made an effort to smile at the group. "Looks like we've finally got the perfect number for meals."

Piper pulled out a chair across from her and sank down into it. "It is sure going to be nice not to eat off our laps while sitting on the ground. I'm tired of roughing it."

"My idea of roughing it is going without hot water. That brings me to the final stops on the tour. Behind the staircase there is a bathroom with a shower and tub and over there is the kitchen. You should figure out where everyone is going to crash. Basement has two singles, up here are the two single daybeds and the sofa. In the first bedroom is a double bed and the second has the queen." Jay looked at the silent group. "How about you all talk it over and I'll start dinner?" Without waiting for an answer she escaped into the kitchen.

Stirring the coals in the stove, Jay added several pieces of wood before turning to fill a large Dutch oven with water, then filled the teakettle while she had the water running. Humming softly to herself, she reached to the back of the counter and pulled out a crock of sourdough starter. She took out a portion and deftly added flour, salt and olive oil to the bowl before she scooped a cup of water out of the pot. She went to the sink to wash her hands and began to knead the bread, stopping only when the kettle screamed.

Tapping her index finger to her upper lip, she selected a bag of mint tea and poured the water into a pitcher with the single bag. Jay returned to kneading until the dough was elastic. She then coated it with more olive oil, returned the ball to the bowl and set it to the side to rise. Muttering darkly over how few tomatoes were left, she chose several and set them near the green beans. Emptying her mind while her hands worked, she snapped the beans.

She glanced up when Susan came into the kitchen. "Do we have a solution?"

Susan nodded. "Yeah. Martha and I will take the queen. Doris will take the double, Carol and Eva will share the basement and Cody will take a daybed and Piper will take the sofa."

"Great." Jay swallowed. "Uh, Susan?"

"Yes?"

"I really am sorry about what happened up there. I don't know what came over me."

"You were scared, honey. It had to be appalling to hear your fears put into words." Susan came closer and pulled her ex-lover into a hug. "I believe that if it is at all possible that Harmony will come back to you."

"You really think so?"

"I do. I know that she loves you very much and that she knows that you love her."

"I miss her so much." Jay butted her head against Susan's shoulder.

"I bet you do. You've been alone a while."

"I've been fine."

"It must have been terribly lonely."

"Sometimes. I keep busy. There's nearly always something to do."

"Well, hopefully, we'll be able to take some of the burden off your shoulders." Susan kissed her forehead. "I also want you to know that you're not alone anymore."

"It may be hard to adjust."

"Let us help you." She squeezed Jay tightly and released her.

"Thank you."

"*De nada, chica*. We should be on our knees thanking you for letting us stay."

"I meant what I said. The offer is as good as the day I made it. This is your home too."

"Don't think we're not grateful."

"I don't. So why don't you all get settled in your space? There is time while the dough rises for you all to shower. It's a pretty large hot water heater, so if no one is too greedy you should all get at least a warm shower."

"Sounds divine. I'll tell them."

CHAPTER FIVE

One of the first ones out of the shower, Cody peered into the kitchen. His damp hair was plastered to his skull and he grinned at his honorary aunt. "What can I do to help?"

"You look like a drowned rat."

He looked wounded. "I combed my hair."

"But did you think of drying it?"

"The girls wanted the bathroom."

"Last time I checked, towels were portable."

"Whatever. Did you want some help or not?" he asked.

"Sure. You remember the secret room?"

"Through the pantry?"

"Yeah."

"Totally."

"Think you can get into it on your own?"

"I remember the rhyme—one if by land, two if by sea, six sets you free."

"Good for you. I've basically turned it into a wine cellar. Can you go down and bring us up a bottle?" She glanced at

Piper, who was taking the stones out of a handful of olives and chopping them. "You want to see something really cool?"

"Trust her, it's the bomb." Cody's voice broke on the final word and he blushed.

"With such a buildup, how could I refuse?"

Cody was nearly dancing in place. "Excellent, come into the pantry." He stood at her shoulder while she washed and dried her hands. "Come on."

"Hold your horses. I'm coming."

Practically dragging her into the small room at the end of the kitchen, he asked, "See anything out of the ordinary?"

Piper looked into the well-appointed pantry. Along each wall, from floor to ceiling, were wire shelves packed with brightly colored mason jars filled with different fruits and vegetables. She glanced at the tile floor and the back wall where a mop, a broom and other cleaning supplies hung. Having studied everything, she shrugged. "No. What's the big deal?"

The young man brushed by her and pulled a thin piece of metal wire out of a jar of junk on one of the upper shelves. Making a production of rolling back both sleeves, he went up to the back wall. Concentrating, he counted over two holes and then down six holes on the pegboard that covered the wall from floor to ceiling. Gently, he guided the wire into the sixth hole and pushed. He both heard and felt the click as the locking mechanism disengaged. Bending over he counted the same number of holes up from the bottom and side and repeated his motion with the wire. Stepping back, he laid his palms against the wall and, with a little pressure, a portion of the wall opened.

Piper gasped as a doorway appeared. The opening was completely dark. "You're right, that's pretty neat," she said, grinning at him.

"Oh, you haven't seen everything yet." Cody beamed at her. He looked around briefly before calling out to Jay, "Is there a flashlight, candles or something?"

Jay answered from the other room. "Feel around for a shelf about shoulder level on the left side. You'll find a couple of those forever lights."

"Forever lights?"

"They don't take batteries. You shake them to build up a charge."

"Oh." He felt around until he found two. "Got it." Cody shook one of the flashlights and handed the second to Piper. After thirty seconds of shaking, he turned his on to reveal a flight of stairs leading into the basement. "What kind of wine do you want? Red, white or sparkling?"

"It's after the apocalypse, boy. There aren't that many options." There was laughter in her voice. "Okay, okay. See if you can find a Shiraz."

"One bottle coming right up." He looked at Piper. "You want to see what's downstairs?"

"You bet I do," answered Piper. She followed him down the steep stairs to a fairly large room. She shone her light over the undecorated concrete walls. Directly under the stairs and behind a curtain, she saw a small sink and toilet. Next to the stairs, stacked floor to ceiling, were cases of prepackaged meals from military surplus. She hadn't been much of a fan of MREs when she was in the army, but the familiar packages were a comforting sight to see.

Along one wall were two pairs of bunk beds. Three beds high, she could see that at least six people could sleep comfortably in the room. Each bed was made up and had an extra blanket at the foot. The far wall was covered with a wine rack that was at least eight feet tall. "This is incredible," she whispered into the silence.

Cody had been watching her explore the space. He said, "When I saw that movie, *Panic Room*, I thought that Jody Foster had nothing on Jay."

"She had this built with the house?"

"Yeah, Jay's a little paranoid. She built this space back when everyone thought Y2K was something to worry about." He laughed as he shook the dimming flashlight back to full strength. "I think she was secretly a little bummed that nothing came of it." He walked over to the wine rack. "Let me grab a bottle."

Piper took the time while he searched to continue her study of the room. Completely self-contained, with water and food, it would enable someone to live down there for months. "You ever spend any time down here?"

"When we were kids, Mom used to ship us up here for part of the summer. We used to all come down here and tell ghost stories and eat that army surplus food."

"You mean Meals Ready-to-Eat."

"Whatever." He made a face. "Cheryl and Carol liked the grape Kool-Aid packs that came with them, but I never really cared for anything but the turkey dinner."

"I was partial to the spaghetti and meatballs."

"We only had to do it for one night per stay, so it wasn't so bad."

"Just think of having to live on them."

"Did you?"

"Sure. When we went out in the field, that was our only food."

"Too bad for you." Cody pulled out a couple of different bottles before selecting one. "Here we go." He raised the bottle and examined it by flashlight. "Cool, it's from Australia."

"Incredible. I can't even begin to imagine the amount of planning that must have gone into this." Piper murmured softly. "What a woman."

Cody led the way upstairs and carefully secured the door and returned the wire to the jar. He put the bottle on the counter and wiped his hands on his pants. "What now?" he asked Jay.

"How about you start collecting dirty clothes and separating the loads?" She smiled fondly as he bounded off. "Ah, to be young again."

"I don't know. I wouldn't do it if I had to live through high school again."

"Amen, sister." Jay handed the corkscrew and bottle to Piper. "Would you do the honors?"

"Of course."

"So," she began. "You used to work with Martha?"

"Yeah, we went to the academy together."

"Did you like being a cop?"

"Most of the time. I really enjoyed that it was a job that was both a physical and mental challenge. That's why I loved the army so much."

"Ooh rah."

"It's the marines who grunt like that!" Piper retorted.

"Sorry. What did you do in the army?"

"I was infantry for the most part. Did some time in the Special Forces."

"Any problems with your orientation?" Jay jerked her head up. "Sorry, you're just pinging my gaydar, so I figured."

"Oh, I'm bent all right. I had a few brushes with jackasses, but I mainly kept my head down. It was easy as I was single the whole time and never aspired to be a lifer."

"What have you been doing since the fall of the empire?"

Piper laughed. "I was a rent-a-cop."

"From all I've heard, that's a pretty dangerous thing to do."

"You're right on that. Defending the few haves against the starving have-nots wasn't really the way I wanted to go."

"What do you bring to the table?"

Piper tilted her head. "Excuse me?"

"Susan says you kept them in meat."

"I'm a good hunter. I've never farmed and fishing is boring."

"True, but fish are oh so tasty." She punched down the rising dough and molded it into two loaves before sliding them to the side to rise again before their trip into the oven. Jay checked the large pot of water and saw that it was boiling. She tossed in two boxes of pasta. "You ready for a new task?" she asked Piper.

"Whatever you need."

"In the fridge should be a paper bag of mushrooms. Get a couple handfuls and chop them up."

"Done." Piper took the mushrooms to the sink for a quick rub down. "What shall I do with the stems?"

"Put them in the bowl with the ends of the beans. When you go down to the garden tomorrow, you'll see the compost area."

"I can hardly wait," she said dryly.

Carol and Eva stepped into the kitchen. Carol hugged Jay. "It is wonderful to have hot water for a shower."

"Glad you enjoyed it. I'm proud to offer all the comforts of home."

Eva shook her head, whipping dark strands of hair around. "Better than home or at least what was left after the crazy Christians were done," she said angrily.

"Well, you're safe here now. Make yourself comfortable."

"Do you need us to do anything?"

"Would you set the table? There are plates in the sideboard and utensils in the drawer."

"No problem."

Jay smiled her thanks as she slid the sliced and cored heritage tomatoes under the broiler for a quick roasting. When they were done, she put the risen loaves of dough in the oven. Pulling out a skillet, she drizzled in some olive oil, some minced garlic and the green beans. She sautéed the ingredients for a few minutes before tossing the tomatoes and chopped olives into the skillet.

The group of refugees were milling about, so she had them pour water and iced tea for those that wanted it and red wine for the adults. She strained the pasta and put it back in the pot and poured the contents of the skillet into the mix. Jay had Susan stir everything together and take it to the table while she pulled the bread out of the oven.

Taking the empty pasta pot, she filled it with water and put it back on the stove for the water to heat during the meal for them to have to wash dishes afterward.

Once everyone was seated and served, Jay raised her glass. "I'd like to propose a toast." The lifted glasses of the diners sparkled and refracted the rich, red wine. "To new beginnings."

"Hear, hear."

Susan lifted her glass again. "To prior planning. You're a lifesaver."

Inclining her head, Jay accepted the accolade. "I'm glad you all finally made it up here."

"Better late than never."

"Too true. I hope your sojourn here is peaceful, and you all find what you need to flourish."

"Just looking at the meal before us, and I can tell you that we're already so much better off," responded Martha.

"Good. Why don't we all dig in?"

For a while, the house was quiet except for the sound of silverware on plates and appreciative moans. Once the first hunger pangs were assuaged, Jay asked the group, "So, what's new to report?"

"Do you have any idea where we're coming from?" Doris asked.

"I've heard stories. After the attacks, I went to Sacramento to see if I could help." She shuddered. "Things were bad, but there was still stuff available. I made a couple of trips to bring more supplies up and I haven't been more than fifty miles from here since." Jay twisted the stem of her wineglass in her fingers. "What about you all?"

Martha nodded her head. "Sacramento was hit pretty bad but nothing like San Francisco. The militia targeted it as the new Sodom and basically wiped it off the map."

"I haven't heard anyone making it past Daly City since the bombing, and with all the bridges out there is no other way in but boat," Piper added.

"How about your area?"

"We were pretty lucky," said Piper. "Oakland only took a couple of hits. The problem was that the port received the brunt of the bombing."

"Even without the trade sanctions imposed by Japan, there was no way for supplies get ashore."

"Japan?" Jay asked. "I heard about Canada and Mexico closing their borders, but I didn't know that anyone else was against us."

Doris's voice was strident. "Everyone is against us."

"Yeah, seems Japan didn't take particularly kindly to a tidal wave destroying Osaka." Wiping her mouth, Martha added,

"But it's not like they're alone. The international community was not well pleased about the UN building taking a direct hit."

"How could they tell? I thought New York City was carpet bombed."

"It was pretty much leveled, but I understand that those who know can tell. It wasn't an accident what was targeted."

"The fact that we've been isolated is why there's been no significant recovery." Susan drained her wineglass. "The Confederacy managed to alienate the entire world. There was a lot of nongovernmental aid in the first years, but we all know how much humanitarian assistance was being financed by US dollars. Without cash, there's no help."

Piper added, "The world economy may never recover from the financial market crash."

"So I can finally get rid of my paper stocks?"

"It's not a joke," Doris replied tartly. "The New York Stock Exchange, NASDAQ, the Chicago Mercantile Exchange, the American Stock Exchange are all gone."

"A lot of worldwide banks were based in US cities. I guess the lessons of 9/11 didn't sink in so well because when the bombs fell, the banks collapsed."

"Do you know how many regimes around the world depended on our money for survival? We heard that most of Africa and South America have fallen into conflict."

"Of course, it doesn't help that Fort Knox is under Confederacy control." Carol spoke up for the first time since the conversation turned serious.

Cody burped, looked apologetic and interjected, "Yeah, who knew they'd be stupid enough to try and link their new currency to the gold standard."

"What do you know of monetary policy, cub?" Jay asked with a smile.

"Enough to know that William Jennings Bryant was right not to tie us to an impossible standard."

Martha interrupted, "In any event, we haven't even gotten to the human cost of the war."

"I never expected that Doctors Without Borders would ever be needed in our country," Piper said in a low voice. "And then they had to withdraw when the Confederacy threatened to extend their targets outside of the country."

"Can they do that?"

"You bet. They've got more than just what the bases had." Martha looked disgusted. "They've got control of the ICBMs and you know that no one wants to take on maniacs with nuclear weapons at their fingertips."

"We're a rogue country now. No one wants anything to do with us."

"Frankly, I always wondered why we're not occupied."

"What do you mean?"

Jay shrugged. "Why haven't Confederacy troops appeared on the horizon? We've got no way to stop them, no outside allies, nothing at all to even slow them down."

"I heard that they accomplished what they wanted." Piper played with the salt and pepper shakers. "They wanted to create a pure, Christian land. The bombings weren't to soften us up for their missionaries. They were to form a moat along each coast. A boundary for their complete and total isolation from the mud people and degenerates of the world."

"That does make a certain, perverted sense." Jay nodded as she drained her glass of wine.

"But why?" Eva was nearly in tears. "What did we do to them?"

"Our very being threatened them, honey." Martha opened her arms and allowed her niece to climb onto to her lap and into her embrace. "They wanted so badly to have right on their side, and when we wouldn't accept that or their vengeful god, they decided that we shouldn't be allowed to live."

"But we wouldn't have done anything to them."

"That's the downside of tolerance, Eva. When your opponent isn't bound by the same sense of fairness and acceptance, you are at a decided disadvantage. For all their talk, they certainly didn't do what Jesus would have done."

"Why can't it be like it was?" Carol cried out. "Why did Cheryl and Mr. Matlan and all the others have to die?"

"I can't explain it because even I don't understand it. We just have to go on from here." Susan spoke soothingly to her daughter.

"Maybe we should find something else to talk about," Doris said. "It's too upsetting."

Susan looked around the table of clean plates and empty bowls. "That was a great meal, Jay. Sorry we ruined it with all the depressing talk."

"Yeah, thanks for what you're doing for us," Piper added.

"You're welcome. I'm glad everyone enjoyed it. I have to say that I don't think open discussion is a bad thing." Jay rubbed her eyes. "When I was growing up, we used to come close to blows at meals. It might not have been the best thing for our digestion, but I'm better for having taken part in regular discussions about the events and issues of the day."

Piper nodded. "I agree. We've got a chance here to start our own traditions. I'd like for mealtime to be a place to share anything."

"Well, I don't want my daughter in tears at every meal."

"Mom," whined Eva. "It's hardly likely that every meal will make me cry."

"I think that everyone is tired and emotional after the journey. Why don't we table the discussion until everyone has had a chance to regain some equilibrium?" asked Martha.

All around the table, heads nodded in agreement. Jay smiled. "Excellent. Now, why don't the kids take the first turn at dish washing?"

"I second that motion," Martha quickly said.

"And how about the adults follow me outside? I want to show you another perk of this place."

Intrigued, the four women trailed behind Jay through the French doors to the patio. She walked to the side of the building and pointed at a large shape.

Piper was the first to speak. "Is that what I think it is?"

"Yep." Jay walked over and lifted the lid. "One genuine California hot tub, at your service."

"Unbelievable."

"I've got a special enzyme concoction that keeps the water soft and clean naturally and lasts for a super long time. Those solar panels over there collect enough energy to power the heater and the air pump." She turned and faced the group. "The big rule is that you have to shower before getting in. The system works better if no body oil or soil makes it into the water. And definitely no peeing in the tub!" Cocking her head at the kitchen window, she added, "I also think we need to have a clothing rule with the youths around."

"Agreed. There are some things that Cody doesn't need to see."

"What are we to wear?"

"T-shirts and shorts should do it." Jay set the lid back down. "I'm going to turn in, but feel free to use it before y'all head to bed."

With a smile and a wave, she walked back inside to a chorus of "Goodnights."

CHAPTER SIX

The household woke in the morning to the scent of fresh-baked bread. Almost as one, the travelers crawled out of their beds and followed their noses to the dining room.

Turning the corner out of the kitchen, Jay smiled at the tousled heads and sleepy eyes of her new household. She held out a jar of blackberry jam and a jar of honey. "Here are the spreads to go with the biscuits I made," she said, pointing at a towel-covered wicker basket.

"Wow," Cody enthused as he threw himself into a chair. With gusto, he smeared jam on the still warm bread and stuffed more than half of it into his mouth. "Dude, this is really good," he said, spraying crumbs.

The women acted less like starving wolverines but were no less eager to eat the hot biscuits. Moaning in pleasure, the group inhaled the contents of the basket in record time. Jay laughed at the worried looks that were shot her way when the basket became empty.

Walking back into the kitchen, she pulled out a second tray of biscuits and slid them off into the basket. She put it on the table and quickly stepped back. Ostentatiously counting her fingers to make sure they were all still attached, she invited, "Try the honey. It's from very local bees."

"How local?"

"Over on the other side of the pond."

"You've got beehives?" Eva asked.

"Yup. At the end of the month would you like help me prepare the hives for winter?"

"Sure. That would be so cool."

"Where did you get the jam?"

"There's a guy farther up the mountain who puts it up. I never had the patience to stand out there collect enough berries to make jam." Jay ate a biscuit. "Though, to be honest, if I didn't eat so much while I'm picking, I'd probably have plenty."

Jay was sitting at the head of the table, and she looked out over her new household. "How did everyone sleep?" Following the positive chorus, she stuck her finger in the honey pot and licked it off. "Feel free to switch around, there are plenty of places to crash."

"Having a bed at all is wonderful," replied Susan. "We've been on the road almost two months and, before that, living out of the only two undamaged rooms in our old house. We are used to sleeping on floors and the ground."

"Well, I'd be happy to scrounge up some rocks to toss between the sheets."

"No thanks."

Martha pursed her lips. "The luxury of it all is delightful after all we've been through."

"I think you might be amazed at how quickly you fall back into the habits of civilized life."

Piper nodded. "We'll be spoiled in no time."

"We deserve some spoiling after the last few years." Doris set her mug down sharply. "You might have been living rather well up here, but it's been horrible for us."

"At least you have your health." Jay smiled to take the sting out of her words. "Millions lost their lives, you didn't. You've made it safely here, enjoy the peace."

"I don't appreciate you making jokes of our suffering."

"I'm just saying that things have been tough all over."

"Not here."

"I'd be the first person to call our isolation a blessing." She raised a hand against Doris's interruption. "I also would defend my level of comfort because I was smart enough to plan for disaster."

"Well, forgive us for not predicting the future."

"In any event," interjected Martha, "we're here now." She looked around the table. "You said something last night about what we need to do. Why don't we discuss a plan?"

Susan agreed. "Good idea. We need to know what to do first."

"Well, as I see it, we've got a couple of priorities. The first one is getting more wood chopped. I had more than enough for me to make it through next year. But now we'll need a lot more just to make it through the winter."

Doris asked, "Why?"

"The stove is a wood hog. Cooking and heating for an additional seven people takes more than doing the same for one."

"How much more?"

"Three or more cords."

"That's a lot." Martha scratched her chin. "Will it have time to season?"

"I took down a couple of trees that I was planning to leave for another month or two. They won't be completely dry, but it's what we've got to work with."

"How do we get it here?" Carolyn asked.

"Working together we can just go up and fetch them down. Teamwork and all that jazz will make quick work of getting a log from Point A to Point B. Once it's in the yard, we'll have a good old-fashioned chopping party." She pushed her plate back. "How are y'all with an ax?"

Susan looked around. "I think everyone should take a turn. This is all fairly new to us."

Flexing his bicep, Cody declared, "I was born to wield an ax."

"That's fine, sweetheart. It will be good for everyone to give it a try. While I think we should find our own comfort level, we all need to learn the basics."

"Everyone agree to that?" There are nods around the table. "That brings me to the second point. Food."

Doris crossed her arms over her chest. She asked, "Don't you have plenty downstairs?"

"Not if you want well-balanced nutrition. Most of what's stored is staples and canned vegetables. We need protein in the form of meat and that means hunting and fishing."

"I saw several deer on our way up here," Piper interjected.

"Yeah, the herds have really made a comeback. You won't have to go too far to get a good buck or two. Of course, there are more things with meat that don't have hooves. There are fish and birds and other animals. I've got some snares and traps in the basement that I haven't used in a while. I've also got fishing supplies." Jay turned to Martha. "Am I right in remembering that you used to fish?"

Martha grinned. "Oh, yeah. I really like fly fishing."

"Excellent. I've got several rods and reels in the closet. Check them out and see if they are good to go."

"And if they're not?"

"We'll base the trip to the river on the number of complete sets we've got. With a little cobbling and disassembly, we should have enough for a successful jaunt."

"When do you think we should go?"

"The sooner the better. How about in a couple of days for a fishing trip?"

"That shouldn't be a problem."

"Hold on," Doris exclaimed. "Why the rush? We're all exhausted and need to take it easy for a while."

"Because we need to take advantage of the good weather. It'll be getting colder soon and food will get harder to find."

"I don't see that a couple of days will mean starvation come winter," Doris whined.

"Don't worry, you don't need to kill yourselves. Believe me when I tell you that with everyone's cooperation, I think you'll be working less than you did to survive in Oakland."

Martha added, "I think I speak for everyone when I say let's err on the side of caution. I definitely want to have more food than we need, and we can always stop hunting and fishing when we reach storage capacity."

"Agreed." It was only one word from Piper, but the glare she shot across the table at Doris was unmistakable.

"In that case, I'll take you down and show you a good spot. There's also a smoker near the camping area, so you can stay down until you get a good haul."

Martha nudged her lover and waggled her eyebrows. Susan coughed and said, "I volunteer Martha and myself to be the adults who go fishing."

"Oh, I suppose you think a little holiday is in order?" Piper laughed. "Have we been cramping your style?"

"Stop it." Susan's blush covered her face and neck. "New topic. What are we going to do today?"

"I figure that Doris is right that you all could use an easy couple of days." Everyone nodded gratefully. "There is still the rest of the tour to get through too."

"You've got more than what we've already seen?"

"We didn't do the outside. There's the garden, greenhouse and the rest of the land. If everyone is done with breakfast, why don't y'all come with me down to the garden?"

With universal agreement, they formed a procession, walking out the back doors to the edge of the cliff. On the way out, Jay picked up a plastic container of kitchen waste to add to the compost pile. She set it in a small box that sat on rails on the top of the cliff. She then pulled off the tarp that was covering an old exercise bicycle. The chain from it was attached to a pulley that in turn was attached to the cart.

"What's that for?" Susan asked for them all.

"I don't know about you, but I figured that hauling all the veggies up those stairs was too much work." She stood near the crumbling edge and pointed to the rails that led down to the base. "It takes a bit of leg power, but you basically pedal the cart up the rails."

Jay led the group down the steep stairs that were cut into the cliff face. At the bottom of the stairs was a large open plot surrounded by a fence. "The only real problem I've had is with deer. I put the fence up to discourage them from eating all my hard work."

"Can anyone see it?"

"No. This part of the mountain is far enough from the road and inaccessible enough that it's pretty secure. You have to be higher than us to see it and the next closest mountain is too far away."

"It looks safe," said Doris.

"It also gets southern exposure." Jay waved them forward to the first of the rows. "That way, we can have two good seasons of crops from here. I was alone this past year, so I only did one planting." She pointed to a hose. "I even put in an irrigation system from the creek on the other side of the house." At everyone's look of amazement, she grimaced. "Just count yourselves lucky that you missed the fun of hauling and laying pipe by hand."

She began to walk the end of the rows, gently touching leaves as she passed. "We've only got a few plants that are still producing. In the next months we'll need to haul a few loads of compost and turn the soil over to rest for the winter."

Turning back to the cliff face, she moved over to a tall, square box. It was painted camouflage to resemble the lichen-covered rock. She knocked on the side and smiled at her audience. "I bet you're wondering what this is?" After receiving nods, she opened the door to reveal a short, wide toilet. "It's a new generation outhouse."

"What do you mean?"

"It's a carousel composting toilet. Four composting chambers rotate as each chamber is filled. With the power from the solar panel on the roof, it warms the waste and, with a little help from some microbes, turns it into a rich mulch." She opened one of the chambers and pulled out a spoonful. "Dry, fluffy and odorless. Great, huh?"

"Is this what is up at the house?" The look of distaste on Doris's face was almost comical.

"No, those are part of a low-flow system with two flush options. For liquid waste, you get half the water as when you flush solids." She put her hands on her hips. "Don't get me wrong, we had originally planned on incorporating this system everywhere but, as it was, we didn't get around to installing them. Trust me, we have a pretty advanced septic system that requires very little maintenance." Jay looked around at everyone. "Hey, I thought you'd be pleased that you didn't have to climb all the way back to the house if you needed to go. This outhouse is damn convenient and incredibly efficient."

"Yes, it's wonderful all right." Susan tried to sound enthusiastic.

"I can't believe you guys. What system were you using back at home?"

"Stinky, smelly outhouses," Cody answered for everyone.

"This is so much better, right?"

"It is. It's just the reality of still having to handle our waste that is hard to get our minds around," Susan replied diplomatically.

"It was so much easier when we could just flush."

"Unfortunately, Doris, we no longer have the benefit of a sewage treatment plant to handle it for us," Jay answered. "At least with this system, our impact on the environment is minimized."

"I guess." Doris didn't look convinced.

"I told you it wouldn't take you long to get spoiled." Jay rapped her knuckles on the outbuilding. "By the time you actually handle this stuff, it is quite a distance from actually playing with poop."

"And remember," Carol and Cody said in unison, "everybody poops."

Everyone laughed at the potty-training reference and Jay stepped away from the port-a-john. She walked over to an overhang area of the cliff and indicated that the group should follow her. When she got to the rock, they saw a recessed door in the shadows. Opening it, she showed them the shed that had been built into a shallow cave. Inside were floor-to-ceiling gardening and farm tools. There were scythes, rakes, shovels, hoes, augers and a number of unidentifiable things.

Cody pushed a wheeled machine with one finger. "What's this?"

"It's a seeder that opens the soil and drops the seeds a set distance apart. Works great for long rows so you don't have to spend all your planting time on your knees."

"Where did you get all this stuff?" Martha explored the packed shed. "I've never even seen half of these things."

"All I can say is thank goodness for the Amish and Mennonites. I found a number of companies aimed for that niche market who still made things that don't require any gas or electricity. I stocked up well before things came to a head."

"You knew this was going to happen?" Doris's tone was derisive.

"Actually, I thought a massive earthquake was far more likely. I did think that the direction the country was going was worrisome, but who knew that anyone was crazy enough to launch a sneak attack against the blue states?" She opened up a five-gallon container to reveal a bunch of cotton gloves. She handed out pairs to everyone. "How about we pick everything that is ripe? Tomorrow we should go ahead and can as much as possible."

The group spread out over the rows and quickly filled up the baskets. They were all sweaty and dirt-smudged by the time they loaded the last basket into the cart. Jay sent Cody up to pedal the cycle to pull the cart up the hill. He was huffing when Piper made it to the top to relieve him.

Once everyone made it topside, they divided up the load of vegetables and carried the produce up into the house. Jay made them another salad for the midday meal.

After lunch, they walked around the pond. Martha tossed a couple of pebbles into its brown water. "How deep is it?"

"It's just a little over my head in the center."

"Are there any fish?"

"No, it really isn't healthy enough to support life." Jay widened her eyes. "That's an idea, though. Any of you know anything about water gardens?"

"Nope," answered Martha.

"It might behoove us to learn, although I've always just enjoyed floating on the water."

She led them over to an oddly shaped building on the other side of the pond. Surrounded on three sides by trees, it looked like a large golf ball partially sunk into the ground.

Opening the door into the geodesic dome, Jay held it for everyone to enter. The temperature inside was slightly higher than it was outside. Bracketing the door were two trees. Around the outer edge were raised beds, with a range of plants in various stages of growth. The center area looked like an island with six seven-foot tall trees surrounded by a moat. Floating around the island were several sizes of plastic yellow ducks. While Jay waited for everyone to finish exploring, she pulled one of the ducks out of the water and made it squeak several times before replacing it.

Leaning her foot on a pipe that trickled water into the tank, she began speaking. "Water flows down from the stream in pipes. I buried the pipes about a foot deep but they're made of polyethylene, so they can freeze and thaw without rupturing. The water flows into this moat and the water mass helps to maintain an even temperature year-round."

She walked over to one of the walls and thumped it with one finger. It sounded like a drum beat. "The polycarbonate panels only let diffuse light into the dome. That means that it rarely overheats. There are solar-powered vents for when it gets too hot. It basically works like a chimney. The bottom vents open to let in cooler air and the roof ones release the hot air." She pointed her thumb outside. "The trees I planted around it are deciduous, so they lose their leaves in the winter and let the dome get more of the available sunlight."

"That means you can grow stuff year-round, right?" Piper was sitting on the bridge that led across to the island and trailing her fingers through the water.

"Yeah, that's why the beds are raised." Jay bent down and opened up one of the panels. She pointed at the pipes that disappeared to run under the dirt. "There is an exhaust fan that blows warm air through the pipes to keep the soil warm."

Cody stepped over Piper to walk around the island. He reached up and pulled a lime off one of the trees. "Is this what I think it is?"

"You betcha." She grinned at them. "I thought that living in California meant that everyone got their own citrus trees. I was shocked to learn that they couldn't grow up here. I decided not to accept that and researched until I found a way to circumvent geography. I've got two Satsuma, two lemon and two lime. They're a hybrid dwarf variety, so that is as tall as they'll grow."

"How much do they produce?"

"Not much fruit yet, but I have high hopes."

"What are these trees?" Standing by the entrance, Susan shook the trunk of a tree that was almost twice her height with oval dark green leaves.

"Those are avocado." She held her hands up, surrendering to their stares of disbelief. "A girl can hope, can't she?"

Martha asked, "What else can you grow in this place?"

"Year-round I've got herbs growing in here. See those boxes there against the north wall? That's basil, parsley, sage, rosemary, dill, mint and oregano. In summer, I grow stuff that needs a hotter environment like beans, peppers, more tomatoes, cucumbers and edamame. In winter, I primarily grow onions, garlic, broccoli and lettuce."

"I'm floored at the variety," Martha mused. "I never had a clue what you had going up here."

"Oh, and I've got some mushrooms going, but I get most of them wild."

Susan shook her head as she took a circuit of the dome. "I'm noticing a pattern here. Where're the rest of them?"

"What do you mean?"

"You never were much of a vegetable eater and I don't see that you're growing anything you don't like." Susan put her hands on her hips. "Fess up, Jay."

"So there aren't any carrots, spinach, collards or peas. No big deal."

"Do you have seeds for them?"

"Well, duh. She could reseed the garden of Eden, right, Jay?" Doris asked sarcastically.

"Actually I do. There are jars of seeds up at the house."

"Why?" asked Piper.

"Why what?"

"It sounds like you don't particularly care for any other vegetables. Why would you have them?"

"Because I always knew that someday I'd get called out on my selection. Besides, I wouldn't want to disappoint the nutrition police." She smiled at Susan. "Come springtime you can plant what you want. Even beets."

"I'll hold you to that."

"I said I'd let you plant them. Nothing was said about me eating any of it," warned Jay.

Laughing easily and teasing one another, the group continued to talk as they walked back to the house to start dinner preparations.

CHAPTER SEVEN

Doris appeared in the kitchen late the next morning, wiping her brow. "Where is everybody?"

"They're out and about," answered Jay. "The morning is almost over and you're the last one up."

"Why is it so hot in here?"

"I've got the wood stove fired up."

"What's going on?"

"I'm just gearing up for some canning." Jay finished filling another pot with hot water and placed it on the stove. "Since you're here, you get to help."

"Why me?"

"Martha and Piper have already left to gather some firewood, and Susan is collecting herbs. You snooze, you lose."

"What are the kids doing?"

"They're out swimming. No reason to trap them in this steam room."

"But it's fine for us?"

"Sure. We're real women." Jay flexed liked a body builder.

"I guess."

"If you want to eat, you'll help." Jay's voice was sharp.

"Wonderful. Do I at least get breakfast first?"

"If you can eat it on the fly. As you can see, I've covered the table with canning necessities."

Doris walked over to the table and lifted an empty jar out of a box of empty jars. The tabletop was nearly covered with boxes of quart jars and lids. Putting the jar back down, she opened up a large paper bag. She stirred the band rings inside and asked, "What do we need all this stuff for?"

"We've got to put up the vegetables we took out of the garden yesterday."

"It has to be done now?"

Jay suddenly appeared behind her. At Doris's startled squeak, she grinned, "Now's as good a time as any." She handed her a jar of honey and the basket of biscuits. "Not much but it should take the edge off."

Doris sat down heavily and pushed some jars out of her way. She flipped the towel off the basket. "I can't believe this is all that's left."

"Next time get up earlier."

"This is the first chance I've had to sleep in forever."

"You slept later than everyone else, so don't bitch about the chore choice or lack of breakfast."

Doris glared up at her as she stuffed part of a honey-covered biscuit into her mouth. "So rude," she mumbled under her breath. Louder she asked, "Is there any tea?"

"You can scoop some water out of one of the pots, if you want. It's clean and boiling."

"What about the teapot?"

"There isn't space on the stove for it right now."

"I get the feeling that there would be space if I was someone else."

"Since you're not, I guess we'll never know the accuracy of that." Jay cracked her knuckles. "Hurry up. We've got a ton of washing to do."

"Give me a minute."

"The clock is ticking." Jay went back into the kitchen and began sorting the vegetables out onto the counter. She hummed "You Are My Sunshine" to herself as she waited for Doris to join her.

Finishing off the final biscuit, Doris returned to the kitchen. She put the basket with the others over the stove and shook the towel out in the sink. "Now what?"

"To start with, we've got to think clean. None of us can afford a case of food poisoning. We've got to wash the vegetables and sterilize all the supplies. That will be your job."

Doris huffed dramatically before beginning to wash.

Susan came in with a basket of basil. "Morning, Doris. Here, Jay. I cut almost all of it."

"Great." Taking the basket, Jay dumped the contents into a colander and tried to hand it to Doris.

"What do you want me to do with that?"

"Just rinse it."

"I'm not done with washing the tomatoes."

"You can interrupt the process to run that under the faucet."

With bad grace, she took the colander. "What do we need so much for?"

"It'll be packed with the tomatoes," replied Jay. "I did plain tomatoes earlier in the season."

"So what's the plan?" Susan asked.

"Well, we need to pressure cook the green beans and get the skin off the tomatoes. I'll make a sauce with half the tomatoes and we'll can the rest."

"What about the peppers?"

"There'll only be enough to add to the sauce and for dinner tonight." Jay wiped her hands. "Could you take the ends off the beans?" she asked Susan.

"No problem."

"Once you've done so, you can pack the beans into the clean jars. And I mean pack. They need to be in there pretty tightly, as they're going to shrink." Filling a large bowl with cold well water for shocking, Jay began to blanch the tomatoes.

Doris finished washing and paring the vegetables. Standing behind Jay, she tapped tentatively on the still warm glasses. "These look dry."

Jay glanced over. "Good. Now run your fingers across the top to make sure there aren't any chips."

"I could get cut."

"Not likely. If you don't do it, you're more likely to get sick from food poisoning."

"From a chip?"

"From the air that gets in through the space. That's why you have to pack them tightly. You can't give air and the bugs who live in it any room."

"These are all fine."

"Great. Pass them on to Susan and you can start peeling the tomatoes. Put twenty-four in that bowl there and then hand me the rest for stuffing into jars."

Jay turned back to the stove and put the pressure cooker on the open burner. Adding a little bit of water, she waited until it began to boil before she started taking the green bean jars and loading them in.

"I remember my grandmother boiling the jars to seal them." Susan chewed thoughtfully on a basil leaf. "I don't think I've ever seen a pressure cooker in action."

"We'll boil the tomatoes and sauce."

"Why not for everything?"

"Safety reasons. Open kettle cooking doesn't get hot enough for the beans."

"What do you mean?"

"Water boils around two hundred degrees. Steam gets much hotter. High acid foods like tomatoes already make it hard for any germs that make it through the heat to get a foothold. In low acid foods like the beans, the environment is ripe for germs to have a field day."

"Why don't you just do everything the hottest way?"

"Because heat kills flavor." Jay wiped her face on a hand towel. "Did you ever walk away from a pot of green beans on the stove and come back to most of the water gone and the damn things limp as a noodle?" she asked. "That's what would happen if we boiled everything."

"This is so much work!" Doris complained. "Can't we freeze them or something?"

"The freezer space is pretty finite. What room we've got needs to be saved for whatever game we can get."

"Can't you can meat?"

"Not easily."

"So what do you do with it?"

"Smoke, salt or freeze it. And we don't have enough salt to spare."

"I'm ready for a new task."

Jay handed Susan a knife that she first dipped into the boiling water. "Chop four onions and three green peppers."

"What for?" asked Doris.

"Look, I'm getting pretty tired of having to explain myself to you." She poked Doris in the chest. "I wasn't even talking to you."

"I was just asking a question."

"Why can't you just do what I ask?"

"Why can't you just answer the question?"

Susan stepped closer. "Jay, give her a break. You know that you wouldn't want to do something without finding out why first."

"I know, I know. I guess I've been on my own for too long."

"Your manners certainly show that," responded Doris nastily.

Jay threw her hands up. "I was trying to apologize."

"Doris sometimes doesn't know when to give it a rest."

"Hey!" Doris exclaimed. "Stop insulting me."

Susan shrugged. "It's true and you know it. Now, how about we all take a deep breath and finish this task so we can go outside where it's cool."

"Fine with me."

"Agreed." Turning to the pressure cooker, Jay placed a rocker over the steam coming out of the vent on the top.

"What are you doing now?"

"I wanted to make sure that the cooker was filled with steam. That gauge keeps the pressure steady at ten pounds."

"Don't those things explode?"

"That's why the gauge is on. It will keep the contents at a certain poundage of pressure. If things get too hot, the steam will blow the gauge off and release the steam."

"So it's safe?" Doris was still standing well away from the stove.

"Completely." Jay looked over and saw that Susan had diced almost all the ripe tomatoes and peppers. "You can chop the green tomatoes."

"And then?"

"Tossed with vinegar and some spices, we'll have the perfect sauce for pouring over rice, beans or pasta." While she was talking, she was taking the bottles of tomatoes that Doris had packed and putting them in the pot of boiling water.

Susan called, "Everything is chopped."

"Okay." Checking her watch, she moved the pressure cooker away from the stove.

"Now what?"

"We wait for it to cool on its own. When you can take the gauge off and no steam escapes, then the lid can come off and the jars can be taken out." Jay went over to the door and picked up a couple pieces of firewood. She slid them into the firebox and stepped back to the door. "Man, this place is a sauna."

"How many times a season you do this?"

"Three or four for the veggies." Jay wiped her face. "Since Harmony went south, I haven't planted as much. We can do a lot more with more bodies."

"You do anything else?"

"We'll be pickling the last of the cucumbers shortly. And we can plan on jam making next year."

"Do you sun dry or dehydrate anything?"

"Sun drying takes too long." Jay rotated her shoulders, trying to work out some of the strain. "And I hate picking out the bugs from the tomatoes when they make it past the screens." She smiled at Doris's look of disgust. "I do dry mushrooms and herbs over the stove. I've got a dehydrator if anyone wants to make jerky."

"Mushrooms?"

"Sure. I've got some growing in the greenhouse, but there are a lot of wild mushrooms that I pick when I'm out wandering."

"Is that safe? I mean, I've heard such bad things about mushrooms."

"Oh, Doris. Where is your sense of adventure? I pick only what I know is safe."

"How do we know that you know what you're doing?"

"I'm still alive, for one thing. I've got field guides to mushrooms, if you'd like to confirm it yourself." Jay smiled. "Of course, some of the descriptions are ambiguous. I guess that you'll have to stay on my good side to avoid getting poisoned."

"I don't find that very funny."

"You wouldn't."

"Where do you go when you wander?" asked Susan, trying to redirect the conversation. "Is there much to see and do?"

"Mainly around the mountain. I like to know what's going on around the place. I go up to see the neighbors sometimes and see what trees are ready to come down."

"Are we going to meet these people?"

"Eventually."

"Why not now? Are you ashamed of us?" Doris accused.

"Not at all. But with the fishing trip planned for tomorrow, introductions will have to take a backseat." Jay pushed off from the door and came back to the stove. "It isn't something we can rush. Most of the people came out here years before the Cleansing to get away from everything rotten out there. They were off the grid long before it became fashionable and don't take kindly to strangers, especially when those strangers haven't proven themselves." Taking a pair of tongs, she began lifting jars of tomatoes from the pot to the towel. Lightly touching each lid, she felt to see if a seal had been made. Nodding to herself in satisfaction, she was startled when Doris spoke.

"Don't you people look out for each other?"

"To an extent, yes. The first rule out here is to take care of yourself first. I can afford to be a lot more generous than the rest of my neighbors because I had the funds to stockpile supplies for all occasions. The rest of these guys are certainly better off than those in the big cities because of the abundance of natural resources, but they would be careful about sharing with people they don't know."

"They know you."

"And it took me almost three years after I first started building up here to get any of them to say more than 'hello' to me. They didn't respect me until I'd been up here for a full year and showed I was capable of surviving."

"What happens when you run low on supplies?" Susan asked.

"You do without. You don't go knocking on their door for a cup of sugar."

"What about emergencies?"

"We help each other when we can. Just last month, I had to give the last of my Tylenol Three with codeine to Carlos after his wife got all tore up from a breech birth. Knock on wood we don't have any emergencies of our own until we can restock." Jay finished testing the last of the bottles and looked around. "Any other questions?"

Cody popped his head around the corner and asked, "The girls sent me to ask what's for lunch?"

"Well, I figure dinner will be venison and mushroom-stuffed peppers, so lunch should be lighter. Maybe rice and beans?"

"All right." Cody disappeared as quickly as he came.

"You going to help with lunch?"

Sighing, Doris asked, "What do you need me to do?"

Jay handed her a mixing bowl. "Downstairs there are several five-gallon buckets. The content labels are on the lids. Bring up about five cups of black beans." She stirred the pot of vegetarian chili for a moment before getting another pot and filling it halfway with water. Placing it on the back eye of the stove, she glanced up to see Susan staring at her.

"What?"

"Nothing." At the look of disbelief, she shrugged. "Okay, I was wondering just how hard this is on you."

"What do you mean?"

She waved her hand. "It must be hard with all of us just descending upon you. It's just been you for such a long while."

"I'll deal the way I've always dealt."

Grinning, Susan shook a finger at her. "Running away is not an option."

"I know. If things get too close, I'll go off for a bit by myself into the woods. Or I shall hide up in my bedroom with the covers over my head until the urge to murder you all in your sleep passes."

"Not that I don't entirely empathize, but could you let me know when you're getting close to the edge?"

"I can try." Jay dumped the big pot of water out in the sink over the dirty knives and bowls. She filled a smaller pot and put it on the stove in readiness for Doris's return with the beans. "Don't mistake me, Susan. I don't regret y'all being here at all."

"I know. I won't take it personally." With a saucy wink, she headed out of the kitchen. "Let me go check on the kids."

"Excellent. Bring everyone in for food in about two and a half hours." Jay took the beans from Doris and put them on the back of the stove to stay at low heat for a quick soak to soften.

"What about the rice?"

"I've got a canister here."

Doris poked around the kitchen. "What are you going to put on them?"

"We've got a jar of sauce that didn't seal. I figure that everyone can add the amount that they want."

"So we're finished?"

Jay answered, "For now. I'll need help with dinner, but you're free until then."

"Finally," Doris said as she flounced from the room.

Shaking her head, Jay finished making lunch and tidying up the kitchen while lunch cooked. She called everyone in and, after they all found seats at the table, she said, "I think that we can work tomorrow morning on getting everything ready for the fishing trip. If we head down around lunch, we should be able to catch something for dinner."

Martha asked, "It's not that far?"

"Not really, we're just going to the other side of the mountain. I'll spend the night with you and head back the next morning."

"You don't want to stay out longer?" asked Susan.

"No. I agree with Piper: fishing is boring. I'll leave it to you."

"I'm surrounded by Philistines," complained Martha. "If you'd only give it a chance."

Laying a restraining hand on Martha's wrist, Susan hinted, "Honey, I thought we were going to enjoy our time together with the kids."

Martha exchanged a significant look with her partner and nodded sagely. She turned to Jay. "Of course, I completely respect your opinion on fishing. We'll let you show us the best place to go and then wish you well for your trip back."

"Good answer."

The meal finished with continued banter and joking. The members of the household went their separate ways after the meal to find their own ways to relax the rest of the day away.

CHAPTER EIGHT

"So, what kind of fish are in these waters?"

"At this time of year, mainly trout."

"What else?"

"Salmon and steelhead." Jay pushed back from the breakfast table. "All right. Martha, you work with Cody and Susan to see what of these rods and reels we can take with us." She opened the closet to reveal a mess of fishing supplies. "You may have to cannibalize a couple."

Muttering darkly to herself about people who don't take proper care of their equipment, Martha began to empty everything out of the closet. In quick order she was hip deep in tackle boxes, rods, reels and flies.

"Oh, and you might need to sharpen the hooks."

Ignoring the commentary that her comment engendered, Jay took Carol and Eva downstairs with her. "Okay, Eva, why don't you grab a first-aid kit? I make it policy not to go anywhere without one." She directed Carol into the storage area and had her hold a small sack that she filled with cornmeal. "You like fried fish?"

"How much of a choice do I have?"

"Well, you'll be down there a week. By the end of that time, I expect you'll be like Forrest Gump's friend and know plenty of ways to cook our fishy friends."

"You really think we'll catch that much?"

"I don't really know. I certainly hope so. We need some smoked for the winter, but I think that five of you should be able to reel in plenty."

"What sort of sides should we take?"

"What have you got?"

Jay walked around to several large bags. "We've got a lot of rice."

"That would go great with fish," agreed Eva.

Filling up another sack, Jay handed that one to Carol as well. She scratched her head for a moment. "You guys want to take some potatoes with you?"

"You've got potatoes too?"

"Of course, you know those barrels in the laundry room?" When Eva and Carol nodded, she grinned. "I plant one in March and have potatoes now, and I started the second at the beginning of this month." She saw the looks on their faces and grinned. "Come on, let me show you."

Jay led them over to the two tall barrels. One was filled with compost and had pretty shoots with pink flowers coming out the top. There were doors located all along the side. She knelt down and opened the bottom sliding door.

"What's that?"

"It's a specially designed container." She pointed to the spuds that were revealed. "The roots are strong enough to keep the dirt in. All you have to do is reach in pull out what you need."

"Can I pull one out?"

"Why don't you both get ten each? We'll leave a couple here for your mom and Piper and take the rest with us."

The girls reached through the sliding doors and felt around for the spuds. The treasure hunt through the rich dirt was fun and rewarding.

"Why don't you grow these outdoors?" asked Carol.

"A couple of reasons. They rot easily if frost hits them, and they suck all the nutrients out of the soil they grow in. If I planted them with the rest of the garden, I wouldn't be able to plant anything else in that area for a couple of years. By keeping them in here, I've got potatoes at hand almost all year round."

"What do you do with the dirt afterward?"

"I mix it with the composting pile to let it recharge." Jay looked around. "I think this is a pretty good haul for your trip."

With their hands full of cornmeal and rice, potatoes and the small medical bag, the three went back upstairs to add it to the supplies that were to be packed down to the river.

After a pleasant lunch, they donned the packs and headed out. Jay led the way around the mountain. She spoke over her shoulder. "Where I'm taking y'all is where the Trinity River divides into several tributaries. There's generally plenty of trout and salmon running." She looked back at Martha. "You can speak better on any differences in catching them."

Martha took a deep breath, but before she could begin speaking, Susan interjected. "Remember that we are trying to encourage them to want to fish."

"Are you saying that my explanation lacks interest?"

"Not exactly. It's more that we need to be staying awake in order to hike safely."

Over the good-natured laughter that ensued, Jay spoke. "When we get down there we will need to do a couple of things. First, we need make a small dam where we can trap the fish we catch."

"We're keeping them alive?"

"The smoking will take a bit of time, but it helps if we have the whole thing full." The group stepped over a rusty chain. Jay pointed at an overgrown trail to their right and explained, "That way leads to the other homes on the mountain."

"Are they going to be upset that we've come?"

"Not as long as we pull our own weight and don't bring any unwanted attention to our presence here." Jay shrugged. "You'll meet them soon enough."

"What else will we need to do when we get to the river?"

"Check out the smokehouse, collect wood and make camp." Jay led them across the road and down another incline. "I can do all that while you give them a fishing lesson, Martha."

"Sounds fine to me."

"All right, then."

As the group continued their descent to the river, Martha spoke to them about fly-fishing. She enthusiastically shared stories from her past fishing trips. After a while, her voice trailed off.

"Don't sweat it."

Martha jerked at the apparent *non sequitur*. "Excuse me?"

"There'll be plenty of fish," Jay answered.

"How did you know that was what I was thinking about?"

"It didn't take a psychic. You were chattering away and then you went all deep and thoughtful." Jay glanced over her shoulder. "Trust me. You'll have time to fool around with your lady too."

"I hope you're right. I don't want to let everyone down."

"Not gonna happen, but if it did, we'll find another way."

Taking a deep breath, Martha tried to relax her tight shoulders. She felt a small hand clasp hers, and she glanced down at her lover.

"You okay?"

"I will be. Jay talked me down off the ledge."

"She's good at that."

"Yeah?"

"Yeah." Susan squeezed her lover's hand. "I'm glad we're doing this. It's still unreal to me that we've fallen into this perfect world."

"It's far from perfect," Jay interjected. "And things aren't always going to go so smoothly or easily."

"Our lives are definitely not about to be as brutish and short as they would have been had we stayed in Oakland."

"I can't speak of the horrors you've seen, but I say that things are looking up. We're here," she said, raising her voice so everyone could hear her.

After climbing over a couple of fallen logs, the group stepped past the last stand of trees and arrived at a small beach. The cleared area was about the size of Jay's house. The six people walked across the sandy ground to look closer at the river.

Martha squatted down at the river's edge. She trailed her fingers in the fast-moving water and picked up a couple of smooth stones. "It's cold."

"Yeah, there's a lot of mountain runoff in there."

"It's not a bad thing. Trout hang around the surface when the water's cold."

"You're right, the fish seem more active when the water is colder. However, y'all might find it a little too chilly for your taste. I think you should fish in shifts. Some of you stay and tend the fire and get warm and dry. The others wade in and pull in what they can before hypothermia sets in."

Looking around, Martha noticed that, besides the beach they were on, the banks of the river were obscured by underbrush. "Is there any place that doesn't have as many trees near the water's edge?"

Jay thought for a minute. "Down that a way about three hundred yards. Why?"

"I'm thinking that teaching them to cast will be easier if they are allowed to stay on dry land for the learning."

"I would like to second that," Susan said, waving a hand at the two of them. Behind her, the three teenagers waved their hands in the air as well.

"Well, you've got a majority." Jay dropped her pack on the ground. "Why don't you all go down and start the lessons and I'll make camp. On the way back, y'all can start gathering the wood for smoking."

"What are we looking for?"

"You need to make sure that you choose green wood for smoking. However, never ever use any evergreen branches. Pine smoke is oily and poisonous. See those trees over there? That's a stand of birch trees; they would be the best to use. It will give a sweet taste to the fish."

The group dumped their packs on the ground and grabbed up the rods. Martha led them upriver to a larger clearing. She grinned at the looks of trepidation on the faces of the teenagers and her partner. "Hey, gang. Loosen up," she chided before stepping to the water's edge.

"Okay, you want to watch where the sun is, so that you can keep your shadow off the water."

Cody asked, "I thought you wanted an area without trees?"

"That was just so none of you snagged a tree when we practice casting. We're going to work on you all being able to put your hook where you want."

"Why?"

"Trout like to hide behind rocks and let the water swirl their food right to them. Look for eddies in the water and cast just upriver from the eddy. Then, let your bait bump by and you might get a strike."

"Bait?" Eva asked with a moue of distaste. "I don't want to have to put worms on the line."

"No, no. We're using artificial baits." Martha opened up the gearbox and showed them all the assorted flies.

"How come there are so many different types?"

"Depending on what you're catching and the time of year, you change your bait. Trout like flies of various sorts and salmon like worms."

"I thought you said no worms," Eva nearly wailed.

Martha reached into the bottom of the box and pulled out a handful of neon rubber worms. "I did. We're going to use these."

"Oh." Reaching out, Eva took one of the slightly sticky worms. "They feel weird."

"They're designed to move with the current to mimic how a live worm would wiggle." Martha handed out a worm to everyone and showed them how to attach it to the lines.

The lessons progressed smoothly and they were able to catch a couple of fish for dinner. They returned to the camp, grateful for the fire that Jay built. They dried their clothes while the potatoes cooked.

Dinner was a congenial affair. Without Doris's sobering influence, the conversation among the group was free-flowing and filled with laughter. Cleanup was quick and easy, and everything quieted down as the fire started to die out.

"We should hang the rest of the food." Jay's voice carried on the night air.

"There a problem with scavengers?"

"There are bears out here. The smell of the smoker may draw them, and there is no reason to give them any more food than necessary."

Working together, the adults secured the rest of the potatoes, the cornmeal, rice and other staples in a large bag and hoisted it about twenty feet above the ground. With that accomplished, they all went back to their positions in front of the fire.

Martha sat with her back against a fallen log with Susan snuggled up with her. She looked across the glowing coals of the campfire at Jay, who was leaning on one elbow and tossing small sticks into the embers. Carol and Eva were sitting cross-legged next to each other, giggling about the happenings of the day. Cody was almost asleep, nodding off after overexerting all day in an attempt to burn through all the testosterone running through his system.

"I think we should start a school." Susan's voice carried on the night air. She ignored the "Aw, Mom!" from her kids and went on, "All of us have information that we should pass on before it's too late."

"Good idea, sweetie." Martha tipped her head for a kiss. "We also need to share knowledge between ourselves. Everyone needs to know how to do at least the basics."

"I've never taught before. Training was Harmony's job, you know."

Martha pointed a finger at her. "What do you think you've been doing since we got here? You've been an extraordinary teacher."

"That's more sharing than teaching."

"Call it what you will." Susan rubbed her cheek against Martha's thigh. "I think we should all make a list of what we know and what we feel capable of passing on. Jay, you should do an inventory of your books."

"What makes you think I don't already have one?"

"Of course you do," Martha muttered.

"What was that?"

"Nothing, honey," she said, patting Susan's head. "I used to enjoy teaching the self-defense classes. I'd be happy to help."

"You're not going to make us attend classes?" Cody whined.

"We'll all be sitting in on some of them. The world as we know it may have ended but that doesn't mean we have to forget everything we ever knew. Besides, it will be a way to keep busy during those long winter days."

"Let's call it a night, everyone. We can discuss our plans for the future later." Jay stood up and banked the fire before she headed to the area they had dug for waste. Speaking over her shoulder, she called, "Susan, your and Martha's tent is the one furthest from the rest."

The teenagers fell over themselves laughing at the blushing adults. They ignored the mock glares and went to their separate tents.

Cody was bunking with Jay and the two girls were sharing the tent next to them. It meant he would have a tent to himself for the rest of their stay at the river. Asleep almost before his head hit the pillow, Cody didn't even stir when Jay entered the tent and crawled into her sleeping bag. She quickly joined him in slumber.

The clearing was quiet except for the occasional giggle from the girls' tent and low moans from Susan and Martha's. Soon, even those noises stilled and the camp slept to the sound of the river rolling past.

There was a chill to the air the next morning. When the teenagers were rousted from their tents, they saw Jay and Martha over by the smokehouse. It was a box about two feet square and five feet high. The top three quarters was solid, except for an inch gap near the top.

Jay pointed to the pit under it. "You build the fire and let it burn down to embers. Only then do you fill the box with fish that have been gutted and filleted. We don't want to cook the fish, just smoke it. You close the top section, and then you feed the leaves and green wood into the fire. Don't forget, it will need to be tended regularly through the day and night."

"How long is it going to take?"

"Depending on the thickness of the meat, three days should be sufficient."

Martha divided her attention between the box and her fishing students. "So, you figure two days of heavy fishing, three days of smoking and fishing for our dinner and then home?"

"Something like that." Jay used her ax to chop off the branches from a large limb Cody had dragged back to the camp. "If you want to explore, there is an apple orchard and an old mill upstream a ways. It was still abandoned the last time I was through here, but you should always be careful of squatters."

Susan looked at the eager faces and nodded. "We might give it a try."

"Keep as many of the fish you're not smoking alive as long as you can in the live buckets. We can freeze what isn't smoked."

"Great. Are you going to head back now?"

"No, I'll gather some more wood while the first shift fishes."

"You're going to steal our product?"

"You betcha. I plan on taking up enough for dinner tonight."

The camp ate a cold breakfast and started work with Cody helping Jay find wood for the smokehouse. The sun was climbing in the sky when she called out to Susan that she was ready to go.

"You have enough fish?"

"Yeah, Martha's been on fire. She got five without breaking a sweat."

"Considering the temperature of the water, I'm not sure that means anything."

Jay smiled affectionately at her. "I'll be heading up now."

"Okay, we'll be here."

"I'll start looking for you in five days. Either Piper or I will come looking for you at seven." Jay lifted the string of fish. "Thanks for these. I'm sure we'll enjoy them tonight."

"Bye, Jay," Cody, Carol and Eva chorused.

"Hey! Eyes on your lines," yelled Martha. She winked at Jay as the teenagers focused their attention back on fishing.

CHAPTER NINE

Jay came back from the fishing camp with four fish on a string. She came up the old hunting trail and surprised Doris and Piper, who were sitting on the porch in silence. "Sorry. I didn't mean to startle you."

"Maybe we should tie a bell around your neck."

Piper shook her head at Doris's testy remark. "Good to see you back. I was just thinking how good it would be to see a friendly face."

Laughing, Jay held up the fish. "Well, I'm back and I brought dinner."

"I guess I can take it that the fishing trip is going well?"

"You certainly can. The kids have taken to it like, well, fishes to water."

"That's just awful." Piper dried her suddenly damp hands on her pants. "Although, perhaps, not as awful as what happened."

"Oh?"

"See, Doris had a movie going last night when the power went off. I didn't know what to do, so we've gone without since."

Jay pinched her nose. "I hope you've kept the fridge and freezer closed."

"Of course. We're not idiots," Doris replied.

"If you didn't bother to do the basic arithmetic to figure out capacity before use, then I'd have to say you actually were." Jay set the fish in the sink. "Come on downstairs with me."

At the panel in the basement, she flicked the large breaker switch. There was an immediate hum as the freezer turned on. Picking up the calculator, she said, "Let me go over this again. The freezer uses 500 watts and its 600 for the fridge. Add 818 watts for the water heater. Finally, plug in the requirements of the system itself. The total of those are 30, which is the combined wattage of the battery regulator, equalizer and inverters. Our current total usage is 1948." She pointed at the readout from the solar panels. "There's only about a hundred watts left to play with now, and, at night, the television and DVD could easily have exceeded the battery capacity, causing the short."

"Did having it cut off harm anything?" Piper asked.

"If the freezer and fridge stayed closed to keep the cold in, it should be okay. Anything longer than forty-eight hours and we'll have a lot of spoilage on our hands."

"Did it hurt the equipment?"

"It's not good for the system to get shut off like that. Too many hard resets and we could blow out the motors of the appliances. It's not like we can run out to Walmart to replace any of this shit." Jay tapped the notebook. "That's why it is so important to first check here where I've written down what everything in the house uses."

"I didn't mean to do anything wrong."

"I know that. I wasn't assigning blame. I was merely trying to impress on you better behavior in the future." Heading back upstairs to the kitchen, she took out a thin-bladed knife and cut the fish into fillets.

Doris and Piper followed her and watched her deft movements with the knife. Clearing her throat, Piper asked, "How are you going to cook them?"

"I haven't decided yet. What would y'all like?"

"What are our choices?"

"Fried or grilled."

Piper smacked her lips. "I'd like grilled."

"Excellent. Let me put these in the fridge until dinner."

"What shall we do until then?"

"Oh, I'm sure that we can find something to do."

"I'm enjoying sitting here in the quiet," Doris stated.

"I know," Jay said, clapping her hands. "Let's go bring down a tree."

Piper grinned at her. "I'm game."

"Excuse me? A tree?" Doris looked concerned.

"Yep."

"What do you expect us to do?"

"I cut a couple of trees that were dying this spring. I was planning on letting them dry in place until the end of winter but needs must. They're up the hill a couple hundred yards."

"What do we need?"

"You mean, other than brute force? Come back downstairs and help me gather what we need." Jay led the other women down into the basement. She handed out a saw and an ax before grabbing a pair of wheels and a couple of straps.

"What are those for?"

"Well, we can roll the log part of the way, but there are a lot of other trees up there. It's a pain to be constantly forcing it around the obstacles. It'll be easier if we drag it."

"Drag it? You expect us to drag a log?"

"Duh. How else did you think we'd get wood for the fireplaces?"

"There are only three of us. We should wait until the others come back." Doris tried to hand the saw back.

"We don't need them. Hell, I've brought logs down with just me and the dogs." Jay fondled the ears of two of the black mutts that hadn't left her side since she returned to the property.

"Then use them. Don't bring us into it."

"No." Piper's tone was sharp. "We're in this together. We'll go and we'll work together." She glared at Doris until she nodded.

Jay smiled in thanks. "Let me get a basket."

"What for?"

"You never know what you may find that you'll want to carry back home. I take a basket anytime I go wandering. It keeps my pockets from getting too dirty." She glanced at her companions. "Ready? Okay, follow me." She flipped the straps over her shoulder and whistled to the pack of dogs. Tossing a ball out before her, she laughed at the melee that ensued.

Amazed that the dogs could chase the ball and run uphill, Piper spoke quietly, "You've had the dogs for a while."

"They're a family group. My neighbor from the other side of the mountain has a male lab. I've kept a female from each litter and sold the rest to other neighbors."

"They are well-trained."

"I've had plenty of time to teach them to do what I want them to."

"Do you plan on getting more?"

"Replacement only. They're starting to eat me out of house and home."

"What have you been feeding them?"

"They're natural scavengers. I feed them leftovers with supplements from the animals I've killed. I don't eat the intestines or bones and the dogs love them."

"So I should make sure I bring the offal back?"

"Yeah. I've found a way to use most everything. If possible, bring the whole animal back and we can bleed it on the rack near the house and dress it there."

"No problem."

"You say that when you don't have close to two hundred pounds of deer over your shoulder."

Doris caught up with them. She was panting. "How much farther?"

"Not much." Jay pointed up. "See the patch of sunlight over there? That's the space that was created when it came down."

Stepping into the clearing, the three women walked around the fallen tree. Piper spoke for all of them when she said, "That's awfully big."

"Indeed it is. Just think of all the dinners and cozy nights it'll supply." Indicating the branches, Jay asked Doris, "You start sawing off everything on this side and Piper will chop off on her side."

"What are you going to do?"

"I'm going to see if I can find any other deadfall trees. No reason to waste energy chopping trees down when some are already on the ground." Jay whistled to the dogs and began hiking farther up the side of the mountain.

"I don't know who she thinks she is, leaving us with all the work."

"I'm sure that she'll be doing her fair share." Piper reassured Doris between strikes of her ax. She quickly developed a rhythm and dropped into a trance state. When she finally looked up toward the sky, she noticed that at least a couple of hours had passed. Glancing over to her workmate, she saw that Jay had replaced Doris at the saw.

"Didn't see you come back."

"You were working awfully hard."

"Find anything?"

"Yeah, there is a dead tree about five hundred yards east. I also saw a few dead standing trees. We can come back up and cut them down in the next couple of days after we've dealt with this one." Stopping to wipe her brow, Jay added, "I also got a basket of mushrooms."

"Don't expect me to eat anything so unsafe!" Doris interjected.

Her lips tightening in annoyance, Jay looked around for the other woman and saw her sitting on the stump. "Why don't you make yourself useful and collect the branches?" she asked. "We need them for kindling."

"Good idea," Piper agreed.

With ill-concealed reluctance, Doris stood up and brushed off the seat of her pants. She moved very slowly and tossed the branches into a haphazard pile.

"Should we tell her that it would be easier if she stacked them properly?" asked Jay in a soft voice.

"Doris has never struck me as being particular open to new ideas or to long-term planning."

"So I'm coming to see." Jay put down her saw and measured the width of the tree.

"What's the plan?"

"We've got these straps that go over our shoulders. We need to pick up the top end and slowly pull it forward over the wheelbase here. Once I secure that to the log, we head down hill at our best pace and let gravity do the real work."

"It can't be that simple."

"Trust me, it isn't elegant but it does the job without breaking our backs."

The three women were able to work well enough together to get the log in motion. Despite Doris's tendency to drop her section at the most inconvenient times, they made great progress.

After they had wrestled the log through the trees and down the hill, Jay went into the house and brought out a chain saw from the basement. On her way back out, she grabbed one of the already split logs. Brandishing the split, she said, "The wood has to be no longer than this if it is going to fit in the stove."

Piper hefted the chain saw. "This works?"

"Yeah. I've got a little gas left."

"You have gasoline?"

"Yep," answered Jay.

"Why didn't you have that up there when we were having to saw off the limbs."

"Because the limbs aren't that much work." Jay shook her head at the look on Doris's face. "I use the saw to bring down trees and to cut it into manageable pieces once we get it down here. We'll chop those segments by hand. If I used it on every task, I'd have run out of fuel years ago."

Piper unscrewed the cap and sniffed appreciatively. "Boy, the smell of that takes me back."

Jay laughed. "Do you miss the smog too?"

"No, just the conveniences that used to run on it."

"I hate the smell." Doris crossed her arms over her chest.

"Did you hate being able to drive where you wanted to go when you wanted to go there?"

"Not really." Doris glared at each of them before spitting out angrily, "One of the best things to happen was the end of all those horrible, gas-guzzling cars."

Piper nearly dropped the saw at her outrageous comment. "Are you nuts? You think the death toll was worth getting cleaner air?"

"All that pollution was damaging the environment."

"And you don't think those bombs or the rotting corpses or the release of toxic waste constitutes a bigger environmental tragedy than the exhaust from vehicles?" Piper was outraged. "You're insane."

"No, I'm not."

"I don't know where to begin to disagree with you."

"I just know that things couldn't go on like they were." Doris turned to walk back inside. Suddenly, she whirled back. "If you were honest with yourselves, you'd realize that the best thing to happen to this country was the Confederacy."

"How can you say that?" Jay asked, aghast.

"Didn't your husband die, along with those other millions?" asked Piper.

"Things had to be sacrificed to return a sense of decency to this country. At least they were willing to die for their faith."

Piper spat on the ground. "I guess that's where my problem is. They weren't the ones doing the dying. They were doing the killing."

"People like my husband, who accepted Jesus into their lives, would have been taken into heaven. We will be reunited in the promised land." She whirled and flounced into the house.

Piper and Jay stared at one another. Jay drawled, "Why do I get the feeling that she did not go in to fix us a nice cup of tea?"

"I bet she won't be around to bother us for a while."

"Thank god." They both spoke at the same time.

Jay laughed. "Jinx. You owe me a Coke."

"Put it on my tab. When I get one, I'll pay you back."

"I get the feeling that you aren't entirely serious about your debt." Jay shook her head sadly. "Back to the chain saw. It should only be used during the middle of the day. It's almost too late to use it now but we'll take the risk."

"Why?"

"Sounds don't travel as far at midday. There are few enough around to hear, but we shouldn't borrow trouble."

"No, there's enough of that to go around."

Jay primed the chain saw and pulled the cord. Indicating for Piper to hold the split, she made a quick cut. Together they worked their way down the entire log, cross-cutting it to size.

Finished, Jay turned the saw off and set it next to the house. "Now, we have to split these."

"What about the limbs?"

"Let me go inside and get Doris to go and fetch them down." Jay went into the empty house and found Doris sunbathing on the patio. "Hey."

"What do you want now?"

"I need you to head back up the hill and get the limbs." She held out a folded cloth. "You can use this."

"What is it?"

"It's a tarp. Just put it down and fill it with branches. Fold it over and you should able to drag the whole thing down hill."

"Aren't you going to help?"

"No. Piper and I will be chopping the tree." Jay stared down at her. "Of course, if you would rather chop…"

"That's all right." Doris stood up and snatched the tarp from Jay's hand. "I'll go."

"I expect it will take at least two trips. Don't expect dinner until you've brought them all down."

"Whatever."

Doris followed her back outside and huffed her way back up the hillside. Piper and Jay set their backs to reducing the split log into manageable pieces. The two of them worked together until dusk, with only the thunk of ax meeting wood to be heard.

"What now?"

"We need to stack it over there." Jay pointed to an area about twenty yards from the house.

"Why so far away?" asked Doris.

"In case of wildfire." Jay waved at the cleared area. "I've made sure that there is a firebreak around the house. We don't want to undo all my good work by putting fuel too close to the structure."

"Is that really a danger?"

"Don't you remember hearing about those massive wildfires that swept California? Given a really dry summer anything can happen." She pulled around a two-wheeled cart. "Using this will help."

It was almost full dark and they were tired and sweaty when the last piece of firewood went on the stack. They grinned at one another as they silently admired their accomplishment, their teeth white in the gathering darkness.

"Are we done yet?" Doris asked from her seat on the patio.

"Yeah. Why don't we all head in and take showers?"

"What about dinner?"

"I'll start the potatoes baking and you can start the outside grill." Jay wiped her hands on her pants. "Once we're all clean, I'll do something with the fish."

Doris clapped her hands. "Sounds good to me."

Jay's hair was still damp from her shower when she started to brush the dirt off the mushrooms.

"Are you sure these are safe?"

Looking over her shoulder, Jay watched Doris poke the mushrooms. "You can skip that course if you don't trust me," she said mildly.

"I'm just asking."

"Haven't poisoned myself in the past five years, but if you want to check on me, there is a book on mushrooms in the bookcase nearest to the bathroom. I think it's on one of the lower shelves." She shook her head when Doris left the room in search of the item.

Glancing through the French doors, she saw that Piper had the fire going. Putting the lemon-pepper-sprinkled fish and clean mushrooms on a platter, she carried everything outside, along with a bottle of olive oil and a brush.

Jay quickly brushed a coating of oil on the fish and mushrooms and placed everything on the grill.

"How long?"

"Just a couple of minutes," answered Jay as she turned to go back inside and check the potatoes. "Oh, I do have a lemon in the crisper. Cut a couple of thin slices, and when you turn the fillets over, put the slices on top."

"Sure thing." Piper moved gracefully past her to the refrigerator and rummaged around. Her hands were swift and sure with the sharp knife as she sectioned the lemon.

The two women worked quiet and companionably while they finished the cooking. They only exchanged a couple of words before the food was on the table.

"Mmmm. This is good," Piper said. The whites of her eyes almost glowed in the candlelight from the tapers in the center of the table.

"Fresh is best."

"You eat this way all the time? I still can't believe it."

Jay sighed before answering Doris. "Not all the time but regularly. Remember, there aren't that many people up here fighting for scarce resources. If you're willing to work, you can eat like this as much as you want."

"I can get used to this," Piper sighed in satisfaction.

"It's too isolated." Doris scowled down at her plate.

"What?" Piper finally asked.

Looking up in confusion, Jay raised her right eyebrow. "I'm sorry?"

"It just looked like Doris had something else to say."

She shook her head. "I was just thinking that's it's all right for people like you, but this isn't good for me or the children."

"What are you talking about?"

"How do you expect them to grow up properly?"

"I think they've done pretty well so far."

Doris sniffed. "You would."

"What do you mean by that?"

"Just that it's obvious that you don't have children of your own or you would understand."

"I understand that you're a narrow-minded twit."

"Piper," warned Jay. "There's no need for name-calling."

"Thank you."

"Wait a minute." Jay set her utensils down with deliberation. "I certainly don't agree with you. Everything I've seen about those kids has been wonderful. Considering all they've gone through, they are the most normal and well-adjusted children I've had the pleasure to know."

"Hear, hear." Piper echoed. "Martha and Susan are great parents, and Eva is smart as a whip."

"Why, thank you for noticing." Doris refilled her water glass. "It's all right now but without a proper male influence, those children will be doomed."

"I think that's a little harsh."

"You only think that because you share the proclivities of my sister."

"Possibly. Or I could just have seen plenty of well-adjusted single-parented and gay-parented children and more than my share of piss-poor straight parents when I was on the force. Besides, it isn't gay parents that leads to homosexuality."

"Oh, really?"

"Really. My parents were straight. Weren't yours, Jay?"

"As arrows."

Doris shook her head. "In any event, I'm not sure how long Eva and I will stay here."

"It's safe here, Doris. Whether or not you agree with our life choices, you can't seriously think it's better to live in the chaos that was Oakland?"

"No, I don't want to go back there. I think that there are other communities out here that would be better. Right, Jay?"

"There are towns on the coast that are surviving and even thriving. I just don't see why you would put yourself at risk when you don't have to." She ate another bite of fish. "I guess I would feel differently if I were uncomfortable with my surroundings."

"Well, it's not like I need to make a decision immediately."

"No. Why don't you take it easy through the winter and reassess in the spring?"

Doris nodded and the rest of the meal passed in silence.

CHAPTER TEN

After dinner, Piper pulled her rifle out of the closet and set about cleaning it. Jay watched her from her place in front of the fireplace. "You planning on going out tomorrow?" she asked.

"Yeah."

"Cool. You want to go and find something on your own or do you want me to go with?"

"Why don't you show me the good hunting ground?"

Jay pushed herself to her feet. "No problem. Let me go and make you a picnic basket. How long will you want to stay out?"

"How far is it?"

"Just a couple of miles."

"Then just for the day." Piper wiped her hands. "I can always go out again the next day and so on until I get something."

"Oh, I don't think you'll have much trouble." Jay walked toward the kitchen. "I'll set you up with a morning snack and lunch."

Doris came in from the hot tub while Jay was slicing meat and wrapping it with bread. "What are you doing?" she asked. "You're not still hungry, are you?"

"No, I'm making up a picnic for Piper and myself for tomorrow."

"Where are you going?"

"Piper is going hunting. I'm just going to show her a good place to make a stand, and then I'll wander a bit before coming home."

"You two are going to leave me here alone?"

"I'll be back for lunch."

"You didn't even ask me if I wanted to go."

Jay looked up at the still-damp woman. "Did you want to go hunting?"

"No, but I don't think that you should just walk out without saying anything."

"We haven't gone anywhere yet. Considering how late you stay abed, I doubt you'll even miss me."

"I can't believe you. I slept in once." Doris stood glaring at Jay with her hands on her hips. "I should have been consulted before you two came up with this idea. I would have told you that this is a bad idea."

"What's so bad about it? We need meat and I need air."

"I don't know where to begin. Either of you could have an accident out there, and I'd be left here all alone."

Piper came into the kitchen and leaned against the counter. "Chill out, Doris. Jay will be back before you know it."

"I don't even know her."

"Do you want a copy of my résumé? I think I've got one around here somewhere."

"Don't mock me."

Shaking her head, Jay finished packing. "I'm not trying to fight with you, Doris." She pointed a finger at her. "You've got a choice. You can either join us at o'dark thirty tomorrow morning, or you can deal with being in the house by yourself for a few hours. We're going hunting with or without you."

Doris looked affronted. "I'm not going hunting."

"Fine," answered Jay. "Sleep tight, y'all. I'm going to turn in early."

With a chorus of answering "good nights," they headed to their separate bedrooms. The house was still and quiet in no time at all.

It was cold and dark when Jay stumbled downstairs the next morning. Piper was already sitting at the table, finishing a mug of tea. "Did you want some tea?" she asked.

Jay shuddered. "No, thanks. My body doesn't know it's awake yet. I'm not going to do anything like eating or drinking that will speed up the discovery."

"I take it you're not a morning person."

"Oh, I don't have a problem with morning. It's this still-dark-outside-when-you-get-up thing. It's just wrong."

Piper laughed. "How do you handle the darkness of winter?"

"By staying in bed as late as I can and turning in as early as possible." Jay settled and adjusted the pack on her back. "Thank goodness I now have a house full of people who can take over doing the morning tasks."

"What, no milking cows for you?"

"You've got it." Jay buckled a little pack around her waist. "There'll be no dairy farming around me."

"What's that?"

"It's a basic first-aid kit and a holster for my 9mm." Jay illustrated the dual function of the pack. "I never leave home without it."

Piper shrugged into her jacket and pulled on her backpack. Picking up her rifle and a bandolier of shells, Piper waved for Jay to precede her out of the door. "After you, Bwana."

"No, no. You're the great hunter."

The two women stood for a moment to let their eyes adjust to the darkness. The dogs circled around them, sniffing. Jay knelt down and roughhoused with them, grabbing their muzzles and pulling their ears. Standing up, she told them to guard and then glanced over at Piper. "You good to go?"

"Yeah. Let's do this thing."

Together, they walked in companionable silence down the trail to the old rest stop building. Instead of going either direction on the road, Jay went directly across the road and down the hillside. Once across the stream, she showed Piper an area where the grass was beaten down and led away from the water.

"See, here is a game trail." Jay pointed at a narrow path between the trees. The path looked almost man-made; it was so clean and well kept. She pointed to a crumbling pile of dung. "Something has been using it recently."

"How far does it go?"

"It leads almost directly to the river from that mountain over there." The mountain she indicated was a little larger than the one on which they now lived. "You can follow the trail nearly all the way across the valley."

They began walking in single file slightly to the side of the path. They had to walk carefully in the rough bush alongside, trying not to make too much noise.

The predawn light was gray and cast odd shadows through the trees. Piper split her attention between the woods they were walking through and the trim outline of the woman before her. She was startled when Jay stopped short.

"Check up there," whispered Jay. She pointed up at a forty-foot oak tree. "I put a stand in that tree and in another about three hundred yards further on." She tapped the first of four steps nailed into the trunk. "Will you need help? The seat is very narrow."

"Naw, I'm an ace at climbing trees, especially when someone's gone to the trouble of giving me hand- and footholds." Piper swung her pack off her back and onto one shoulder. She tightened the gun sling before making the short climb to the stand. Squirming on the seat, Piper adjusted her rifle across her knees. As comfortable now as she could make herself, she reached down for the pack that Jay passed up to her.

"I'm going to walk the trail and take the long way back to the house." Jay touched Piper's boot. "Good luck."

"Thanks. I'll see you later tonight."

"If you get something, there's a clearing just to the east with a good tree for hanging. I put some rope in the other pack."

"Good plan. I'll take out the intestinal sack, and we can come back and get the carcass in the morning."

With a wry grin, Jay responded. "But not so early."

"No, we can wait for sunup." Piper winked at her.

"Fine. I'll see you later." Jay headed down the path.

She decided to walk partially around the base of the mountain and through a meadow where she knew she would find wild onions.

After only an hour in the stand, Piper took down a smallish buck. She waited in the tree before coming down and following the deer's trail.

About twenty yards away, she found a bright splash of blood and followed it into some brambles. Piper grabbed the dead animal by the back legs and pulled it from the covering brush and dragged it in the direction of the clearing Jay had spoken of earlier.

Tying the rope around its front legs, she was able to hang it by the front hooves. Piper pulled out her long knife, cut the jugular vein and removed the intestinal sack. She went back to the river to wash up.

Glancing up at the sun, she decided to eat her lunch before returning to the house. Making herself comfortable on the bank, Piper enjoyed the sandwich Jay had made for her. When she finished her meal, she placed everything back into her pack and strode back to the house.

She found Jay and Doris in the living room. They were seated as far apart as possible while still being in the same room. The silence was deafening. Both of them looked up, grateful, when Piper returned.

"You look like you got lucky."

"I got a buck." She shrugged. "It's only about a hundred and fifty pounds."

"Where is it?"

"I hung it where you told me to." Piper kicked off her shoes and hung her jacket up in the closet. "You two want to go with me and bring it back?"

"Sure."

Doris shook her head, "Right now?"

"Yeah. There's plenty of daylight left and it's an easy hike."

"I don't know."

"I thought you didn't want to be left alone," Jay responded snidely. "I found some onions today. I figure to slow cook them with some pork belly I found in the back of the freezer."

"Sounds divine. I need a shower. I'm itchy from the blood."

"You want to bring the venison back before you get clean?"

"No. I'll take another one after we come back. I haven't gotten my fill of hot running water yet."

"No problem. You give a holler when you're ready." Jay went into the basement and came back up carrying two long poles. "We can use these to cart him home."

"Why not just one?"

"Displace the weight onto both shoulders."

"Oh." Doris watched as Jay buckled on the fanny pack. "You always take that with you?"

"Yeah. You were right last night when you worried about something happening when we're away from here. I always take this so I have a gun and a first-aid kit if something bad happens."

"Has it? I mean have you needed it?"

"Not for anything major. You want me to make you one?"

"No. I don't anticipate going anywhere where I'd need it."

"That's kind of the point. You've got to expect the unexpected."

Piper joined them, dressed in clean clothes, catching only the last part of their exchange. "Is that how you can keep from getting disappointed?"

"No, it's how you keep yourself alive." At Piper's odd look, she patted her fanny pack. "I was just speaking of the merits of being prepared."

"Okay." She shrugged. "Are we taking the dogs?"

"Sure. We won't go hunting again for a few days, and the dog smell should be gone by then."

The trio journeyed to the hanging carcass, Piper in the lead and Jay at the back of the line. Sticking to the middle, Doris wasn't looking where she was going. She walked into Piper when she stopped to grab the second pack from the tree stand.

Doris looked from the stand to the trail. "Doesn't the deer see you in it?"

"No. Like most animals, deer don't look up," answered Jay.

"I doubt I'll ever have need of that little tidbit." Doris followed them over to the deer. She threw her hands up when both women started to speak. "I know, I know. You never know." She sighed. "What are we going to do now?"

"Untie it and lower it from the tree. We'll use the same lines to tie it to the poles. We can take turns lugging it up the hill." Jay nodded at Piper and they worked swiftly to make the transfer.

The trip up the hill took almost three times as long as it did to come down. Doris only hiked a few yards with the two poles on her shoulders before she began whining. Neither of the other women were in a particularly good mood when they came within sight of the house.

"Now what?"

"We'll hang it there." Jay jerked her head toward the area behind the hot tub.

As they brought their burden near, Piper could see a frame built between the trees. "You've obviously done this before?"

"Yep."

"Are we having this for dinner?" Doris asked.

"No way. We're going to let it hang here for a day before butchering it."

"You're just going to leave it out there? It's going to rot and waste all the food." Doris look appalled.

"No, it's not. The meat is aging. If we took it out now, it wouldn't be as good."

"That can't be right."

"When you bought meat from the grocery store, it wasn't fresh killed."

"I thought that was because it had to travel."

"No. The enzymes in it have to break down. Trust me it will taste a whole lot better once some time has passed."

"How are you going to keep the animals off it?"

Jay picked up a roll of chicken wire. "Easy. The dogs can't get through this and they'll keep everything else off." She brushed her hands off. "Let's clean this day off ourselves, as we'll be busy tomorrow."

The next day passed in a blur as they worked to butcher the meat. Piper was successful in removing the hide in one piece. Jay and Piper were bloody and cranky by the time all of the meat was processed. Doris, very cleverly, managed to make herself scarce until meal times.

Once all the edible parts were packaged, Jay worked with Piper to collect the hooves to be boiled to make glue, and the inedible tendons strung up to dry so they could be used as ties. Finally, they gathered all the bones to be pressure-cooked until they were soft and then put them through a food mill. It was hard work to grind everything together, but the resulting sludge was a high protein supplement to the dogs' food.

They decided to forgo the clothing rule since the kids were away and take a soak in the hot tub.

"Damn, that was a lot of work," Piper said with a sigh as she leaned back to let the jets pulse water against her lower back.

"We got a lot of useful materials off of it."

"I know but I think I'm getting a little old for this shit."

"You're not old."

"I've got more than ten years on you."

Jay opened one eye and looked at Piper. Her short hair had very little gray and there were laugh lines around her eyes and mouth but she had no other signs of her age on her face. Her body was compact and muscular without too much excess weight and very little sag. "You wear the years well. Really well."

"Why thank you. I'm so glad you noticed."

"I didn't mean to say that out loud. I'm just going to sink under the water now."

Piper laughed. "Don't drown on my account. Would you be less embarrassed if I confessed that you weren't the only one doing some noticing?"

"No but thanks for saying so." Jay slapped at the bubbles. "Can we pretend this conversation never happened?"

"If that is what you want, sure."

They sat quietly and stared up at the night sky. There was heaviness to the air, but the stars had yet to be hidden behind clouds.

"You think it's going to rain soon?"

"In the next day or so." Jay's eyes closed.

"I wondered if I should go again."

"After the rain is soon enough." She stretched a little bit.

"You okay?"

"Yeah, I've just got a twinge in my upper back."

"You want me to massage it?"

Jay opened her eyes and looked across the bubbling water at the dark-skinned woman. She saw Piper looking guilelessly back at her. "If you don't mind?"

"No, I'll just expect a repayment at a future date to be named later."

"I can handle that."

Half floating, Piper moved across the hot tub. "Turn around and try to relax."

"Ooh," Jay murmured as strong fingers sought out the knots of tension in her back and neck. "That feels good."

"I'm no expert."

"Maybe not but it's been a while since I've had anyone give me a rub down."

Piper worked silently for a while. "How long have you and Harmony been together?"

"Twelve years." Jay took in a deep breath and released it slowly. "'She was my North, my South, my East and West. My working week and my Sunday rest.'"

"What's that?"

"It's part of a funeral poem from W.H. Auden."

"You think she's gone?"

"If she's still out there, she'll come back to me. I haven't given up hope yet."

"I don't think you should."

Jay turned slightly and looked over her shoulder. "Really?"

Nudging her back around, Piper nodded. "Really. It took us a month to get here from Oakland and we had a general idea of where we were going. It would have taken her at least three times that just to make it to the Los Angeles area. I can't imagine what would be entailed in searching the city for a single survivor."

Jay reached up and wiped away a couple of tears. "Thanks. It's good to hear someone else's voice saying things like that."

Patting her on the shoulder, Piper leaned back and watched Jay return to her side of the hot tub. "I just said what I believe. Besides, she would have to work to find food and shelter and that will add even more time to it." Seeing Jay's hopeful smile let her know that she had said the right thing.

"I don't know about you, but I'm ready to turn in."

"I'll come inside in a bit."

"All right." Jay stood up and stretched before gracefully climbing out of the tub. "I'll see you in the morning," she said as she pulled a towel around her shoulders.

Piper stared at the strong and capable woman walking away from her and croaked a "good night." She sighed when the door closed behind Jay. She stretched out and enjoyed the feeling of the water coming from all directions and hitting different parts of her body. Running her hands across her breasts, she luxuriated in the sensation of cool night air, warm water and tickling bubbles.

The night sky was dotted with lights, and she floated for a while with her eyes on the countless stars. There was something freeing about being outside and submerged in the warm water. The intriguing stimulation of the water against her skin had her turning in the tub to position herself directly in front of one of the jets so the water pressure could hit her most sensitive places.

She let the water fondle her between her legs before slowly rolling over so that the jets were hitting her from behind. Groaning, she braced one hand on the edge and used the fingers on her other hand to sift through her pubic hair. There was just a trace of slick juices that hadn't been washed away. Slowly Piper slid her fingers back and forth across her clit while the jets continued their pulsing action on her pussy and ass. She lifted her upper body slightly out of the water so the bubbles could burst and tease her nipples.

Feeling the impending orgasm, she rubbed harder on her clit. As her body shuddered, Piper moved slightly so that the water jet hit between her fingers, prolonging her pleasure.

Rolling over, she stared up at the glimmering lights and caught her breath. As the stars crawled across the sky, she wished on one of them to help her find a love of her own.

CHAPTER ELEVEN

Everyone was stuck indoors as the rains came down for the third straight day. It was no gentle summer shower but a sky-opening deluge. The small pond had flooded to almost twice its usual size, and small tributaries were developing in the rest of the yard.

Piper paced around the living room, moving from window to window as she monitored the spread of the water. Occasionally, she would fling herself down on one of the daybeds. Those periods of inactivity would never last long.

"Could you just rest a while?" Martha finally asked.

Susan agreed. "Yeah, you're making the floor dizzy." They and the kids had returned early from fishing. They had tried to stick it out, but once the beach went underwater, they gave up on smoking any more fish and came back to the house.

"Sorry," Piper answered, not really meaning it. "I'm just a little stir-crazy."

"I totally understand." Meeting Piper's eyes, Susan smiled at her. "After all this time, I know how hard it is to be stuck inside."

"I'm glad we're back," said Carol.

Cody fiddled with his letter tiles. "I am so glad to be dry and warm again."

"My fingers and toes are still a little pruney," added Eva, holding up her hands.

Piper began pacing again. "Once the rains started, we couldn't work outside because the ground was simply too muddy."

"Chopping any more wood was out unless one of us wanted to risk losing a limb to an ax." Jay laughed at the glaring Piper. "Take it easy. You deserve a break what with processing the buck and an entire tree by yourself."

Sighing, the stocky woman went over to the fireplace and added another log. "I know I'm being a big baby, but I'd really rather be doing something."

"How about reading a book?"

"Or joining our game?" Cody asked. "I'm getting killed on this one and would love to have the tiles reshuffled."

Cody, Carol and Eva were sitting in front of the fireplace, playing Scrabble. Piper looked from them to Martha and Susan, who were snuggled up on the couch. In the easy chair, Jay was reading.

The cozy scene was enough to bring a slight smile to her lips. A smile that dimmed when the next voice spoke.

"We are running out of things to wear," Doris complained as she tried to repair a split seam on Eva's pants.

Jay looked up from her book. "What kind of clothes do you need?"

"Everything. I don't think we have anything that doesn't have a tear or a rip in it." She held up a shirt and another pair of pants and put her fingers through the holes.

"I might be able to help with that."

"What do you mean?" Doris laughed. "In all the other stuff you've got in the basement, you've got a clothing store too?"

"No. Just the raw materials." Jay put a bookmark between the pages of her novel and stood up. Walking over to one of the daybeds, Jay lifted the mattress shelf to reveal several bolts of cloth stored in a cabinet underneath. She pulled them out, calling out the materials. "I've got flannel, wool, denim and several different bolts of cotton." She stopped and glanced over her shoulder. "That's cotton twill for pants, broadcloth and jersey for shirts and unmentionables." She walked over to the other daybed and motioned for Piper to stand up. Under that mattress were several more bolts and a couple of boxes. "I've got stuff in each of the daybeds. Upstairs are skeins of yarn to make sweaters and socks. In this box are buttons, zippers, elastic and Velcro. The other is filled with spools of thread and needles."

"This is freaking cool," enthused Piper. She ran her fingers over the colorful cloth.

"Thanks. I'm glad this stuff will find some use before the bugs get to it."

"I don't know how to make clothes." Susan shook her head. "I've never had to do this before."

"It's all right. The bottom shelf of that bookcase has pattern books." Jay pointed to bookcase near the front door.

Carol went over to the indicated shelf and pulled out several titles. "Neat, see all these different shirts." She handed one of the books to Eva and they cross-legged on the floor in front of the bookcase. "Awesome, we can make dresses."

Jay shrugged at the raised eyebrow from Susan. "That pattern book was Harmony's idea."

"I like the fit of these pants," Cody whined.

"You can also take apart things you like and use them as a template for a new set," Jay said, attempting to reassure him.

Susan's eyes filled with tears. She stood next to the Martha, who filled her arms with different bolts. With a watery smile, she said, "Jay, this is fabulous."

"I'm sure."

They all looked at Doris.

"What?" Jay asked, confused by her sarcastic tone.

"This is all well and good, but why are you only showing it to us now."

"What do you mean?"

"We've been here for almost a month, and you've kept this from us this whole time."

"Not even two weeks and, I beg your pardon, but you didn't tell me you needed new clothes until now," Jay answered reasonably.

"What else are you keeping from us?"

"I'm not keeping anything from you."

"What do you call hiding things we need?"

"They were hardly hidden. Those are built-in cedar chests."

"And how were we to know that?"

"You could have asked." Jay shook her head in bafflement. "What is your malfunction, Doris?"

"That's rich. You're in the wrong, and you accuse me of having a problem."

"How am I in the wrong?"

"You're hoarding stuff."

"Doris, I hardly think I need to justify my actions to you. Yes, I collected materials for the end of the world as we know it. Anyone else could have done the same thing. I owe no one an apology for planning ahead."

"Why didn't you tell us that you had it?"

"It's not like we've had a chance to go over every inch and inventory every item in this house. Trust me that as you tell me what you need, if it's here, it's available."

"I'm tired of being a pitiful pawn that you play with."

"Doris," Martha shouted. "Enough."

"No, it's not. You all act like lap dogs, sucking up to her."

Jay's voice was calm. "I don't ever recall asking anyone to kiss my ass."

"Oh, you never ask. You are all lady of the manor and we're here at your mercy."

"This is ridiculous. Everything I have is yours."

"But how do we know what you have if you keep hiding things?"

"I'm not hiding anything. I don't even remember all the stuff that's all over this house, unless I need it."

"We shouldn't keep finding things out like this."

Piper spoke up, "Doris, she's been more than generous to open her home to virtual strangers. What more do you want? What would make you happy?"

She sniffed in disdain. "I'll be happy if we had more say in the running of our lives."

"You can have all the say you want. Just get the hell off my land first."

"Your land," she said in triumph. "See, I told you that she doesn't consider us full members of the household."

"And why should she? We've brought her nothing but trouble," Susan angrily answered. "She's had to work double hard to provide food for us. She's offered us much more than we can ever repay."

"I'm not seeking any repayment, Susan. Frankly, I've generally liked having most of you on board."

"Out with it."

"What?"

Tapping her foot impatiently, Doris asked, "What is it that you want? Everything has a price and I am tired of waiting for you tell us what it is."

"A little courtesy would not be out of order."

Martha grabbed her sister by the shoulders when she would have spoken again. "Just shut up." There was a tense silence while the two sisters stared at one another.

Blinking first, Doris took a step away from Martha. "I don't know why you all are always mad at me. I'm just saying what you're too afraid to say."

Susan shook her head. "You don't speak for me, and I'd appreciate if you'd stop insulting my friend."

Trying to change the subject, Piper looked from the bolts of cloth to the pattern books. "Who knows how to sew?"

"I do, but I'm not about to sew everybody else's clothes," answered Doris.

"Who said you had to?" Piper asked. "I'm willing to learn, if it means new clothes."

Doris turned to look at Jay. "Well?"

"Well, what?"

"You seemed to have thought of everything else. Don't you have a machine?"

"You are quite the piece of work, Doris." Jay shook her head. "Under that cactus there." She pointed at what they had all thought was just an ornate table. She opened the top to show them a foot-pedal-operated sewing machine hidden inside.

"Do you know how to work it?"

"Yeah. When you're ready, I'll show you what to do."

"Jay, I can't tell you how great this is." Martha stepped toward her.

Jay flinched away out of reach.

"What's wrong?"

"I'm sorry. Just a little claustrophobic right now."

"Oh? Can I help?"

"No," she said. "I think I'll take a walk."

"But it's getting dark."

"It'll be better than being in here." Jay slammed out the nearest door and called the dogs. They had been curled up in their houses, but they all leaped out at her command. Encouraging them to jump and bound around her, she set off down the driveway. At the fork in the road, she turned uphill, deciding to climb up to the remains of the old fire-watching station.

With each stride, she muttered curses against Doris and her ancestors. "How can such different people come from the same parents?" she asked her doggy companions. "And how has she managed to live so long? I would have killed her years ago." Splashing in the puddles, she muttered, "I can't imagine the kind of gall it takes for her to spew her guts out at everyone else when she's such a piece of work."

The pack wound their way up the mountain. Growing tired of the quick pace, Jay sighed and slowed down. She asked her canine companions, "You guys don't think I'm only doing this because I want something, do you?"

Only doggy grins answered her. She balanced her way across a broken-down bridge while her dogs ran down the culvert and across the small stream before joining her on the other side.

Out loud, Jay said, "I'm glad to have people in the house. Really, I am. I was getting lonely." She thought about that. "Okay, maybe not all the people that are currently in the house would I ever had invited before the bombing, but I'm not about to kick any of them out. How dare she accuse me of having ulterior motivations?"

The dogs had no answer. Coming across a pinecone, she kicked it and the dogs chased it down. She watched two of them try to share carrying duties before dropping the pinecone at her feet for her to kick again.

"I do resent having to spend my stash on her, though. She works my last nerve." Jay laughed, shortly. "Of course, that would be the only work she does without duress." Kicking the thoroughly chewed cone again, Jay watched the dogs race each other to it.

When the wind blew the rain off the surrounding trees and onto her, she cursed Doris again. "She's nice and dry in my house while I'm out wandering in the rain. Who's the smart one here?"

"Fuck me!" Jay yelled at the top of her lungs. The dogs whined around her. She sat down under the low branches of a young redwood. The dogs crawled around her to lean against her body.

"Sorry for shouting, guys. She makes me so angry." Rubbing and petting the closest dog, Jay told the chocolate lab mix, "My mama told me that you shouldn't wrestle with a pig because you both get dirty and the pig likes it. Do you suppose she knew somebody like Doris?"

She sat for a while on the log, watching the moonrise from behind the storm clouds. Her sweater clung to her, and her butt was cold and wet. Jay sighed when the rain picked up and wearily climbed to her feet. Reluctantly, she headed back to the house.

* * *

Martha had waited for a few moments after Jay stormed out before whirling on her sister. "Where do you get off?"

"Yeah. You are the living end." Susan was still stroking her hand over the bolts of cloth. "This stuff is just fabulous and you treat it and her like they demean you. If you've got such a problem, why are you even here?"

"Where else can I go?" Doris wrapped her arms tightly around her body. "You've got them and her," she said, waving her hand and Cody, Carol and Martha. "What do I have?"

"You mean, other than your daughter and sister?"

"I mean that I'm tired of being alone and having to do everything myself. I want someone to take care of me for a change."

"Listen, Doris, I don't know what they're smoking on the planet you're living on but, I've got to tell you, you don't have a reason to be tired. You don't do half the work the rest of us do, and I'm including your daughter in that. We have all been taking care of you for a long time." Susan took a deep breath. "You are lucky Jay's been too generous to call you on your shit. I'm not. Start pulling your own weight and keep your mouth shut around Jay unless you've got something pleasant to say."

"Oh? So I don't even get to talk anymore?"

"I can't deal with this." Susan threw up her hands and turned to her partner. "Martha, you need to talk some sense into her. I'm going to soak in the hot tub."

The tall woman looked over at her sister. "You and I are going to have to talk about your behavior."

"Why is everyone on my case?"

"Because you've been entirely too selfish."

"I can't believe you'd say that to me."

"I should have said something earlier. You don't have any idea of your effect on other people."

"I don't have sit here and listen to this."

"Yes, you do." Martha was implacable. "You and I are going to have a sit-down tomorrow."

"Why don't you just dump on me now like everyone else?"

"Because all of our tempers are running too high right now. We need a breather, or someone is going to say something that will be unforgivable. Why don't you go to your room and think about what you're willing to do to be a part of this family."

"You're sending me to my room?"

"I'll be heading to mine as well."

Susan came out of the bathroom and asked, "Anyone care to join me for a soak?" Without waiting for an answer, she padded toward the door.

"Do you care that it's raining?"

She laughed at Piper's question. "It's not like sitting in the hot tub is a dry activity." Glancing over her shoulder, she asked her lover, "Are you going to join me?"

Martha shook her head at Susan's back. "No. I'm going to take a book to bed."

"Your loss. Try and stay awake until I come to bed, okay?"

"I'll try." Martha nodded at others. "You kids head to bed when you're ready. Clear the room when Piper wants to go to sleep."

"Don't worry. I want to stay up until Jay comes back," answered Piper as she tied her do-rag over her hair. "Are you sure you shouldn't go after Susan?"

Martha smiled. "No. She'll talk when she's ready. I've learned not to push her. She can be quite the terror when roused."

"I bet. Just try to keep your efforts at détente down."

Trying to look innocent and failing miserably, Martha stuck her tongue out at Piper. "I don't know what you're talking about."

"Whatever." Piper flipped her a salute. "Good luck on dealing with your sister tomorrow."

"Thanks, I'll need all the luck I can get to make it so we can have a little peace around here."

"You always were a good negotiator. I figure you'll find a way to make us all get along eventually."

"From your lips to God's ears," Martha answered. She pulled a book off the shelf near the bedroom. Waving it to the room at large, she called, "Good night, everyone."

CHAPTER TWELVE

As the rains started coming down harder, Susan sank deeper into the warm water of the hot tub. With only her nose and eyes above the surface, she did her best crocodile impression.

"Having a good time?"

Susan threw herself sideways as she startled from the voice. "Who? What?"

"Sorry," Jay stepped out of the darkness and closer to the tub. "I didn't think before I spoke."

"Damn you. I think you've taken off ten years from my life." She raised her eyebrow. "You also need to get into some dry clothes before you catch your death."

"I should be so lucky."

"What do you mean?" Susan eased her way across the hot tub and rested her chin on the side.

Jay couldn't meet the eyes of her friend.

"Tell me, Jay."

"I'm tired of the fighting."

"Martha will read her the riot act." Susan splashed her hands in the water. She forced herself to ask, "Do you want us to go?"

"God, no." Jay held her hands up. "Not at all. Things just got close."

"I'm sorry about that."

"Don't be. She's a bitch. I just have to stop letting her get to me."

"Well, once you figure out how, tell me. I've been trying since she showed up."

"Was she like this before?"

"Before the bombs?" Susan clarified. At Jay's nod, she shrugged. "I don't know. She wouldn't give Martha the time of day before the world ended. I had never met her."

"She's quite a piece of work." Jay sent the dogs back to their houses and turned back to Susan. "What's the rest of Martha's family like?"

"They disinherited her after she came out to them. Except for religious pamphlets on her birthday, we had no contact with them."

"Martha is an amazing woman to escape that indoctrination."

"Don't I know it."

"Just make sure that you don't forget to show her." With a flash of white teeth, Jay headed into the dark house. She nodded gravely to Piper before climbing up to her room. She stripped in the bedroom and quickly warmed up in a hot shower before heading up directly to bed.

Susan soon followed her inside. Quietly, she went into the bedroom and clicked the lock on the door behind her. In the dim light, she stood for a moment just looking at her lover.

Martha had gone to bed with a copy of *Foxfire 3*. Glancing up, she watched Susan watch her. "Was that Jay I heard?"

"Mmmhmm. She made it back safely."

"I'm glad."

"Me too, darling," Susan drawled. "I was not looking forward to getting a search party out to look for her. I wouldn't even know where to begin to look."

"She can take care of herself."

"Yeah, but what about accidents?"

"Jay knows this area like the back of her hand. She knows well enough to avoid the danger areas."

"But with this rain, the ground is soaked. What if she slipped and fell in a ravine?"

"She made it back. Don't dwell on worse-case scenarios."

Susan sighed and finished drying her hair. "All right, I'll let it go." Her voice muffled under the towel, she added, "Although she did look a bit like a drowned rat when she came back."

"You should know. I can't believe you were out in the hot tub in this weather."

Susan pushed away from the door and stepped close to the bed. "It wasn't bad at all. You should have been there." Slowly, she dropped the towel. "I would have been less lonely with you in there with me."

"Sorry. I sort of thought that you were mad at me and I wanted to do some reading."

"I wasn't angry at you, dear. I was just frustrated with the whole situation and needed to relax." Running a hand down her naked body, Susan licked her lips. "I considered doing something while I was there."

Martha stared at her. "You wouldn't."

"If I thought that was the only way to go." She pouted. "Are you planning on doing any more reading tonight?"

Sighing dramatically, Martha tossed the book onto the nightstand. "Well, I suppose, with sufficient inducement, I could be finished for tonight."

"That sounds like a challenge." Susan crawled into bed and curled her body around Martha's larger frame and rested her head on Martha's chest. She felt the pulse speed up under her ear. "I get the feeling that you can easily be induced," she said. Tugging on her partner's sleep shirt, Susan told her to take it off.

Martha quickly complied and laid back onto the bed as Susan settled herself on top of her. Leaning forward, she shivered as Susan deliberately exhaled over her bare left breast.

"My, what have we here?"

"I've wanted you all day," she admitted.

Smiling faintly, Susan moved the hand that was resting on Martha's stomach to the other woman's warm hand. Grasping it gently, she guided it up over her head and closed the fingers over the spindles in the headboard. She kissed Martha and moved so that she could reach Martha's other arm. Lifting it, she lightly stroked the muscles that quivered under her touch.

"Susan?" the other woman gasped, only to fall silent as fingers shifted to brush her lips.

"Trust me, baby," Susan whispered.

Martha's arm shifted ever so slightly, and a strong hand closed over her wrists. Not to restrain her in any way, but as a gentle reminder to keep right where she was. Susan squeezed and released before trailing her hand down the taut frame.

"But..." Martha began.

"Shh. No talking," Susan breathed, her voice a gentle rebuff. Then, there were no more words as she started kissing Martha with all of the passion in her heart. Hot lips converged. With uncommon skill, she incited and teased relentlessly.

Continuing the butterfly kisses, Susan trailed her hands over Martha's upper body. First stroking lightly and then scraping with her nails, she alternated her touches with no particular rhythm. She continued the delicious torment until Martha was writhing helplessly. Susan trailed her lips down her lover's throat, randomly placing kisses and bites along the sensitive flesh.

"Please," Martha moaned low in her throat.

"I said no talking," Susan warned softly. She lifted her fingers to brush her lover's mouth. "If you wake the others, I'll be forced to stop." She kissed Martha again and inhaled her lover's soft whimper into her mouth. "You don't want that, do you?"

Martha nearly answered before enough brain cells worked out that shaking her head would be a better response.

"Very good, sweetheart." Flattening her palm over Martha's sternum, Susan marveled at the rapid beat of her heart. Wanting more contact, she pulled Martha's panties off, exposing Martha to her appreciative gaze.

"You're so beautiful," she stated in awe. She continued her fingers' rambling journey and traced her way to the curve of a firm breast. "Here is so soft," she breathed as her mouth slid lower to press kisses onto flesh that goose pimpled in their wake.

Martha released her grip on the headboard and brought her hands down to her sides. As her lover explored and teased, Martha thrashed in pleasurable agony and gripped the sheets. When Susan's lips wrapped around a taut nipple, she gasped in surprise and need.

"And here you're hard," Susan drawled. She swirled her tongue around the erect tip as her fingers followed her tongue's movement on Martha's stomach. "You want more, don't you, love?"

"God, yes."

"Good," Susan said with a smirk. "I'd hate to think that you were bored."

"Never bored," gasped Martha. "You enthrall me."

"I'll have to reward that answer," promised Susan. She slid her hand down and brushed Martha's inner thigh. She was pleased to hear the gasp Martha couldn't contain.

Muscles quivered under her light touch, and she guided Martha's legs farther apart. Raising herself, she settled her hips between her lover's and applied gentle pressure. Martha bucked beneath her, trying to grind against her thigh.

Susan stroked a thumb against her lover's mouth. "Shh, my love...I'll take care of you." Lips worked against her thumb and teeth scraped, drawing it inside. "Trust me," she promised, pulling the digit free with an audible pop.

Swirling her tongue against Martha's nipples, she smiled as Martha's entire body seem to ripple with tension. "Do you know what I'm going to do?" she murmured.

"I'm hoping," Martha confessed.

Her eyes lifted to pierce into Martha's. "Well, I think you're going to enjoy what I have planned," she promised.

Martha whimpered, her fingers digging into the sheets. At the sharp contact of teeth against her belly, she bucked again, in desperate need of more contact. The tenderness of Susan's tongue soothed the area almost as soon as she had registered the pain. "Please," she begged as her heart tried to pound out of her chest.

"Soon," Susan promised. Sharp teeth bit again, just hard enough to leave a mark, then Susan washed her tongue over the small injury. Riding the slow rise and fall of Martha's hips, she dipped her tongue into the faint depression of her lover's belly button.

Martha looked down as Susan looked up, staring into eyes that seemed to be almost black with hunger. Her fingers ached to stroke and caress her beautiful partner.

"Don't let go yet," Susan requested. "I promise you it'll be worth it."

Martha was trembling as muscles flexed along the length of her body. She tangled her hands into the sheets and gasped, "Oh my god."

Susan slid lower and let her lips play along her lover's hip bones. She nudged her lover's knees farther apart, then tasted Martha's inner thigh. She nipped at the tender skin hard enough to leave a mark.

Martha jerked her hips in an attempt to meet the lips that were now zeroing in on her aching need. "Please," she whispered, the words a supplication.

Strong hands stroked Martha's inner thighs, purposely drawing things out. Martha was so ready that when that gentle contact finally came she was close to exploding. She was so sensitive that the warm breath against her intimate flesh made her arch and cry out loud.

"I love you," Susan breathed, using the passage of air to tease the sensitive flesh before her. Gentle fingers caressed lightly before she flicked once with her fingernail. Martha bucked and lifted her head. Their gazes met for a searing instant before Susan relented.

Martha held her breath, afraid that her lover was going to make her wait even longer. With the first, direct touch of Susan's tongue, she arched off the bed. Panting unsteadily, she cried out, "Don't stop. Please don't stop."

Fluttering her tongue, Susan focused on the small bundle of nerves in Martha's clit. With a rough scream, her lover's entire body froze as she climaxed. Shuddering, Martha cried out, "I love you."

Susan quickly climbed up the bed to enfold her lover in her arms. "God, how I love you," she murmured into the dark hair as she gentled her through the aftershocks.

Her face wet with tears, Martha returned Susan's embrace. She kissed her essence off Susan's lips and face. "Thank you, darling."

"You're so very welcome." She licked salt off her lips. "Are you all right?"

"I can't remember a time when I was better." Martha kissed her partner. "I'd like to return the favor."

Susan nearly purred when her lover's long fingers trailed down her body to play with the dark, damp curls. "It was my pleasure, honey." The hand stilled and she laughed. "But I'm not going to stop you."

"So wet," Martha exclaimed, as she pressed onward. She shifted slightly and inserted her knee between Susan's legs. Lifting slightly, she was able to sink her two middle fingers into the tight channel.

Gasping at the intrusion, Susan clamped down and jerked her hips. "Oh god. That feels good."

When Martha tried to turn them both, Susan held her tightly. "No, sweetheart. Keep holding me tight. I need you to hold me right here."

Obeying her lover's words and needs, she began to thrust the hand between Susan's legs. She bent her thumb to make contact with her clit. Susan was so wet, she slid a third finger in effortlessly.

Martha lavished kisses on Susan's exposed neck and wiped with her tongue against the fast-beating pulse.

"So close." Susan panted. "Don't stop."

"Never, my love," she promised. "I'll never stop loving you."

"I can't believe how ready I was," Susan said a few minutes later with a self-conscious laugh.

Martha eased her hand out from its warm cocoon and brought it to her face. She breathed in the musky scent before sticking out her tongue and licking each finger clean. "I love that you are so responsive to my touch and touching me." She brushed sweat-dampened hair off her still-trembling lover's cheek. "I love you. Go to sleep."

The gentle command worked its magic, and they both slipped into a dreamless slumber.

CHAPTER THIRTEEN

After lunch two days later, Jay called out to Eva as she walked by with some dirty dishes. "You wanted to know more about the bees?" she asked.

"Oh, yes, please." Eva almost tossed the dishes at Cody before hurrying back to the dining room. "I'm ready."

Grinning at the eager girl, Jay told her to go and change her clothes to pants and a long sleeve shirt. When Eva returned, she asked, "You aren't allergic, are you?"

"Nope."

"Good." Jay held out several rubber bands. "Here. You'll need these."

"Um, what do I do with them?"

"Use them to keep your sleeves and pant legs together."

"Why's that?"

"We're going to check on the hives. And these," she said, plucking on the rubber bands sealing her own sleeves, "will keep the little buggers from crawling into places that bees just don't belong."

After Eva complied, the two of them walked over to the other side of the geodome. There was a small windowless metal shed under the trees. Sliding open the stiff door, Jay handed out a hat with netting around it.

"Here. Put this on."

"I thought you had to wear a whole costume when you did something to bother the bees."

"When you bother them, you do." Jay put on her own hat and fluffed the netting around her face. "The beekeeping I do is pretty low-key. It causes a lot less stress on them and results in more honey for us."

Picking up a small crowbar, Jay led the way out to the ten boxes spread out under the trees. Jay waved her hand to encompass the area. "This is called an apiary."

"How many bees do you have? Why do you have so many houses?"

"Because I do everything to excess." Jay shook her head at the look on the teenager's face. "Joking. I didn't know when I'd be able to get resupplied, so I just bought everything in bulk."

"How come you've got two different kinds of beehives?"

"Because I want different things from each of them." Jay tapped the V-shaped box. "This is called a top bar hive. I get less honey but a lot more wax." She walked over to one of the yellow, plastic boxes. "This is called a super. It is what is known as a standard ten-frame hive. From it, I get a lot of honey and just a little wax."

Using the pry bar, she opened each of the hives and showed Eva the few bees inside.

"I expected to see more."

"That's why we're out here in the heat of the day. Most of the workers are out gathering nectar."

A number of bees flew out and around them until she settled the two parts of hive back together. They stood quietly until the bees shifted their attention back to caring for the queen.

"What are we doing now?"

"We are looking for capping." Jay lifted another lid and put it to the side. She pulled up one of the frames. "See how the honeycomb tops are open? You know it is ready to harvest when around ninety percent of them are capped."

"Then what do you do?"

"I extract the honey."

"You mean you take their food." Eva put her fists on her hips.

"You shouldn't think of it as stealing, the bees sure don't. In actuality we're only taking their spit after giving them a great place to live with room for all their young. I should have been so lucky when I was scraping rent up during graduate school."

Jay replaced the frame and lid and moved onto the next box, where she repeated the operation. Taking the three frames she had collected, she led Eva back over to the shed.

Pointing at the machine that dominated the shed, Jay said, "I can put up to five panels in this extractor. Then all I have to do is close the lid and turn the crank. The centrifugal force flings the honey out, where it slides down the sides of the chamber to the holding tanks."

Jay put Eva to work turning the handle. "Do you really see this as stealing?" she asked after a while.

"Not really, I just don't know what else to call it."

"Harvesting honey is just good husbandry. We offer them some benefits, and, in return, we get a sweet reward for our efforts."

Eva seemed a bit disappointed by the little honey that they were able to collect. "Is that all?"

"Don't worry, kid, this is nothing. I do the big harvest at the end of July. That gives the bees plenty of time to make enough storage for winter."

Bending down, Eva looked at the cloudy liquid. "Um, it looks a little gross."

Jay used a squeegee to remove the remaining honey from the extractor. "We've got to strain the honey into the tanks and let it sit for a couple of days for the air and impurities to rise to the top or sink to the bottom. The honey is then ready for bottling."

"What is that machine?"

"It is a squeeze press. For the other type of hive, we will cut off the comb. I only need to leave about an inch at the top for them to start building a new one. We'll place the comb in here and squeeze out all the honey. The wax is then ready for use."

"Like what?"

"All sorts of things. I use it primarily to rustproof metal and make candles. You can also use it as the original tie-dye."

"What do you mean?"

"You've heard of batik? It is done by painting designs in melted wax on cloth and then dying the fabric."

"How do you get the wax off?"

"Boil the cloth."

"Can we do that?"

"Sure. That'll be a good thing to do during the winter."

"Sweet."

Jay took the empty frames and leaned them up against the side of the shed.

"Don't you need to put those back then?" asked Eva.

"To prepare for winter, the colony needs one full super. I've spread that among a couple of hives. By removing a couple of frames, it forces them to consolidate what they have."

"They don't die out?"

"No, in fact they'll stay remarkably warm. The hive is extraordinary. They air condition it in the summer if it gets too hot and their little bodies generate enough heat to keep it warm all winter long."

"That's pretty cool."

"Yeah. They're some of the most efficient and complex insects. They communicate with each other about where to find food with dances." Jay worked quickly to return all the items she had used back to their places in the small shack.

"Why do you keep everything way out here?"

"It's easier to have the whole operation close together. That way, you don't have to walk very far with sticky, drippy things." Jay winked, conspiratorially. "Honestly, though, I moved the extracting operation out here after Harmony threatened to kill me because of all the honey I tracked into the house."

Jay handed Eva the strained bottle of honey. "Carry this back and set it downstairs near the water heater. After a couple of days, we can pour it into bottles." She directed the teenager outside and closed the door. She threw an arm around Eva's shoulder for the walk back to the house. "Pretty neat, doing all that and not getting stung, huh?"

"Yeah. I thought it was more dangerous than that."

"Just remember to come out during the hottest time of the day to check the hives. That way, most of the bees are off collecting more nectar and not hanging around looking to sting you."

"Have you been stung?"

"Several times, in fact. But not lately." Jay pointed at her foot. "The last bee that stung me did so because I stepped on him."

"You should watch where you're going."

"Or wear shoes." They laughed.

Going down into the basement, Eva put the jar aside while Jay grabbed a bag of squabs from the freezer. "How about we do a honey glaze on these birds for dinner?"

Eyes bright, Eva nodded enthusiastically. "Sounds great. Can I help?"

"Can you? My dear child, I insist."

"What do you insist?"

Jay nearly jumped out of her skin. Doris had snuck up behind her before speaking. "Damn, woman. You scared me."

"What have you been doing with my daughter?"

Looking confused, Jay pointed at the jar of honey. "We've been charming bees out of their stash."

Doris turned to her daughter. "Is that true? Is that what happened?" At Eva's nod, she asked, "Are you sure that's all?"

"Now wait just a cotton-picking minute here." Jay drew herself up and glared at the taller woman. "What the hell are you implying?"

"Not a thing. I would just appreciate it if you would get my permission before you disappear with my child."

"I'd hardly think that walking over to the other side of the pond is disappearing."

"Mom, it's okay. Jay was just showing me her beehives and all about extracting honey." Eva put herself between the two women. "It was really neat. I can hardly wait until the summer, and we get to do it for real."

"I'm not sure I want Eva to have anything to do with that."

Eva's face fell. "Mom, it's not dangerous at all. The bees didn't even come close to stinging me."

"It really is very safe, Doris."

"I'll be the judge of that—just as I'll be the judge of any other activities that involve my child."

"Whatever." Jay patted Eva on the shoulder and walked by her to the stairs. "I hope you let her out of jail long enough to help with dinner."

Doris looked at her daughter. "I don't care for her attitude."

"You insulted her, Mother."

"Don't take that tone with me."

"Of course. You just take that tone with everyone else."

"Eva Maria Matlan, you go to your room. There is just no talking to you when you're like this." Turning her back on her daughter, she stalked after Jay. "It's obvious that you know nothing about raising children."

"I didn't do anything with her that I haven't done myself."

"You have the experience to make such decisions for yourself, not for a minor child."

"Nothing happened to her!" Jay nearly shouted in her frustration.

"This time. What about next time?"

"She'll be just as safe next time as she was this time."

"If you can't be responsible, I'll need to insist that you keep away from her."

"That might be a little difficult as we live in the same house." Jay stomped upstairs.

Doggedly, Doris followed her. "You need to respect my decisions regarding my daughter."

"Frankly, I'm finding it hard to accord you any respect at all." Jay pulled open one of the doors to the sideboard and pulled out a bottle of tequila. Pouring herself a shot, she downed it with a cough.

"That's fine coming from someone with a drinking problem."

"I don't have a drinking problem. I have a problem with you and I'm drinking. Big difference."

"Hey, what's going on in here?" Martha stepped out of her bedroom and looked between the two women.

"Oh, your sister seems to think that letting her daughter be alone with me will either kill or corrupt her." Jay poured another shot. This one she savored with her eyes closed.

"Hey, is that Patrón?"

"Yeah. You want some?"

"Damn straight."

Jay giggled. "No, that's why we're having issues." She pulled out another shot glass and filled it with the pale liquid. Pushing it across the table, she grinned at Martha.

"I don't think that your drinking is going to solve anything," Doris hissed.

"There's only one way to solve this, and until that happens, my drinking might just be what saves your life."

"You're threatening me?"

"No. No threats at all." Jay raised the bottle and an eyebrow at Martha, who shook her head. She recapped the bottle and put it back on the shelf. "I've tried to be patient and give you the benefit of the doubt, Doris. But you seem bound and determined to make the lives of everyone around you miserable."

Looking at her sister, Doris asked, "Are you going to let her talk to me like this?"

"Shut up, Doris."

Jay nodded a thank-you to Martha. "I'm tired of these almost daily clashes. I get that you're not happy, but that's no reason for poisoning the air for the rest of us."

"What are you saying?"

"I'm saying that from now on you need to apply yourself to the principle that if you don't have something nice to say, you say nothing at all."

"You're silencing me?"

"Since you don't seem to have the ability to do it yourself, yes."

"You can't do this."

"You're right. I can't. You have to." Jay glared at her. "And if you don't, I'm not sure I can be held responsible for my actions. You've already had a taste of what happens when I lose control."

Doris stood staring at her with her mouth open. Taking the two empty glasses, Jay dropped them off in the kitchen before she headed out the door.

In her wake, the sisters just looked at each other. Martha waited for Doris to blow up.

"I can't believe you just stood there and let her say those awful things."

"Doris, I can't protect you anymore. You promised me when we last talked, less than forty-eight hours ago, that you'd try to get along. Falsely accusing Jay of being a pedophile doesn't show me that you're making any effort at all."

"I am trying. It's just so hard." Doris started to cry. "All of you are against me."

Martha crossed her arms. "No, we're not. We're all in this together. You are the one keeping yourself apart."

"But I have to."

"Why?"

"Because my eternal soul depends on it."

"Sister, you've lived with me and mine. You've seen the love in my life. How can you possibly think that I'm not made exactly the way God wanted me to be?"

"Because the Bible says so."

"Exactly where? After the passages about it being okay to sell your daughter into slavery? Or the ones about it being okay to rape someone if you offer to marry them afterward?"

"I just know what I've been told," she wailed. "I don't want you to go to hell."

"What you've managed to do is make this a hell on earth." Martha begged, "Please, leave the judging to God."

Doris threw herself into her sister's arms. "Don't hate me!"

"Sweetheart, I don't hate you. Life is hard enough without hate." Martha patted the sobbing woman's back. "Just try to be a little more accepting." Stepping away from her, Martha pointed a finger at her sister. "From this point forward, no more snide remarks, no more baiting and absolutely no more boundless accusations."

"I don't know if I can."

"Take this seriously, Doris. If you don't change, I won't protect you anymore."

"I can't believe you're taking their side over your own sister."

"I'm taking the right side. The side you could be on if you would take those shackles off your mind and your heart."

"I'm as our parents made me."

"I managed to unmake myself from their hate and bile and you'd do well to do the same."

"What should I do?"

"Well, if all else fails, you could you simply try to keep your distance from Jay."

"If you say so." Doris wiped her face. "Um, Martha?"

"Yeah?"

"Do you think we should have alcohol left out like that?"

"Like what? She put the bottle back in the cabinet."

"There is no lock. Think of the children."

"I trust the kids."

"There's no need to put temptation into their way."

"It's not like they're ever left alone in the house. I don't think you need to worry about it."

"That's the difference between the two of us. You don't worry enough and I worry too much."

"No, the real issue is that you tend to worry about things that don't matter in the grand scheme of things. We're working for our very survival here, Doris. We don't need to waste our time getting wrapped around the axle about something that doesn't matter." Martha began to pace. "We need to make sure that we have enough food to feed us through the winter and enough firewood to keep us warm. An open bottle of booze is not the end of the world."

"It's how things start. Don't you get it? The same thing happened in the country. Every blessed person willing to turn a blind eye to sin."

"No. The way things started is that some people refused to accept that they aren't the center of the universe. Just because you're white and hold as truth a particular version of the Bible doesn't give you the right to force your ideas down everyone else's throat."

"You can't tell me that you don't believe that there aren't moral absolutes."

"Not really. I believe that you should do unto others as you would have them do unto you."

"That's it?"

"Yeah, everything else is relative. I've stolen to feed my family and I'll kill to protect them. I guess you could say that my ethics are situational." Martha pinched the bridge of her nose. "We've gotten a little off topic here. Your issues with the state of our souls notwithstanding, you need to do your fair share without us having to tell you and to keep a civil tongue in your head."

Gritting her teeth, Doris nodded. "Fine."

"Good. Now, how about you come with me to chop the rest of the log out front? We need to get that area cleared so that we can bring another log down." Martha led her sister out of the house and into the sunshine.

CHAPTER FOURTEEN

"Oh, man. You should have seen it!"

"Seen what?" Susan asked. She came out of the kitchen to see Piper and Martha roughhousing in the living room. "What are you two doing?"

"You're looking at two of the baddest hombres on the mountain." Martha boasted as she got the other woman in a headlock.

"Really? What have you done now?"

"We just brought down that mondo log."

"What?"

Piper blew a raspberry on Martha's side and grinned when she was pushed away. "Yep. It's over by the pond. We couldn't get it any further on our own."

"I thought we were going to leave that one until everyone could go up and help bring it down."

"Help? We don't need no stinking help," cried Martha in a bad Spanish accent.

"You two are in amazingly high spirits for people who are about to get a lecture on safety and teamwork," Susan stated as she set plates down on the table. "I don't even know where to begin…"

"Well, you could just forget about it," Piper said hopefully.

Susan shook her head. "No way. I'm not just going to ignore your doing something potentially dangerous and extremely foolish. Now sit down for lunch."

In a small voice, Martha asked, "Are you really mad at me?"

"I'm a little disappointed, darling, but I'm sure we'll work it out." To erase the sad look on her lover's face, she leaned over and kissed her soundly. She then had to wipe her lips with the back of her hand. "Wow, you're salty."

"It feels good to be active again."

Flexing her arms, Piper kissed each of her biceps. "I'm so glad the rains stopped, and we could get out there and use these babies."

Jay took her place at the table. "What are we going to do with you two when winter hits?"

"Oh god. I hadn't even started to think about that." Susan shook her head.

"May I make a request?" asked Doris.

"Um, sure." Jay looked curiously at her.

Doris had been very quiet for almost two full days after their argument. This was the first meal she had taken with them since then.

"I would appreciate it if you would refrain from using the Lord's name in vain."

Trying not to roll her eyes, Susan agreed. "Sorry, I just don't know where my head was."

"Thank you. I've made every effort to keep quiet, but there are just things that I can't turn a blind eye to."

"Right. We'll try to watch our language," Martha said. "Right, guys?" She received a round of agreement from everyone sitting at the table. Trying to change to subject, she asked, "So, how's the soil turning going?"

"Why don't you ask Doris?"

"Pardon?"

Susan cleared her throat. "We were making good progress on the field until we lost one of our workers."

"Why are you all picking on me? I've been doing what you've asked me to do."

"You know this stuff needs to be done. We shouldn't have to ask you to help."

Martha put her head in her hands and worked on breathing deeply. She was almost at her wit's end in dealing with her sister. "Doris," she started to say.

"I can't believe that you're taking their side without hearing mine." She pushed her chair back and stormed out the French doors.

Piper stood up. "Let me go and talk to her." As no one else wanted the job, she was on her own when she left the house in pursuit.

Catching up with her at the woodpile, Piper asked, "So, you want to tell me your side?"

"You don't really care."

"If I didn't care, I wouldn't have followed you out here."

"You're just like the rest of them."

"Unfortunately for you, I don't find that to be an insult." Piper leaned against the pile. "What can it hurt to talk to me?"

"It won't do any good. You stick together like some lesbian club."

"It goes with the secret handshake. Now, it seems to me that you're just defensive because you know you're in the wrong." When Doris didn't respond, Piper went on. "Cat got your tongue?"

"I never!"

"No and that's one of your problems. You've cut yourself off from one of the most fabulous experiences on the planet."

"You are so full of yourself. You've got nothing that I would ever want," Doris hissed vehemently.

"I think the lady doth protest too much."

"What are you saying?"

"Just that I don't think that you'd have such a problem if you'd just get laid properly." Piper straightened up and stalked toward the other woman.

"I beg your pardon?"

Taking hold of Doris's upper arms, Piper leaned forward and whispered, "You heard me."

"You're disgusting and you better get your hands off me!" Doris's eyes were wild as she looked into Piper's eyes.

"Shut up while I kiss you." She proceeded to do just that, putting her entire body into the interaction and moving her left hand up to cradle the back of Doris's head.

"What the fuck!"

Both women took a step back from one another, Martha's shouted question like a bucket of cold water thrown into their faces.

Doris's hand flashed out and she slapped Piper. "I can't believe you did that."

"Oh, like it's my imagination that you were responding to me." Rubbing her cheek, Piper grinned at Doris.

"I think, as a cop you'd be familiar with the phenomena of rape victims physically responding to their attackers." The words from Doris's mouth were coated in ice.

Piper looked like she'd been hit in the gut. Her face turned ashy, and she swayed slightly.

Stepping between the two women, Martha asked, "What the heck just happened?"

Doris hissed, "I don't want to talk about it."

"Speak to me, Piper," Martha demanded. "What the heck were you thinking?"

"I don't know what came over me," she mumbled.

Doris stomped her foot. "I hate you all. Just leave me alone."

"All right, I understand. Why don't you stay out here and cool off while I take Piper inside."

"No."

"What do you want to do?"

"I don't want to be around any of you right now." Doris was shivering. She rubbed her hands on her bare arms. "I need to get out of here."

"Well, I don't like the idea of you wandering out there by yourself."

Stepping outside, Susan called. "Why don't you go with Jay? She won't let you get lost but will let you get as far away as you need." She studied the chalky tone of Piper's face. "I think a little distance will do both of you some good."

Jay was standing at her shoulder. "Are you out of your mind? You want me to go with her?" she asked in a whisper.

"She shouldn't be alone right now."

"I don't think that *I* should be left alone with her."

"You just have to go and keep her out of trouble."

Shaking her head, Jay disagreed. "How do you know she'll be in less trouble with me?"

"You're the local and you've got the survival skills. Face it, Jay, you're the only choice."

"There's got to be a better way."

"No. You have the least invested in this."

"I don't think you should trust me," Jay whined. "Susan, she drives me crazy."

"Please? Do this for me?"

"Don't pull that face on me. It might work on Martha, but I'm immune."

Susan stood looking at her with her arms crossed. She slowly blinked and let her bottom lip quiver ever so slightly.

Jay threw up her hands. "Whatever. But know this, if I come back without her, it wasn't my fault."

Susan walked over to the hall closet and pulled out Jay's crossbow. She handed her the weapon and her fanny pack. "Take these and get her out of here so she can calm down."

"You trust me with a gun near your sister-in-law?"

"Just go with her and when she's done with freaking out, bring her back."

With poor grace, Jay stomped out onto the patio. She looked over at the two pale women and felt a slight pang. "Ready?" she asked Doris.

"I don't need you to hold my hand."

"That wasn't what I was offering." Jay stopped herself and took a deep breath. "Look, you lead the way. You won't even know I'm there. When you achieve inner peace, I'll get us back home. Deal?"

Doris looked closely at her. "You aren't going to try any funny stuff?"

"No way. Scout's honor, I'm just a shadow."

"Okay." Doris pulled on the jacket Eva handed her and stormed past the lake and greenhouse to the secondary trail down the mountain. For a while the only sounds were her labored breathing and twigs snapping beneath her feet.

When they reached the road, Doris stood for a while looking both directions. Finally, she started walking north. They had covered almost two miles when she turned on Jay. "Why don't I ever see animals?"

"What?"

"I never see any of the animals that the others say they see."

Jay shrugged. "You crash through the woods and scare everything away."

"What do you mean?"

"Take just now. All the way downhill, you made a ton of noise. You didn't watch where you put your feet down and everything within a mile radius knew to lie low until you went past."

"You think I walk badly? How should I be doing it?"

"Put your feet down deliberately. Toe first and don't shift your weight until you know that you're not going to break anything." Jay pointed to a trail that led down to the water. "Why don't you follow the trail and try it out?"

The two of them made it down the hill and out into the valley. As Doris continued to walk, she started to talk about all the things that were upsetting her. Her list included the primitive living arrangements, the required manual labor and the fact that lesbians surrounded her on all sides.

Jay wasn't listening to the diatribe that flowed from Doris's lips like water. She was focused on a flock of birds that had taken to the air near them.

"You're not even listening to me are you?"

"Um, you think this is all a bad influence on your daughter?"

Looking at her suspiciously, Doris nodded. "Yeah. Right. What do you think?"

"You seem to forget that I'm one of them," Jay responded, as gently as she could.

Doris stepped back from her. "Oh, yeah. So, I bet you're on Piper's side."

"No. I don't believe in the Trek philosophy of lesbianism." At Doris's quizzical look, she offered, "You know, to boldly go where no one has gone before. I don't believe in recruiting straight girls."

"I'm not questioning my sexuality."

Jay tried to concentrate on the sounds of the forest. "Nobody said you were."

"Then why did she kiss me?"

"Hush for a moment."

"What?"

"I need to listen."

There were no animal sounds. It felt like the woods themselves were holding their collective breaths.

"What for? We're all alone."

"Not anymore, you aren't." The deep voice spoke from the woods. "Now, I have to wonder. What are two nice little fillies doing out here all on your own?"

"We wandered away from the tour." Instinctively, Jay put herself between the speaker and Doris. "We'll just be on our way."

A new voice called out from the other side of the clearing, "Not so fast. We want to get to know you."

"If you're so interested in making our acquaintance, why don't you show yourselves?"

"Forgive our rudeness. We wanted to enjoy the show for as long as possible."

"There's no more to see here, so you can just move along." Jay took Doris's elbow and started to move away from the still hidden speaker.

Another voice, deep with menace, came from the direction they were heading. "It's not nice when meat thinks it can run."

Doris froze and they turned back to face the original speaker. "Show yourselves," Jay requested.

The bushes rustled all around them as four burly men stepped forward. They were dirty and disheveled, as if they had been traveling hard for many days. As Jay looked into their dead eyes, she felt a burgeoning fear.

"Turn around and face the tree." The largest and hairiest of the men spoke as he waved a sawed-off shotgun at the two women.

Raising her hands in supplication, Jay said, "Guys, we don't have anything of value."

One of the men stepped forward and relieved her of her crossbow. "I like this."

"Consider it a gift," offered Jay. "How about you let us go now?"

"Turn around." The largest man repeated the earlier order. "I'm not in the habit of repeating myself," he said with deadly calm.

She looked at Doris and shrugged. "Let's do what they say."

Doris blinked away tears and nodded. Slowly, the two of them turned around.

"Put your hands on the tree."

Doris just stood still. She seemed to be in shock from fear.

Murmuring softly, Jay said, "Hang in there."

"Silence!" he roared. "You do what I say and I order you to shut up."

"What do you..." A crossbow bolt slamming through her back and into the tree cut off Jay's question.

"Aargh," Jay screamed as the pain drove all thought from her head and the breath from her lungs.

Doris tried to lift her up enough so the bolt through Jay's shoulder wasn't supporting her full weight.

"Oh god," Jay whispered through suddenly dry lips.

"Don't blaspheme," ordered Doris automatically.

"We've got bigger problems than my language," she whispered.

Looking over her shoulder at the four huge and dirty men, Doris could see the lust in their eyes. In a hiss, she pleaded with Jay, "Stand up. Please, you're too heavy to hold up."

Jay struggled to get her legs under her. A moan escaped her lips as the shifting caused the arrow to pull at her shoulder.

"Don't leave me," Doris begged.

"Trust me. Not going anywhere," she answered.

One of the men stepped forward and wiggled the shaft of the arrow. Jay's knees buckled. She dug her short nails into the tree trunk and forced herself to stand up again.

"Since you seem to be hung up, I guess we'll start with your friend," he said.

"Leave her alone, you bastards," Jay muttered. She moaned slightly when they pulled at Doris.

Doris released her grip on Jay and began pleading to be let go. Jay heard the sound of clothes ripping. The muffled sobs from Doris tore at her heart and the grunts from the man assaulting her made her blood boil.

Impaled and with her back to the action, Jay braced both hands on the tree trunk and pushed away from it. She was able to pull several inches of the arrow through her. Her jaw clenched tightly against the pain, she did it again. Fumbling into the pouch at her waist with her good hand, she drew out the automatic and released the safety.

She gritted her teeth, knowing that what she was about to do was foolish, dangerous and going to cause an incredible amount pain. Tensing, she dropped her full weight on the shaft. As it snapped, she pushed her free hand against the tree. Her falling body pivoted as she fell to the ground. On her knees and blinking away tears, she brought up the weapon and began firing at the men. Like her old instructor had taught her, she fired twice each into the center of their bodies.

The explosive tips on the bullets had tremendous destructive power. The closest man lost most of his upper body in a shower of gore. Taken by surprise, none of them was able to return fire.

After emptying the clip, Jay ejected the magazine. Bracing the hot muzzle between her knees, she struggled to remove the other clip from her pouch with one hand.

She hefted the reloaded weapon and looked across the clearing. Nothing was moving. Even the afternoon breeze had died, leaving the air thick with silence and the smell of gunpowder.

CHAPTER FIFTEEN

Tentatively, the birds began to sing again. Every muscle in Jay's body was tense as she scanned the clearing. She was looking to see if any more members of this gang were going to respond to the gunfire.

She was kneeling in the patch of sunlight and welcomed the sound of crickets and the hum of bees. A squirrel looked down from its perch in the trees and chattered angrily at the mess.

Jay slid the pistol into her waist holster and forced herself to her feet. She had to confirm that the men were no longer a threat and check on Doris, who hadn't made any attempt to get out from under the body that was pinning her to the ground. Stumbling over to the prone bodies, Jay dropped to her knees again and pushed the almost headless form until it rolled off Doris.

"Hey, are you okay?" asked Jay.

Doris was sobbing silently, her eyes tightly closed.

"Doris! You've got to snap out of it and help me."

There was no reaction, and Jay visually checked the other bodies. She softened her voice and told her, "Doris, honey, they can't hurt you anymore." Touching her gently, Jay pleaded with her. "Please, you're safe now. Come back."

Getting no response, Jay looked up. The sun was well on its journey across the sky. "You've got to wake up. I can't carry you," she muttered. "I can't carry me."

"Jay?"

She blinked rapidly and replied. "Yeah. I'm here. They're dead."

"He was so heavy and it hurt."

"I know, but we need to get out of here."

"I thought I was going to die."

"But you didn't. You've got to hold onto that now. You're alive and you need to help me."

Doris focused her attention on Jay. "How did you get free?"

"I broke the arrow off. Can we go now?"

Doris sat up and pulled the tattered remains of her shirt together. She kicked out at the dead man lying across her legs, nearly sobbing until she was free. She flinched when Jay touched her shoulder.

"We really have to get out of here."

"Why? They're all dead." Doris looked around the clearing at the carnage. Flies had begun to be drawn to the blood and were buzzing around the wounds and staring eyes. "What do we have to worry about? You've killed them all."

"Maybe." Jay tried to get to her feet and failed. She shook her head and pushed against the ground, almost smiling when her knees locked and she finally stood. "We need to go."

"Why?"

"Look around, Doris. None of them have camping gear or packs."

"So?"

"So, it means their camp is somewhere else, most likely, with folks who are going to come looking for these guys because they heard the shots or because they don't return when they are expected."

Doris surged to her feet and looked around wildly. "How many more?"

"I don't know. We just need to get away from here."

Looking down at herself, Doris started to cry again. "My clothes." She tried to pull the torn pieces of her shirt together. Unsuccessful in her effort to cover up her chest, she turned her brown eyes on Jay.

Jay turned to look at her. "Sorry. I thought body shots were best. I didn't want to miss. Take that guy's pants, he's about your size."

"You're kidding me. I can't take his pants."

"Then make do with what you have." Jay sagged against the support of a tree trunk. "Make it quick, though."

Doris scrubbed the heels of her hands over her eyes. "What's the almighty rush?"

"I'm starting to fade. We have to start moving soon."

"What do you mean?"

"I mean that I'm fucking bleeding here and we need to get home before I pass out." Jay had stepped away from the tree when she started speaking. Dizzy, her legs turned to water on the last word.

Jumping forward, Doris was able to take most of Jay's weight and ease her to the ground. For a moment, she stared at the unconscious form in her arms. She panicked and shook Jay, crying, "Wake up! Wake up!"

Jay groaned and tried to pull away from the vise that was squeezing her. When she opened her eyes, she saw Doris's face. "What?"

"Oh, thank goodness. You fainted."

"And you think shaking someone with an arrow through them is a good way to wake them up?" Jay snapped as she cradled her arm against her chest. Glancing over at Doris, she saw her crying in remorse. "I'm sorry. I shouldn't have yelled at you."

"I'm sorry I hurt you."

Jay gritted her teeth and slowly made her way to her feet. "Let's just try to make it back to the house without killing one another, okay?"

"I'm sorry."

Jay didn't answer. She stood swaying for so long that Doris asked, "Hey, I thought you wanted to go." She lightly grasped Jay's wrist. "Hey?"

Raising a trembling hand to her forehead, Jay swallowed. "Sorry. I keep phasing out." She shifted slightly and grimaced.

"What can I do?"

"I need some sort of a sling."

"With what?"

"Take one of their belts."

Doris was reluctant to touch the bodies. Swallowing hard, she rolled one of her attackers over. Anticipating his turn at her, he had undone his buckle. She pulled the belt from the loops in his pants, brought it over and helped Jay move her arm into place.

Once her arm was supported, Jay was better able to straighten up. "Okay. Let's get this show on the road." The women started to retrace their steps back to the path, though Jay was having a hard time walking in a direct line. After she stumbled over a root, Doris took her good arm. She received a flash of a smile in thanks.

On the narrow deer path, they had to walk closely together, and Doris had to support more of Jay's weight. "Can you do this?" she asked before they attempted the steep incline back to the road.

The throbbing of her shoulder made it hard for Jay to concentrate. Her voice breathy, she answered, "It's not like I've got much of a choice."

Both were sweating and panting when they reached the top. Jay was also shivering and mumbling to herself. At the top, her legs buckled again and the two went crashing to their knees.

Looking into Jay's glazed eyes, Doris asked. "Should I leave you here and bring back help?"

"No. Don't leave me." Jay made the effort to regain her footing. With the other woman's help, she was able to stand. "I can do this."

"You're going to kill yourself."

"Nonsense. I'm fine."

"I don't believe you."

"Just watch me." Digging into her reserves, Jay lifted one leg and then the other. Slowly but surely, she lurched the remaining distance to the mountain hideaway.

"Thank you, Jesus," Doris said when the house finally came into view. She practically carried the almost deadweight of the other woman across the clearing. "Hang on, it's just a little farther."

At the pond, she called out. "Help! Hey, we need some help out here." No one came to meet them, not even the dogs.

Using their last remnants of strength, they made it into the house. "Hello? Anyone here? I could use a little help," she shouted. There was no response and she stood there, holding Jay upright and dithered about what to do.

"Put me down," whispered Jay.

"Where?"

"Table."

"I can't get you up on the table by myself."

"No. Sit in chair. Lean on table."

The two of them made their slow way to the dining table. Freeing one hand, Doris pulled out a seat and eased the other woman down.

"Now what?"

"Head down."

Doris assisted the semi-conscious woman in resting her good arm on the table. "Are you going to be okay?" she asked. Not waiting for an answer, she patted the damp, dark head and turned toward the French doors. "I've got to find help, Jay."

"Go. I'm not going anywhere."

Doris went out of the back door at a dead run and scanned the clearing. Not seeing anyone, she headed to the top of the cliff. She nearly sobbed in relief when she spied her family. They were all down in the garden spreading compost and turning the soil under.

"Hey!" she shouted.

Martha looked up. "Hey, yourself. We didn't expect you back so soon."

"You need to help me," she called down to them.

"What's up?" Martha asked, setting her hoe down. "Are you all right?"

"It's Jay. She's hurt." When the other women just stared up at her, she added desperately, "Really bad. She's been shot. Come quickly."

Martha and Piper, reacting immediately to the panic in her voice, led the race up the stone steps. Doris waited only long enough to see that they were responding before she turned and headed back to the house.

Catching up to her, Martha grabbed her arm. "What's wrong?"

Doris shook off the hand. "Let me go. Jay needs you."

"What happened?" Piper demanded.

"Are you hurt? The blood!"

Doris looked down at the bloodstains on her clothes and hands. "No. It's not mine."

"Where is she?"

"In the house. At the table."

"Mama," Eva cried. "Are you okay?"

"I'm fine, baby." She glared at Martha. "Please, go help her." Doris stopped walking, enfolded Eva in her arms and began sobbing.

Piper and Martha sprinted to the house and into the kitchen, coming to a stop over the huddled form in the dining room. The back of Jay's shirt was almost entirely crimson and the feathered haft of the arrow vibrated slightly every time she drew breath.

"I'm going to be sick." Carol, white-faced, was leaning against her brother.

"You two start some water boiling," Martha said. "I need some scissors. And someone...go downstairs and bring up bandages and anything else that might be helpful from the first-aid closet."

She went down on one knee and felt for a pulse on Jay's neck. She swallowed in relief as the woman moaned softly in response to her touch.

Piper took the scissors Cody brought from the kitchen and gently cut away the bloody shirt, exposing Jay's back. She could hardly see skin for all the blood. Biting her lip, she pressed on the area surrounding the entrance of the arrow. She felt the bone give beneath her fingers as Jay shifted in agony. "Her shoulder is in at least two pieces," she said, wincing in sympathetic pain. Looking at Martha, she asked, "You ready to check out her front?"

"Yeah. We'll need to turn her slightly and support her head."

Jay's other hand scrabbled across the surface of the table as she felt herself falling back. She blinked into Martha's startled eyes. "Whoa," she whispered.

"Whoa, yourself. How are you feeling?"

"Dizzy." Jay tried to stifle a cough. "Hurts to breathe."

Martha and Piper cut the rest of her shirt away. "What happened?" asked Martha.

"Four guys. They came out of the woods. It was horrible." Doris was standing in the doorway, her arms tight around her midriff. She began to cry and Susan took her into her arms. "Oh, dear Lord. This is all my fault."

"Shh," soothed Susan. "You didn't make them shoot her. It's not your fault."

"She wouldn't have been out there if it hadn't been for me."

"Hey, neither of you would have been anywhere near there if I hadn't made you run." Piper's voice was filled with self-loathing.

"We can assign blame later," Martha said. "We've got a few more important things on our hands right now." She watched as Doris pulled out of Susan's arms and went out the back door.

"Has anyone ever dealt with something like this?" she asked the room.

"Not without knowing an ambulance was screaming to my location." Piper's voice shook. "I don't know where to start."

"There's always the ABCs," Martha said.

"What?"

"You know, airway, breathing and circulation."

"Yeah, but what about after that?" Piper was very worried. "We don't have the skills or resources to deal with this level of trauma."

"Maybe Jay does." Martha leaned forward. She lightly tapped Jay's cheek and waited for the eyes to focus on her. "Jay, I need your help."

"What?"

"I need to you stay awake and tell me what to do."

"Finally."

Martha was about to respond sharply when she saw the slight smile on Jay's lips. "I know that asking for help is out of character," she responded. "But this is a little out of my league." She took the cloth that Carol gave her and gently wiped at the dirt- and sweat-soaked face.

"It's gotta come out."

"Yeah. I kind of figured that. Why didn't you take it out when it happened?"

"Thought I'd bleed to death if I did." Jay blinked slowly.

"You were probably right about that." Martha touched the broken end sticking inches out of her chest. "Just pull?"

"Your guess is as good as mine."

"All right. What about afterward? You're going to do all that bleeding now. And risk infection too."

"Should cauterize it."

"How are we supposed to do that?"

"A long screw and pliers from the toolbox. Cut arrow haft close...to skin, pull it out...and...put in the screw. Heat it, red hot."

"Pull it out the back or front?"

"Back," Jay panted, coughing weakly. When she tried to speak again, they could see blood on her teeth.

"That's not good."

Jay nodded and winced. "Yeah, think it nicked my lung."

"We're not going to just let you die."

"Good to hear." Jay's eyes fluttered closed, and she sagged sideways.

CHAPTER SIXTEEN

"Jay!" Martha shouted.

Piper moved one of her hands and felt for a pulse. "It's all right. She's still with us."

Martha took a deep breath and dried her damp hands on her slacks. Clearing her throat, she began to issue orders. "Okay, we've got to collect things." She pointed at Cody. "Run downstairs and grab the pliers and a good-sized screw. You know where to find them?" At his nod, she turned to Susan. "I don't know how much blood there will be. We'll need towels and a lot more bandages if we're going to perform an operation."

"What about me?" Piper asked. She continued to hold Jay upright against the back of the chair. Her hands tightened as Jay coughed again and shifted in pain.

"Keep her still. I'm going to go get the propane torch. I'll come back and wash my hands and then I'll relieve you and you can do the same."

"What can we do?" Carol asked, indicating her and Eva.

"Get some water boiling and then get her bed cleared off upstairs."

Cody looked at the staircase. "Why are you going to bother taking her up there?"

"You remember the trap door she showed us during the tour? We can shut it behind us if necessary."

"Necessary?"

Piper nodded. "Maybe they were tracked back here. If we see them coming, we'll be able to defend against anyone approaching the house."

Eva looked out the windows. "Could they be on their way now?"

"I don't know. How about you close and latch the downstairs shutters."

"Until we get the time to work out a better system," Susan added. "We should have the dogs earn their keep. I'll order them to stand guard."

Once everyone had returned from their errands, Martha looked around at the pale faces. "Gang, this going to be hard. If you don't think you'll be able to handle it, you need to leave now. There is no shame in it. Heck, I think I'd head for the hills if I could." There were a few smiles at the comment.

"Let's hope they're right that laughter is the best medicine, 'cause we are sure short on any other kind." She looked around and saw fierce determination in every face. She had never seen her sister look so grim. "Well, let's get to it then."

The extraction was every bit as bad as Martha had imagined. The smell of burnt flesh was nauseating, and everyone was close to exhaustion by the time they wrestled the unconscious woman up the stairs and laid her on her bed.

Susan tucked the sheet around the limp figure and smoothed the bangs on the damp forehead. "I think she's running a fever."

"Some of that could be her body trying to heal, but we won't know for sure for another few hours. We need to have nursing shifts. She shouldn't be left alone." Piper flipped to a blank page of Jay's bedside journal. She made three columns and labeled them Pulse, Respiration, and Temperature. "We should fill this out every few hours to track whether she's actually getting better or not."

Martha continued to dry her already dried hands on a towel. "What for? It's not like we can do much more than we already have."

"Don't say that." Susan's voice was harsh. "Recovery is partially mental. We need to think positive."

"You think you can just *will* her better?" Martha scoffed.

"If you've got a better plan, I'm willing to listen."

"Chill out, both of you," Piper interrupted. "You're both right. Jay's a fighter, but this is bad. We don't have much more than hope and good thoughts to give her."

"At least she has a fighting chance with that arrow out of her."

"It won't matter if whoever did this to her is still out there."

Doris spoke up. "The guys who did this are dead, but she worried about others."

"Did she say why?"

"They didn't have any packs or gear."

Piper nodded. "Good observation. They could have made camp elsewhere and gone out together, but it is possible those animals were the advance scouts of a larger group."

"What should we do?"

Piper and Martha exchanged a long look before they nodded.

"We need to hunker down. I want most of the lights turned off and for us to bank the fire as soon as we get some warm food in us."

Eva and Carol shook their heads. "I don't think I could eat," Carol whispered.

Hugging her daughter, Susan said, "We need to try. I think I'll heat some of those cans of soup."

"Excellent," Piper agreed. "We also need to establish a boundary and check it regularly for any incursions. I'll head out now with Cody and we'll put out some trip lines."

"What are those?"

"Early warning signals if anyone does try to come up to us. There are several rolls of fishing line down in the basement. We'll just attach it to trees and rig some of the empty cans to them."

Cody nodded. "Okay, I'll go down and get the stuff we need."

"Good boy." Martha pointed at Susan. "Those dogs listen best to you. Can you give them signal to guard?"

"Already done."

"Good. We'll need to regroup tomorrow morning and figure out what other measures we can take." Martha looked at Doris. "Can you wait to tell us what happened at a family council tomorrow or should we talk now?"

"Oh, don't worry any about me."

"Doris, please. Don't be a drama queen. Just tell me if it can wait or not."

"Don't sweat it. I'll just sit up here with the patient while you all run around."

"Are you sure?"

"Yeah. I'm not particularly tired." She pushed a pile of clothes off the chair that was set by the bed and sat down in it. "Go on."

Left alone, she spoke quietly. "Thank you, Jay. You're a sinner but I'll pray for God to have mercy on your soul." She spent the rest of her shift praying softly.

It was hours later when Piper was roused from her half sleep by noises from the bed. Jay had kicked off much of the covers, and her head was rolling back and forth. She stiffened and opened her eyes when Piper touched her wrist. "Who?"

"It's me, Piper."

"Water?" Jay licked her dry lips.

"Sure. Here you go. Take small sips." Piper lifted her up a bit and held the mug of cold tea to her mouth. Trickling only a small amount of the liquid at a time, Piper was able to get most of the cup into Jay before she slipped back to sleep.

Jay did not stir again for the rest of the night. The next morning, soon after Martha had started her shift, she had a coughing fit. Things went downhill from there. By lunch, she was breathing in short pants. The family council was canceled while they took turns walking the border Piper had established and sitting by Jay's bedside. As time passed, anytime she tried to take a deep breath, she would begin coughing.

Martha had the idea of raising Jay's upper body up on a stack of pillows. Once they lifted her up, she didn't seem to struggle as much. Martha and Piper took advantage of her improved condition to leave the house and follow Jay's blood trail. They found the bodies of four men laying discolored and bloated in the clearing. They were naked and the area had been stripped of anything else they might have had with them. But there was no other sign of people, be they friend or foe.

Worried, Piper decided to walk the perimeter of the property while Martha returned to the bedside vigil.

As the hours passed, Jay's temperature rose.

It was late evening when Susan jerked awake, wondering what had disturbed her. She looked over at the bed and saw the wet glistening of Jay's open eyes. Jay started when Susan leaned on the bed. "Easy, easy," she whispered as she leaned close. "How are you feeling?"

"Cold," Jay panted.

"You've got a fever."

Weak fingers plucked at the covers. "Not hot. Cold."

"Okay. Let me get another blanket." Susan opened up the cedar chest at the foot of the bed and pulled out a wool blanket. Laying it down over Jay, she sat down beside her. "Can you try and drink something?"

"Don't wanna. Feel sick."

"Would you try?'

Ignoring the weakly shaking head, Susan tried to get her to sip from a glass of water. Jay began coughing deeply after only a couple of swallows. Rolling her to her side, Susan held her as she coughed and vomited up blood and stomach acid. When the spasm was over, Jay's pulse was very faint.

The next afternoon, Piper held a saturated sponge to Jay's lips. She mumbled something and licked her cracked lips. Once the water touched her tongue, her mouth moved, seeking more. Piper slowly dribbled more into Jay's mouth.

After the last try at drinking had led to a coughing bout, they had been doing everything they could to avoid a repeat. The water dripped slowly and steadily from the sponge into her dry mouth. Jay was able to swallow without coughing.

Her eyes opened briefly, blinked and then opened again to study the concerned face looking down on her. "Piper."

"Yeah." Wetting a cloth, Piper wiped her head and upper chest. The water seemed to dry instantly on the fevered skin.

"Not good."

"No, you're not doing so well."

"Back hurts."

"That may actually be from fluid in your chest." Piper dampened the sponge. "Do you want more to drink?"

"Ice?"

"To eat?"

"Skin."

"Good idea. Will you be okay while I go get some?"

"Try," Jay whispered.

Piper clattered down the spiral staircase. She went into the kitchen and began to crack all of the ice cube trays into a towel. She glanced up when she heard a noise from the living room.

"Who's there?"

Doris came around the corner. "It's only me. What's happening?"

The two of them hadn't been alone together since the kiss that had precipitated everything. Piper flinched visibly when Doris came closer and held the freezer door open. "Um. I'm collecting ice from the freezer to try and bring her fever down," she replied as she slid the water-filled trays inside.

Doris debated for a moment before she asked, "Do you need help?"

"Sure," answered Piper. "Grab the towel and let's go upstairs." She led the way to Jay's bedroom.

Piper and Doris worked together to place the ice under Jay's neck, around her head and over her feet and hands. Once that was done, they sat in silence and waited to see if their ministrations had any effect.

It wasn't too long before Jay began to fidget and moan. Piper pressed down on her shoulders. Shivering and moaning, Jay fought against the hands that held her down.

"Stop, Jay. We're not trying to hurt you." Piper brushed her hand across the struggling woman's forehead. "Easy, now."

Responding more to the soothing hand than to the words, Jay slowly calmed. She continued to shiver until they removed the ice melt and wet towels.

"I think she'll sleep easier for a while."

"Why don't you head to bed?" asked Doris. "I haven't pulled a night shift yet, and I suppose it's time."

"Well, if you think so."

"I'll be fine and Martha will be awake soon."

Piper was too exhausted to argue with her and she headed down the stairs. Doris sat on the bed and stared down at Jay. She was struggling for every breath and Doris worried she wasn't going to make it through the night.

Doris slid off the bed and to her knees. Lacing her fingers together, she began to pray for Jay to recover, for her sister and her family to renounce their sins and for the strength to protect her daughter from the evil of the world.

Eventually, she stopped begging God for help and decided to add a few more pillows behind Jay. She was almost sitting up in bed when Martha came upstairs for her shift.

Martha decided to change the blood-stained bandages. The skin was tight around the wound on her chest but swollen where the arrow had entered her back. She manipulated it carefully and was distressed when the blood that oozed out under pressure was watery.

"Jay, wake up. Come on, Jay. I need to talk to you." Martha gently slapped the flushed cheeks until the injured woman responded.

"Why…you hitting me?"

"I need you to help me."

"Kay." Jay blinked owlishly.

"I think your lung has collapsed. What should I do?"

"Dunno."

"I was hoping for a little more than that." Martha clenched her hands in frustration. "Jay, help me here."

"Know how you can find out," Jay said between gasps.

"How?"

"Medic manual on CD."

"Fuck! I forgot about that."

Jay closed her eyes for a moment. Reopening them, she panted. "Also, bottom of the closet…surgical supplies."

"The wound looks infected. What should we do?"

"Poultice. Garlic and onion, hot as…stand it." She lay still and gasped for a moment.

"How do we make it?"

"Boil water, make a paste…put a layer of gauze, then paste, more gauze and wrap in plastic wrap."

"Do I cook the garlic and onion?"

"No. Raw."

"Anything else we can do?"

"Willow bark tea. For the fever."

"Okay, I'll get to work on these. Can you try and stay awake? Susan will talk to you." Martha moved out of the way and let her lover take her place on the bed. When she got downstairs, she waved Piper over. "Give me a minute to flip on the breaker and you can turn on the computer."

"What's up?"

"I think her lung collapsed and you need to figure out what to do."

"Why do I have to do the research?"

"Because you're doing the surgery."

"What?"

Martha held out her trembling fingers. "I can't do it. You have no idea what it took out of me the last time. I don't trust myself." Without another word, she went downstairs. After flipping the breaker, she grabbed the surgical pack out of the closet. On her return, she went over to the bookcase and pulled down a field manual on trees.

Calling the teenagers together, she pointed out the willow tree. "I need you guys to find me some of these. Bring me back some bark."

The three of them studied the book and headed out of the house. "We're going to try down by the creek," called Carol.

"Stay on this bank, that's as far as Piper has patrolled. She hasn't seen any sign of anyone else but be careful." Martha walked over and opened the closet. "Take a weapon each and guard each other's backs."

Walking to the dining room table, she sat down with the surgical kit. She opened up the bag and saw a remarkable array of equipment. She could identify a clear tube, clamps, scalpel, forceps and a retractor.

Piper was peering intently at the monitor. Occasionally, she would take notes on a pad beside her.

Leaning over her, Martha asked, "What did you find?"

"Lots of stuff after I changed my search."

"What do you mean?"

"Collapsed lung didn't bring up anything. She's actually got a pneumothorax. Also, we should have been making her cough."

"It hurts when she does."

"I know, but the manual says that she has to."

"How do we deal with the lung?"

Piper swiveled in her chair to look Martha in the eye. "Oh, it's a snap. We just remove the air from the pleural cavity by inserting a hollow plastic tube between the ribs and attach it to a suction device."

"In English?"

"I basically have to shove a tube into her chest and hope I hit blood before I hit a vital organ like, say, her heart."

"Just follow the directions."

"Yeah, right. I can't believe we're seriously considering this."

"I don't think we have a choice." Martha took a quick look over her shoulder. "She's dying."

"I know, I know. It's the fear talking." Sending the current document to the printer, Piper added, "I don't even know if we have the stuff to do the procedure."

"We do." At Piper's look of disbelief, she nodded. "You should see what's in the surgical kit. I think it's got everything we could possibly need."

"Really?"

"Yeah. Print out anything else you'll need, and let's take a look together." Martha led the way back to the dining room table.

Doris came over and stood with them. "What's happening?"

"We're trying to learn how to do surgery," answered Piper. "Want to join us?"

She let her hands touch the sterile packs. "I've never done anything like this before."

"Join the club. Neither have we." Piper picked up an armload. "Come on."

The three women carried all the supplies upstairs and heard Jay talking to Susan.

"How's Doris?" Jay asked.

Susan looked down at her. "Why?" she asked. "What's wrong with her?"

"They assaulted her. I couldn't get free. She okay?" Jay tossed her head in distress.

"I don't know, she hasn't said anything to anyone." Susan answered, turning to stare directly at Doris. "Maybe she'll tell us when she's ready."

"I'm fine."

Jay shifted slightly on the bed until she could see into Doris's eyes. "You were raped."

"You were shot."

"Sucks to be us, eh?" Jay swallowed and turned her eyes to the others. "What's the plan?"

"I'm going to stick this in between your ribs and we're going to siphon out all the air and fluid that is keeping your lung from reinflating." Piper held up the tube.

"Easy peasy." Wincing, Jay looked at the others. "Got to keep me still. This is going to hurt." She smiled at Piper. "Don't want you to miss."

"You and me both." Piper took a couple of deep breaths. "You all realize that I'm flying blind here, right?"

Martha reached over and began rubbing at the tension in the other woman's shoulders. "Actually, you're flying by manual. It makes all the difference in the world." She turned Piper around and gazed deeply into her eyes. "I have faith in you."

Nodding, Susan stepped up behind her and hugged her. "You can do this."

Straightening her spine, Piper nodded at her friends. "Let's do this thing."

Piper followed the directions from the manual as Doris read aloud to her. After she made the first incision, her hands stopped trembling. It took all the strength of the other women to hold Jay down for the operation. After it was over, Jay was unconscious again. Susan stayed with her while the other women went back downstairs.

Sitting at the table, Martha opened up a bottle of wine. Pouring a glass, she drained it and filled it again before offering the bottle to the others. "Okay, we've got to get something for pain at the very next opportunity."

"What about the aspirin in the bathroom?"

"She doesn't need anything that will thin out her blood."

Doris made a face at the bottle. "I still don't know why we couldn't give her wine or tequila."

"Beyond the fact that it would take a lot to get her drunk enough to cut the pain, the alcohol would make it even harder for her to breathe." Piper was still flipping through the pages she had printed out.

"What about seeing what her neighbors have?"

"You remember what Jay told us. Until we're officially introduced and vouched for, no one on the mountain is going to waste supplies on us, especially something as precious as painkillers."

"Ironic, isn't it?" Doris smirked. "If she had made more of an effort to show us around, she wouldn't be suffering now."

"That's cold, Doris," Piper replied. "She was hurt saving you. Doesn't that count for anything?"

"Not helping, Piper." Martha grimaced. "We'll get to that in a minute. Now, what can we expect next with Jay's recovery?"

"The text says that the lung will usually return to normal in forty-eight to seventy-two hours." She looked at the others. "So, we wait."

Martha nodded. "Maybe while we wait Doris can tell us exactly what happened."

"I told you they attacked us."

"But to be raped…" Martha swallowed thickly. "I'm so sorry, Doris."

"I don't want to talk about it."

"You need to talk about it," Piper said.

"Why? What good is that going to do?"

"It will help you survive."

"To what end?" Doris pushed back from the table and began to pace. "I survived the bombs and look where it got me. I'm in the midst of tribulation. With my soul at risk, what does it matter what happens to my body?"

Martha stood up. "It matters because you matter. I love you."

Backing away a little, Doris shook her head. "I can't hear that now."

"Then I'm going to keep on saying it until you can." Martha sat back down and looked at her sister. "I still don't understand why you didn't tell us."

"Jay needed all your attention. I didn't want there to be any distractions."

"You call sexual assault a distraction?"

"It was only the one and, then, Jay killed him."

"Doris, don't try to minimize it. You were raped."

"She's in worse shape."

"This isn't a hierarchy of wounds." Martha walked over and gently enfolded her sister in her arms. "What can we do to help?"

"I'm fine," Doris insisted as she wriggled out of the hug.

Piper cleared her throat. "I know you have no reason to trust me anymore but if you're ever not fine and need to talk or anything, please come to one of us. No one wants to see you hurting."

"Don't worry about me."

"You're my sister. Of course, I'm going to worry." Martha reached out to her sister, but Doris moved away again. "I'm so sorry I didn't realize you were hurt. Please forgive me."

"I'll be all right."

"I know you will. And we'll be here with you every step of the way." She was about to say more when Cody, Carol and Eva came into the room.

"What's wrong?"

"Nothing," Doris barked. She glared at her sister and Piper.

Unsure about the wisdom of keeping this a secret, Martha frowned. "Um," she began.

Doris shook her head emphatically.

"Fine," she relented. Looking at the others, she said, "Now that we're all here, we've got to set up shifts to see if what we just did is going to help or hurt the patient."

"You're going to let us take shifts?"

"We all need to get a little more sleep each night and more done to prepare for winter during the day. If we spread around all the chores, we'll be able to monitor her and get shit done."

Piper drew out a daily schedule with a to-do list for the next few days and they all took a turn sitting vigil while Jay struggled to heal. The poultice was changed twice a day and, almost imperceptibly and only because they could track the change in the journal, she seemed to recover. Eventually, the infection and her fever disappeared and she was able to sleep through the night.

On the seventh morning after the attack, when Susan came up the staircase with a cup of tea, Piper smiled. "It may be my imagination, but I think she's breathing easier."

"Has she woken up?"

"She has been muttering this past hour. Should be any time now." Piper stretched and opened the curtains. "You've had breakfast?"

"Yep."

"All right. I'm going to get some sleep. Call out if you need anything." Collecting the empty cups and washcloths that had been used that night, Piper headed downstairs.

"We alone?"

Susan was startled by the hoarse question. Sitting down on the side of the bed, she laid a cool hand on Jay's cheek. "Yes, we're alone. How are you feeling?"

"Wiped out." Jay tried to push herself up on her elbows. A sharp pain in her back dropped her back onto the bed, coughing.

"What are you thinking? Stay still, you idiot." Susan helped ease Jay onto her side and held her through the spasms that racked her body. When she stopped coughing and her pulse began to slow down, Susan rolled Jay onto her back and offered her the mug.

Jay drank the foul-tasting drink of steeped bark, grimacing as she did so. "Who was the idiot that suggested this?" she asked facetiously.

"It was yet another one of your good ideas."

"Good thing I'm so full of them."

"Hmm. I always thought that you were full of it but was pretty impressed on what you can do when you're out of it." Susan busied herself taking Jay's pulse. "Without the poultice and tea suggestions, I'm not sure you would have made it."

"How long have I been out?"

"It's been a week. You really gave us a scare."

"Yeah. I think I scared myself. That whole not-breathing thing is a tough way to go."

"Thank goodness you had the supplies and manual."

"Yeah, but I gotta say some antibiotics and painkillers wouldn't have been amiss."

"So you're a dreamer when you're not delirious too."

"Ah, those were some weird dreams." Jay shifted slightly. "Have y'all seen any sign of those guys' friends?"

"No. Piper set up a perimeter immediately after and we all spent some time on guard duty. For the first couple of days, we kept a low profile with no noise or smoke. She and Martha eventually went down to where you and Doris were attacked, but the bodies had been stripped bare and no one else was around."

Jay lay quietly for a while, blinking slowly at the ceiling. "I don't know where those guys came from or where they were going, but I hope any friends they may have had won't want to borrow trouble by coming after whoever killed them."

Susan picked up the washcloth and began to wipe Jay down. "Are you okay about the killing?" she asked quietly. "Doris said you blew them all away."

"I did what I had to do."

"That wasn't my question."

Rolling her head, Jay moved until she was able to look Susan in the eye. "I'm in no condition to second-guess myself. This isn't the first time I've had to use deadly force but it is the closest I've come to dying. Check in with me again once I'm back on my feet. Right now, I am going to focus on getting better."

"I'll hold you to that." Susan laughed. "You know you can always talk to me."

"Thanks."

"No problem. Now, why don't you try to sleep some more?"

As she could barely hold her eyes open, Jay nodded and let Susan tuck the covers around her. Her breathing evened out and her muscles relaxed as she slumbered.

CHAPTER SEVENTEEN

For a long moment after she woke the next day, Jay lay perfectly still.

One of the curtains wasn't closed all the way, and there was a beam of sunlight warming her face. Opening her eyes, she saw the room was empty.

Holding her breath, she rolled onto her right side. Supporting her left arm against her chest, she pushed up and swung her legs off the bed. Hissing softly, she struggled up into a sitting position.

Swallowing against the nausea, she stumbled over to lean against her dresser. Jay opened a drawer and pulled out a pair of sweatpants. Balancing on one leg was a chore, but she got them on. She considered changing her shirt, but the pull from her muscles made her decide to just go out in the flannel nightshirt. She put her feet into a pair of Crocs and made her way down the staircase.

At the bottom, she looked over and saw Doris sitting at the dining table sipping on a cup of tea. For a long moment the two women stared at one another. The ticking of the grandfather clock was the only noise in the house.

Doris blinked first. Nodding silently, Jay went to the closet and pulled out a jacket and a weapon. Gritting her teeth, she was able to slide her good arm into the sleeve and the other side over her shoulder. She missed on her first attempt but was finally able to put her automatic in her pocket with a handful of bullets.

Never turning around, she walked out of the house. When she gently closed the door behind her, the dogs leapt and bounded around her. In a stern voice barely above a whisper, she commanded them to stay and guard. She didn't look back as she walked past the lake and disappeared into the woods.

* * *

"Where's Jay?" Piper shouted an hour later. She almost fell down the staircase, catching herself under one arm on the railing and nearly dropping the mug of tea that she had taken up for the patient.

"She's not up there?"

Piper rolled her eyes at Susan's question. "Do you think the room is so big that I could have missed her?"

"I was just wondering if you checked the bathroom."

"Can she even make it that far on her own?" Piper asked before turning to go back up the stairs.

"She went for a walk." Doris's quiet statement silenced everyone.

"What? She shouldn't be out of bed. How could you let her go?"

"Who am I to stop her?"

"You're right. Perhaps if you had been somebody who gave a thought once in a while to someone other than themselves, we wouldn't even need to be having this conversation." Piper's tone was scathing.

"What are you saying? That this is my fault?"

"Give the lady a cigar. Jay wouldn't be hurt and certainly wouldn't be out wandering around if it wasn't for you."

"Oh, and you had nothing to do with it," Doris sneered. "You kissed me."

"So I made an error of poor taste and judgment. What's your excuse?"

Doris's eyes filled with tears. "None of you have ever made a secret about how little you want me around. I'll just leave."

"Don't be an idiot, sis." Martha was impatient. "This isn't about you right now." She glared at Piper. "You aren't helping things either. Right now, we need to figure out what we're going to do about Jay."

"We need to go look for her."

"I think we should wait." Susan had her arms crossed tightly over her chest. "I think she needed to be alone."

"What?"

"Doris, did she say anything?"

"No. She just took off."

"All right, then. She obviously left under her own power. We need to wait."

"There must have been a reason," Piper wondered aloud. "She hasn't been able to be awake for more than a few hours at a time. Why would she leave?"

"We won't know that until she returns."

"And where did she go?" Piper walked to the French doors. "Maybe her fever came back and she's out there, wandering around, delirious."

Doris spoke quietly. "She seemed to know what she was doing."

"How do you know?"

"Her actions were very deliberate."

"Tell me exactly what happened." Martha took a calming breath before she sat down at the table next to her sister. "Don't leave any details out."

"There isn't much. She had a little trouble with the stairs. We looked at each other, and she went to the closet and got her coat." Doris drew her finger through the water rings on the table. "She put her pistol in her pocket with some ammunition and went out the door."

"Oh, that's just great. She's out there with a weapon."

"Calm down, Piper!" Susan barked. "Have you ever known her to leave the house without some form of personal protection? Her having a gun doesn't mean anything."

"Doesn't it?"

"Not really. I think she just needed time away from us."

"Why? What did we do?"

"Think about it. She's been alone here for a long time. We come and she not only has to babysit us, but she now has to recover from a life-threatening injury. She doesn't like feeling dependent at the best of times."

"Are you sure?" Piper asked. "She may be out of her head."

Susan shook her head. "She wasn't feverish when I checked her last. Knowing her the way I do, I think mine is a plausible explanation."

"I still think we should look for her."

"Give her some time to get it out of her system. We don't want to her to think that she is a prisoner."

"And you're willing to risk her life on your idea that she just wanted a time-out?" Piper asked.

"We have to honor her decisions."

"How long are we to wait while she is out there, dying out in the woods?"

"Give her until after lunch."

"I hope you're right."

"So do I." Susan glanced out the window. "I pray we are doing the right thing."

* * *

When Jay left the house, she headed down the hill, using gravity to facilitate her flight. She was hardly out of sight of the house before she started to struggle, feeling the burn in her lungs and ache in her muscles. She barely made her way down the steep incline to the stream.

Crossing the stream took the last of her energy, and she sank to the ground at the base of a ponderosa pine. Her back to the bark, she closed her eyes and slept.

When she opened her eyes again, the sun had moved overhead. She pulled the pistol from her pocket and balanced its weight in the palm of her hand. The black metal felt almost too light for the amount of power it contained. Gripping tightly, she considered how best to hold it.

She lifted her head, knocking it against the tree at her back. Looking around the clearing, she watched a bird take off. Searching for what had disturbed it, she was surprised to see a large, feral cat staring across the space at her.

"Hello." Jay smiled. "Are you here to bring me some kind of message?" The cat's tail twitched. "You're kind of scrawny for a spirit guide."

The two of them stared at one another for several moments before the landing of another bird distracted the cat. Completely ignoring the woman, the cat stalked its prey. It crouched with only the tip of its tail twitching. With a graceful lunge, the feline landed on the bird and made quick work of it, despite its struggles.

Jay watched the cat eviscerate the bird and carry the remains out of the clearing. She sighed. "Well, that was a pretty confusing portent. Am I supposed to identify with the bird and worry about what happens when I get distracted? Or perhaps I'd be better off remembering that the cat lost one meal before the second nearly landed in his lap." She drew up her knees and balanced the pistol on them. "Harrumph. You're probably just making a statement about the frigging circle of life. The question I have for you is whether I'm coming or going?"

Sitting quietly, Jay listened to the sounds of the forest. She could hear the birdcalls, the music of the river and the wind rustling the tree boughs. Becoming even more intent, she listened to the sound of the insects and the far-off rustling of the cat returning to its den. Peering at the automatic, she grimaced. "Where do I go from here?" she asked.

With deadly economy, Jay fed a round into the chamber and switched off the safety. For the longest time, she stared down the barrel of the gun. The hole seemed to grow until it filled her entire vision.

Closing her eyes to the relief that pressure on the trigger could bring, she turned the weapon away from her face and ejected the unused cartridge. Sliding the bullet and the pistol into her pocket, she climbed to her feet.

She took one last look around the clearing before she turned and headed back the way she came. Stopping at the stream, she made the laborious effort to sink to her knees. Leaning over, she took a long drink from the river before she rinsed her face and hands in the cold stream. The water tasted extraordinarily good and felt refreshing on her skin.

She made her way back to her feet and started back up the way she had come. It was difficult to keep her feet on the gravel road, but she made it to the top without falling.

The effort used up nearly all of Jay's remaining strength. She had to hold onto one of the saplings and gasp for air before she could take another step. Gritting her teeth, she growled to herself before having to laugh. Not even an hour ago she was considering ending it all. Now she was mad when it seemed like she wouldn't make it back to the house. Pushing off, she lowered her head and concentrated on putting one foot ahead of the other.

* * *

Piper stepped out of the woods and saw Jay. Her head was down, and she was cradling her left arm against her stomach. Moving quickly to close the distance, Piper called out, "Jay!"

Jay's steps were erratic, and there was a copper taste in her mouth. She startled when Piper suddenly appeared in front of her. "Hello."

"Hey."

"Where'd you come from?"

"I was looking for you." Piper slipped her shoulder under Jay's right arm. "Where did you go?"

"Didn't I tell you that I had an important appointment?"

"It must have been left off the calendar."

"We need to fire that secretary." Jay had to stop talking to concentrate on staying on her feet.

As they walked, Piper took more of Jay's weight. "Just lean on me."

"Okay."

"Are you in pain?"

"Yes, thank god."

Piper was confused. "You're thankful you're in pain?"

"You bet," Jay panted. "It means I'm still alive."

"Well, I'm glad you're okay."

"Thanks. I appreciate y'all coming out looking for me."

The two of them concentrated their efforts in making their way up the trail. Waving off the worried teenagers, Piper helped Jay up the stairs and sat her on the bed. With an economy of motion, she undressed her and got her lying down in bed.

"You sweated a bit during your adventures. You want me to give you a wipe down?" she asked, frowning at the pale face.

"Thank you. That would be nice."

Piper gathered together a bowl of warm water and a soft cloth. Setting everything by the bed, she began to wash off the day's exertions. Her large hands were gentle in their ministrations.

Jay closed her eyes. The strokes were almost hypnotic, and she eventually relaxed. After it was over, she tiredly refused any food. Between one breath and the next, she fell asleep.

It was full dark when Susan climbed up the stairs to the attic room. "Hey, Jay," she called as she neared the bed. When the brown eyes fluttered open, she said, "I've brought you up a cup of tea."

"Thanks." Slowly and carefully, Jay eased up into a sitting position.

Susan watched her without making any effort to help. Once she was braced, she handed over the warm liquid. "You want to talk about what happened today?"

"Not really." Jay sipped from the mug. Over the tendrils of steam, she watched Susan watch her. "I'm really tired."

"We can do this at another time, but trust me, we're going to talk about this."

"No. I mean it. I'm really tired." Jay shifted against the pillows. She raised an eyebrow. "You know, *tired*."

"Oh, that kind of tired."

"Yeah. I'm also in a bit of pain."

"I think it's more than just a bit, sweetie. I just wish there was something I could do."

"Well, I thought for a brief moment there that what I wanted was to be done with the aches and pains." Her voice dropped. "Permanently."

"I thought as much."

"You're disappointed."

"I wouldn't say that." Susan leaned closer to her. "You're one of the strongest women I've ever met. The fact that you could even consider killing yourself scares the piss out of me." She picked up Jay's hand and held it tightly.

"Well, as you can see, I had second thoughts."

"What changed your mind?"

"A sneaking suspicion that the pain I'm feeling now is nothing compared to the everlasting torment I'm heading for." She laughed, harshly. "No reason to rush to hell."

Susan cocked her head. "You don't really believe that nonsense, do you? You've been listening to the wrong people if you think you're going to burn." She stroked her thumb over Jay's knuckles. "You've fed the hungry, clothed the naked and loved your neighbor as yourself. If anyone deserves to make it through the pearly gates, you do."

"Aw, shucks. Your flattery is going straight to my head." Jay joked, batting her eyelashes.

"I'm serious. You saved us. Tell me what I can do to help you save yourself."

"I fear I'm just a poor patient. I don't do sick or weak well."

"It must be especially hard since you're the one that we've been going to for all the answers."

"Knowledge is power and all that jazz."

"It's still cold comfort when you're feeling ill."

"I'm scared.

"You gave us a scare too."

"Sorry."

"I wasn't looking for an apology. I just want you know that you're not alone."

"I know that. And I'm kind of glad."

"Are you?"

"Yeah." Jay snickered at the look on Susan's face. "I guess you never expected to hear that from me?"

"You never cease to do the unexpected. I need that and I need you." Susan shrugged. "We all need each other, if we're going to make it out here."

"I hate to be the one to break it to you but no one gets out alive."

Susan slapped her thigh. "Don't make fun. I'm serious. We are here for you. You've done so much for us."

Jay blushed and tugged on the blanket. "Yeah, well."

"Well nothing. It's true. Do me a favor? The next time you're feeling impulsive and self-destructive, you'll pause for just a moment and think about how much I love you and would miss you if you were gone." Susan kissed the startled woman on the lips and stood up. "I'll let you go back to sleep now."

"And how exactly am I to sleep after that?"

"Sweetheart, I was just giving you a reminder that you've got something to live for." Blowing her another kiss, Susan turned and went back downstairs.

CHAPTER EIGHTEEN

"Where is she?"

"Outside on the patio." Martha flicked her towel over the bowl to keep the biscuits warm and glanced through the window. "She's been there all morning."

"Do you know why?"

"She said she was cold."

"She's always run cold," laughed Susan. "I remember how she would always have to bring a sweater and coat when we went anywhere because she was sure to freeze."

"She doesn't seem to be able to warm up at all anymore." Martha picked up the spoon and stirred the Dutch oven. "I don't know how much longer we're going to be able to keep her out of the hot tub."

"Do we have to? I mean, it'll make her happy."

"It could kill her. The hot water would raise her blood pressure and cause dehydration. God only knows if all those bits and pieces inside her are healed enough to handle being cooked."

"What are we going to do?"

"Let me try talking to her," offered Piper. She walked through the French doors and sat down in the chair next to Jay's chaise lounge.

Jay turned her head and looked at the other woman. "What's up?"

"Nothing much."

Jay nodded and closed her eyes again. She looked like a lizard, trying to absorb as much heat as possible from the pale October sun.

The two lounged together for the next hour. During that time, Piper took several quick peeks at Jay.

"Out with it." Jay finally spoke.

"What are you talking about?"

"You're as jumpy as a virgin at a sex party. I don't know how I'm supposed to get any rest with your fidgeting."

"Um."

"Spit out whatever's got your panties in a wad."

"I just wanted to know, uh…"

Jay turned her head and glared at her. "What?"

"Do you want a blanket?"

"What?"

"I'll bring you one."

"Excuse me?"

"It'll be no problem."

"I can't believe that all that hemming and hawing was over a blanket."

"Well, yeah."

Jay stared at her with a furrowed brow. "Whatever. I'm fine."

"Good."

"Why is that good?"

"Because if you don't want a blanket, you probably don't want to take a dip."

"Go swimming? No way, it's too cold."

"I meant the hot tub."

"That's a given. I'd give my firstborn to be able to soak again, but I know that it would be a bad idea."

"You're telling me."

"That's right. I am. Now, why don't you tell me what this is all about?"

"I'm sorry?"

"You're going to be." Jay raised her mug of tea. "Don't make me throw this on you. What is going on?"

"We were just a little worried about you."

"You were concerned about me?" Jay waited for Piper to nod. "So, you came out and saw me perfectly relaxed, and you thought that the best thing for my health was to irritate me. Do I have that right?"

"I didn't mean to cause you any stress."

"I see."

"Do you?"

"Not really. I'm just humoring you."

"How are you, really?"

"I'm as good as I can be based on current conditions."

"That's good."

Jay lay back down and closed her eyes. A few minutes and several heartfelt sighs from Piper later, she burst out, "Now what?"

"Are you, uh, are you mad at me?"

"Why would I be mad at you?"

"Because you wouldn't have been out there if I hadn't gotten into it with Doris."

"Remind me later to ask you about that."

"Please don't. I don't think anything you could say would be half as bad as what I'm saying to myself."

"Well, I'm not usually one to refrain from kicking folks when they're down, but you plead so nicely." Jay smiled.

"Thanks. How are you feeling about the whole 'getting shot' thing?"

"I wouldn't recommend it."

Piper nodded sympathetically. "At least the only time I was shot, it was in my arm and I was taken immediately to the hospital for good drugs and competent doctors."

"The doctoring I got was pretty top-notch." At Piper's head shake, she added, "Whatever doesn't kill us, makes us stronger."

"Okay, then, let's talk about the men you killed."

"Why?"

"Because taking a life is hard. Or, at least, it should be."

"It was easy. When those animals went after Doris, I don't think I had a choice. I don't care that they all died at my hands."

"I've never killed in the heat of anger."

"I was angry at them but, even more, I was furious that my own weapon fired the arrow that nearly killed me. I'm not ready to die, and I was pissed that it looked like I would."

Piper's voice cracked. "You came so close."

"But I didn't."

"But you could have."

"Look, we're going around in circles here. Yes, I could have died. I also could have died anytime in the last five years before you came here and you wouldn't have been any more responsible for my death than you are now." Sitting up, Jay looked earnestly at Piper. "You know, I told Susan before we left that I wouldn't be held responsible if Doris died while we were gone. And it doesn't matter how much we disagree, when those guys started on her, all I could think of was how to get both of us out of there alive. That was what mattered. And that's what matters now."

Martha walked out onto the patio. "What matters?"

"We all do."

Confused, she just sat at the end of Jay's chaise lounge. "Of course we do," she said, nodding sagely. "What are your plans for the rest of today?"

"Not much. We seem to be on target with the woodpile."

"Yep, and we've put up the buck Cody brought down the other day." She yawned. "The freezer is pretty full."

"What did he use?"

"The .270."

"How are you doing for ammunition?"

"We've still got some, but it is getting low."

Jay hummed to herself before she began to wiggle her feet.

Raising her eyebrow, Martha asked, "What're you thinking?"

Grinning, Jay answered, "Your saying 'on target with the woodpile' just gave me an idea."

"Well, stow it for a bit," Susan interrupted. "I came out here to bring everyone in. It's lunchtime."

Making faces at each other, the three women followed her into the house and sat at their usual places at the table. Doris and the children were already in their seats.

Jay grinned when Susan set a plate of real food down in front of her. "What? No more broth?"

"I figure that it's about time we started to do things that will stimulate your appetite."

"Well, my stomach and I appreciate it." She began slowly, lifting a forkful of the seasoned meat to her nose. Rolling her eyes in ecstasy, she shoveled the bite into her mouth. "Oh, man. This is good."

Laughing at her obvious enjoyment, the others dug into their own plates of venison stew.

Piper wiped her mouth and asked, "So, what was your idea?"

"It might be time to go back to the basics."

"What do you mean?"

"Y'all haven't done much with bow and arrows, right?"

Piper scratched her chin. "I think I'm the only one who's ever shot one."

"Then it would be a good idea to conduct some archery training for the kids."

"That's a good idea for all of us." Martha opened another biscuit. "I know I could use some help."

"Excellent."

"How do you want to go about it?"

"I've got a target sheet somewhere downstairs that we can lay over one of the woodpiles to give everyone something to aim at."

"I don't want to waste any of my arrows," interjected Piper. "They're not going to last long being fired into logs."

"No worries there. I've got supplies."

"Like what?"

"I've got twenty-, fifty- and hundred-pound bows and a bunch of training arrows." Jay drank deeply from her glass of water. "The tips aren't especially sharp and some of the arrows themselves may not be entirely straight, but it will be enough to get everyone started."

"That sounds good."

"It sounds boring," Cody muttered.

"What's boring about it?"

"Standing around and shooting at the woodpile."

"Didn't you learn how to shoot your rifle by going to the target range and standing around there shooting round after round into paper targets?"

"Yeah, but that was different."

"Not really. If you don't practice, you'll never be able to bring dinner down."

"Why can't I just use the rifle?"

"One day, and that day may come sooner than you think, there will be no more cartridges. Unless you want to chase the deer down and club it with your rifle, you'll need to have something else in your arsenal."

"Won't the arrows run out?"

"Well, we can go out and pick up those that miss and we can always make more when our current batch runs out. The Indians didn't have a Walmart they could run to and they did pretty well for themselves."

"Until the people with rifles exterminated them."

Susan laughed. "Boy, are you in a mood today. Who pissed in your cornflakes?"

"Nobody. I just want to do something more fun."

"Once you've mastered a stationary target, I've also got a graduated series of hoops for you to use."

Cody asked, "What for?"

"It's how the Native Americans taught the braves to shoot. It's like skeet shooting for bows. You work on shooting an arrow through a hoop somebody's sent rolling across the lawn."

Piper looked intrigued. "I'd like to try that."

"Yeah, me too," agreed Cody.

"Great." Jay turned her attention back to her plate. "We can get all the stuff after we eat."

Once the plates were cleared, Martha and children went downstairs to find the target while Jay lay back down in one of the chaise lounges. She was glad she was past the period of falling asleep every ten minutes, but the lingering lassitude was aggravating.

Piper pulled out her bow and restrung it. Wiping a cloth over the fine wood, she asked, "Where should we set up?"

Jay waved at one of the longer stacks of firewood. "I figure that if you center the banner over that, they'll have plenty surface area to hit."

"I don't look forward to chasing down the arrows that miss."

"It's the farthest pile from the cliff face. All the misses should land in the yard."

"From your lips to God's ears." Piper shrugged at Doris's glare. "Sorry, slip of the tongue." She stepped off fifty feet. "Is this far enough?"

"To start with. Since they're not used to pulling too much, we'll start them with the low weight bows and build up from there."

Using her heel, Piper dug a line in the ground. Walking back over to the patio, she rotated her shoulders. "Where are the bow and arrows?" she asked.

"Oh, that's right." Jay struggled to her feet and led the way inside. "Call everyone together."

She waited until the household had gathered around her before she walked over toward the main-floor bedrooms. "I should have shown you all this earlier." She looked up at Doris. "And before you get all righteous, I didn't tell you because I didn't really want to have to deal with it."

"Deal with what?" Susan asked.

"Give me a minute to get it open. I came a little too close for comfort to death, and y'all need to know about the other secret room."

"You never told us there was another one," accused Cody.

"At the time you guys were too young." Painstakingly, she went down on her knees before the bookcase centered between the two bedrooms. She shoved the books on the bottom shelf back to reveal three screws set equidistant apart. Pushing down on them caused the fronting on the base to pop loose. Jay set that aside and wiggled her fingers around in the recess. They all could hear a sharp click.

Jay pulled herself back to her feet. She pressed on one edge of the bookcase. When nothing happened, she put more of her weight onto the edge. This time, it rotated smoothly and they all leaned forward to peer into the darkened recess.

Martha spoke for all of them when she asked, "What do you keep in here?"

Switching on a light, Jay stepped from the front of the narrow room and waved everyone closer for a look. They saw a green metal gun cabinet and several hanging bows. There were cases of ammunition along the back wall and a stack of animal traps.

"It's a secure room. I originally put it in to hide the safe." She pointed at a large, old-fashioned iron safe against the back wall. "I then started storing all the guns and stuff there. Harmony wasn't big on having a lot of firepower in the house. Heck, she was rabid for gun control before the bottom fell out."

"And you weren't?" asked Doris.

"No. I've always thought that gun control meant hitting what you aimed at." Jay smiled and moved further back so that the others could step into the room.

"It's been here the whole time?" asked Cody as he explored the narrow space.

"Yes, it was built with the house."

"And you never mentioned it before?"

"You know what they say? Out of sight, out of mind."

"What's so important that you had to build a separate room to hide it?"

"Well, you all should know by now that I like secret rooms. But to answer your question, I've got the deed to the land here and all of the important documents of my life. Since the collapse of the stock market much of it is just worthless paper."

"But it's bigger than what you would need for the safe."

"I wanted another secure room and, frankly, since I earned the money to pay for it, I did what I wanted."

Piper stepped in and picked up one of the bows. "What does this one pull?"

"Fifty." Jay showed her the boxes of arrows. Some had blunted tips and others, deadly sharp heads. "We can use the blunt ones for target practice."

Moving by them, Martha squatted down beside a metal box. "Is this what I think it is?"

Jay nodded. "Yeah. I was able to get some plastic explosives from the guys working on the highway."

"Explosives?" Doris screeched.

"It's safe enough unless it burns," soothed Piper. "I mean, you do keep the blasting charges separate, right?"

"Of course. Also, the room is entirely concrete. Floor, ceiling, walls. Even if the rest of this place burned, the room should stand." Jay directed Piper to bring out an assortment of bows and training arrows.

"You have all these bows, but I see that you favor the crossbow."

"Yeah. It's a struggle for me to pull the weight and still be able to aim."

"I hear you." Piper handed bows out to the teenagers.

"What are the differences?" Cody asked, looking at the two in his hands.

"One is a twenty-pounder, the other is a hundred-pounder."

"A hundred pounds?"

"Yes."

"Why the difference?"

"Anything below fifty pounds is only good for small game like rabbits or birds. If you want to bring down larger animals, you must have more pounds of pressure."

"Wow! I want to use this one," he said, brandishing the larger bow.

"You need to get the principals down before you attempt the heavier weapons."

Piper looked at Jay. "Shall we bring the whole box of arrows out?"

"Naw, just half." She laughed. "I expect that a number might get lost or ruined. We should keep a few back for the next training session."

Jay came out of the room and secured the hidden door. She glanced up to see Susan coming out of her room.

Putting her hands on her hips, she said, "I never knew that room was there. You can't tell at all from inside."

"That's why the closets are back-to-back. Even if you notice that the rooms aren't large enough, you're fooled into thinking the extra space is explained by the storage area."

"I always knew you had hidden depths."

"Ha, ha. Very funny, Martha," Jay responded dryly. "Are we ready to shoot things?"

"What about the hoops?" asked Piper.

"Oh, those are in the back of the front closet." Jay reached in and pulled out the four-, six- and twelve-inch rings.

"How do they work?"

"One person stands to the right or left and sends them rolling in front of the shooter. The shooter has to get the arrow through the circle for a point."

"What do we win?"

"How about the person with the most points at the end of the day doesn't have to wash dishes for a week?"

"Cool."

With everyone's agreement, Jay sat back on the lounge chair while Piper instructed the others on the use of the bow. Most everyone was eager to learn.

Doris didn't join the others for the lesson. Instead, she dragged a chair into the shade and sat down with her arms crossed.

Looking around for her, Martha stomped over to where her sister was sitting. "What are you doing? You need to get out here, too."

"The heck I do."

"Take a turn, damn it. We all need to know how to protect ourselves and to hunt."

"No, I won't. There are enough killers in this group already." Doris jutted out her chin. "You go and play with your new weapons and I'll be fine over here by myself."

Before Martha could retort, they were joined by Eva.

"C'mon, Mom. It is a lot of fun." Eva smiled at her.

Doris waved off her daughter. "I just want to sit and think but you go and have a good time."

Occasionally glancing back over her shoulder, Eva returned to the lessons. At first, most of her, and everyone else's, arrows flew over and around the woodpile. Over the course of the afternoon, nearly everyone eventually demonstrated some proficiency of hitting the stationary target.

The hoops were another story. At first no one was able to get an arrow through the biggest hoop. They kept at the practice and were amazed when Eva was the first to graduate to the smaller size. She and Carol competed for several more rounds but ended up tied as winners of the contest.

"I'm tired," Jay called. "How about we call it a day?"

Piper agreed. "Yeah. I think that a good start has been made." She unstrung her bow. "We can go again in a day or so."

"Why not tomorrow?" Cody asked. "I still think I can win this."

"Trust me, Cody. Your arms are going to be very sore tomorrow."

With bad grace, the young man put his bow down and joined the others in gathering up the spent arrows.

The sun dipped toward the horizon as the last shaft was brought indoors. The entire group gathered for dinner in better spirits than they had been for days. Eva and Carol sat like queens while the dishes were collected and cleaned.

CHAPTER NINETEEN

"Jay, wake up." Susan put one knee on the bed and reached over to gently shake her arm. "Jay," she called loudly. When the brown eyes opened, she waited until they focused on her. "You awake?"

After clearing her throat, Jay muttered, "I think so."

Lowering her voice, Susan said, "There's some guy outside."

"What does he look like?"

"Big guy. He has some boxes of stuff and he won't come inside."

"Must be time to go a-bartering." She swung her legs off the edge and sat up.

"You all right?"

"I'm fine," she answered automatically. When Susan didn't move or say anything, she glanced up into worried eyes. "I'll be fine," she clarified. "As soon as this vise lets loose of my chest."

Gently, Susan prodded, "You look a little green."

"Sudden movements, like sitting up just now, make me want to throw up."

"Your lung collapsed. You can't expect to return to running around anytime soon."

"Maybe not, but I'd thought after a couple of weeks, I'd at least be feeling a little better."

"You've never had any patience with weakness. Especially your own."

"I've never been this weak before."

Susan grinned. "Right. I'll just take your word for it." She walked over to the window and flung the curtains open. "What shall I tell the guy sitting in the front yard?"

"What time is it?"

"I don't know exactly. It's got to be a couple of hours after lunch, though. Was it bad for us to let you sleep through it?"

Jay scratched her head, trying to stimulate her brain. "No, these naps are draining, but I really needed it." She stood up and stretched, gingerly.

"Uh, the guy?" reminded Susan.

"Offer him a glass of wine. Open the bottle down there in front of him and keep filling his glass."

"Why?"

"We should take any edge we can get."

"What are you talking about? What's going on?"

"Negotiations." Jay took an experimental deep breath. She smiled when she was able to draw in a good deal of air into her lungs. "We want the advantage of being generous with our precious supplies, and if he's foolish enough to let it go to his head, we'll take advantage of that too."

"While I'm getting a perfect stranger drunk in the front yard, what are you going to be doing?"

"Waking up."

"And after that?"

"I'll need a shower." Jay moved to her closet. Pulling down a faded T-shirt and a ragged pair of jeans, she said over her shoulder, "Tell the others that I'll need to see them downstairs in about fifteen minutes."

"Everyone?"

"Sure, we need to decide on a wish list." She started downstairs but looked back to see Susan still standing by the window. "Please and thank you," she offered with a wink.

Bemused, Susan waved her on. "I hear and obey, O Great and Powerful Oz."

"Now you're getting the idea." Jay headed to the bathroom for a quick shower.

Clean and dressed, Jay dropped into her seat at the table and looked around at the expectant faces. "Okay, Josh is heading out for the harvest festival held near the coast. We need to figure out what we need and what we've got to trade for it."

"Like what?" asked Piper.

"Shoot for the moon. I mean, what have you realized that you're missing?"

"You've given us most everything we could ever need."

"Susan, it's been my pleasure, but surely there are things you want. Maybe like different cloth for clothes or patterns that I don't have. There are all kinds of things available during the fest." Jay climbed to her feet. "I need to go out and speak to Josh. Anyone want to join me?"

Piper cleared her throat. "What do we do?"

"He's got some stuff that I told him I needed the last time we met. I can go ahead and finish the transaction. He's bound to have brought some other things to trade. You can look and see if he's got anything you want."

Susan pushed her chair back from the table. "Just show us what to do. We're here for you."

"Thank you. I don't want to overwhelm him, so let's have just a few of you go out with me."

There was a bit of discussion while Jay waited impatiently. Eventually, they reached a decision on who would go out and who would work on their wish lists.

The solidly built, white-haired man was sitting cross-legged on the blanket next to his two boxes. He watched them approach and tilted his glass at Jay. "Glad to see that you could finally join me."

"Hello, Josh. I'm sure that you appreciated the opportunity to have all the wine for yourself."

"Thank you for your consideration."

"Think nothing of it." Jay pointed at the people with her, introducing Martha, Piper, Eva and Doris. She sat down across from him and indicated for the others to sit around her. Silently, they studied one another.

"You're looking a little peaked, Jay."

"It's nothing to worry about." She waved her hand. "I've been a little under the weather, but I'm getting better every day."

"The weather have anything to do with those vultures circling that clearing a while back?"

Jay nodded. "There was some bad shit, but we're here and they're not."

Raising his glass, Josh saluted her. "Here's to the good guys winning one."

Jay smiled and drank deeply.

"Looks like you've got a house full." He watched the others out of the corner of his eye. "Can you speak freely?"

Jay threw her head back and laughed. "They're not holding me hostage, old friend. These are friends."

"All right." He rolled another sip of wine around in his mouth. "Just curious. Were you trying to get me drunk?" Josh asked, waving the half-full bottle of wine.

"Who me? I was merely trying to be hospitable."

They grinned at one another.

Jay asked, "How was your summer?"

"Not bad. I've seen your folks around the area." His eyes trailed over the others.

"Of course, they never saw you." The two shared a grin before Jay shrugged. "Just a few friends from down south decided to join us."

"Us?" he asked. "Harmony's back?"

"Not yet."

Josh stared at her for a long moment. "I'll keep a good thought."

"Thanks." Jay waved her hand. "Let's do this. What do you have?"

He pulled out several pint jars and set them on the ground next to his knee. "Blackberry jam. Trade for an equal weight of honey."

"Not a problem."

After her nod, he lifted out several bags. They were filled with a brown meal. "Acorn flour."

Piper reached across and hefted a bag. "How many acorns does it take to make this much flour?"

"Lots more than you can ever imagine. I sometimes feel that I've looked at every damn acorn on this mountain." The man scratched his scraggly beard and peered closely at Piper. "If you want to see the process, I'm willing to teach."

Before Piper could answer, Jay put her hand on her knee to silence her. "At what cost?"

"Shame, girl. I won't cheat your people." He snapped his teeth at them. "I only bite strangers."

"Accepted. What would be a fair exchange?"

"I need to dig out a new privy."

"One day's work?"

"Maybe three. The ground is all rock."

Jay turned to Piper. "Your choice. It will take three days of hard labor, but in return, he'll show you everything you need to know."

"Just me or could several of us learn?"

"I'm not used to having a lot of folks up in my business. I can teach one, you can teach the others."

Nodding, Piper stuck out her hand. "You've got a deal." She nearly withdrew it when Josh spit in his and reached out. She looked at Jay, who grinned at her discomfort. Gritting her teeth, she spit in her own and they shook on it.

"Come up when I get back and we'll do it then." Josh scratched his bearded chin and held out a bag. "Something new."

Jay took it and opened it up. "Shit, man."

"Yeah."

Jay handed the bag to Piper, who whistled and handed it to Martha. It was filled with homemade nails. "How'd you make these?"

"I finished the forge last winter. Used scraps for those."

"I won't need so many. Just enough for repairs and stuff."

"No worries. Take what you need."

"What do you want?"

"You got a better location for growing things. You and me trade for some of your vegetables."

Running her fingers through her hair, Jay shook her head. "Like what?"

"Tomatoes and beans." He smiled. "I could use some beeswax too."

"I suppose we can spare some," responded Jay with a grin of her own. "Six quarts total and a two-pound block?"

"Done." Josh pulled out several animal pelts and set them in an overlapping pile. "Can I tempt you with any of these?"

Jay looked around. She saw several faces gazing greedily at the fur.

Eva petted the rabbit pelt. "How do you keep it so soft?"

"Make sure all the flesh is off. Air dry and lots of salt. It'll need a soaking then and a bit of scraping and scudding."

"Scudding?"

"I use an old hacksaw blade to scrape and the back of a knife to scud. One takes off the flesh and the other takes off the final tissue layer. If it's not removed, the hide will spoil."

"What about these?" Eva picked up a couple pieces of soft leather.

"After slaughtering, I soak the skin in ashes and water for up to three months. All the flesh comes off and I either work in fat or brains, depending on what it's to be used for."

"Why?"

"'Cause tanning the hide makes it stiff and waterproof. Depending on how you intend to use it, you know, clothes versus shoes, you've got to treat it differently." He glanced at Jay and waggled his eyebrows. "I could teach, but you'd have to supply your own furs."

Doris interrupted, "I don't think that will be necessary."

"But, Mom! Touch it. They're so soft."

Clearing his throat, Josh shrugged. "Don't sweat it. Another time, perhaps."

"We'll let you know." Jay glanced at the remaining boxes. "That everything?"

"Yep."

"You want to stay for dinner?" Jay asked.

"Can you spare it?"

"Sure. I wouldn't offer if I couldn't."

"Okay." Josh stood up and walked over to the pond without another word.

Piper watched him go. "That was interesting."

"He's a character all right," answered Jay. "Let's go inside." Once inside, she brought everyone together. "Cody, could you fetch three more bottles of wine? The cabs in the lower left corner."

Doris spoke for the first time. "Why?"

"We need something to drink with dinner." Jay beckoned the others closer. "He did a good job with those furs. The big question is what would you do with it when you had it and what are you willing to give for it?" She stood up and stretched. "Think about it realistically."

Jay pointed at Carol and Eva. "Hey, could you bring up what we promised him?"

"I don't remember all you said," Eva admitted.

"He's getting four pint jars of honey, six quarts of canned vegetables and a block of wax. It's all down the basement." Jay turned to Piper. "Could you go down to the freezer and pull twelve venison steaks out?"

"Sure."

"What's for dinner?" asked Susan.

"We can grill some steaks, cook a few potatoes and have a salad." Jay went into the kitchen and filled a pot with water for a quick thaw of the meat. "Josh won't come into the house, so we'll eat this as a picnic outside."

Doris stepped into the kitchen. "Why are you feeding that man?"

"He's a neighbor and we just did business together. I won't let him make the trek home on an empty stomach." Jay glanced under her brows at the scowling woman. "I would have thought that you'd be pleased to have a single man at the table."

"What's wrong with him?"

"Nothing. He's just been out here alone a long time."

Doris wandered over to the window and gazed speculatively at the swimming man. "I see."

The dinner that night was a low-key affair as Josh talked about as much as Piper did. Doris flirted shamelessly with him, but he was very gentle in his rejection. He headed back to his home with a promise to return in two days' time.

At the end of the meal, Jay gathered everyone together. "I've got stuff downstairs that I'm willing to spare for a good cause."

"What kind of stuff can we get?"

"Whatever your heart desires and is available for trade."

Martha's voice was low in reply. "Painkillers."

"That is an excellent idea." Jay opened her arms. "Think about what you want. It's very likely that it will be available at the festival. People come down from Oregon and even from across the border. The last couple of years there have even been sailors from China."

"What do you want?" asked Susan.

"Books. I've got a pile that I want to trade. They're mostly trashy novels that I've read once. You all should go through it and anything you want to read can wait to be traded until spring festival." Jay stroked her chin. "I also want to get some nuts. And more salt."

"What about animals?"

"What do you mean?"

Susan ducked her head shyly. "I was thinking that a few chickens might be a good idea. We could have eggs and even the occasional chicken dinner."

"Hmm." Jay pondered on that. "You know, that might be a good idea. I'm just not sure if heading into winter is the best time to start something new like that. It also might be better left for spring when it's our turn to make the trip and get exactly what we want."

"Yeah, you're probably right. We don't even have a coop."

"Don't be discouraged. It's a good idea, and I don't want any of you to think that you can't make plans for this place." Sucking her teeth, she walked over to the bookcase near the bathroom and searched through the shelves until she found a specific volume. She carried it over to Susan. "This book has a couple of chapters on raising birds. Why don't you review it and we can make plans for the new year?"

"Great. Thanks." Susan took the book with a genuine smile.

"So any other ideas?"

"Chocolate," Carol requested. "I haven't had any since we left the Bay Area."

"They still have cocoa down there?"

"If folks have connections south of the border they could get it." Martha grimaced. "It cost an arm and a leg, though."

Jay took hold of Carol's hand. "Come with me." She waved her arm to indicate that the invitation included everyone. "Let me show you something." She led them downstairs into the storage room. On the way in, she switched on the light. At the back corner, she twisted the lightbulb in the socket to flood the dark area with illumination.

In front of them was a narrow rack. The top shelves had boxes labeled holiday decorations, but the rest of the case was loaded with mason jars and cardboard boxes filled with all manner of things. One entire shelf was filled with bottled seeds. On another shelf were boxes of sewing needles, fishing hooks, honing oil and sharpening stones, dental floss and razor blades. Below that shelf was a smaller shelf of water filters, light sticks and packages of wicks and mantles. On the floor was a case of several different strengths of reading glasses.

"I'll be the first to admit that Y2K was blown all out of proportion. But it did open my eyes up to the 'end of the world as we know it' planning of the various militias. Online, I found a number of websites loaded with supply guidelines and suggestions for what would be the most use in bartering."

She looked around the group. "This stuff is better than gold. Think about it. If what you want is available and easily portable, we should be able to have Josh trade for it."

The happy smiles of her housemates convinced her that she was doing the right thing. She left them to their dreams and went upstairs to take another nap.

* * *

The day before Josh was to return, Eva came downstairs to find her mother packing up the side of the bedroom she shared with Carol. "What are you doing?" she asked.

"We're getting out of here."

"What?"

"I need you to find your pack and put this stuff in it."

"Mom, are you serious? You're leaving?"

"We're both going, sweetie," corrected Doris. She tightly rolled up the extra clothes.

"No."

"Excuse me?"

"I said no. I like it here. This place is so much better than Oakland."

"We'll find someplace else. You'll see. You can be happy somewhere else."

"No. You can go if you want, but I'm staying here."

"Don't be silly, Eva. Your place is with me."

"I'm serious. My home is here."

"You're just like your father. You can hardly wait to leave me."

"That's not true, Mother. Dad didn't leave, he died. And I'm not the one leaving; you are."

"Don't you understand that I have to get out of here? This isn't the place for me."

"You could make a bigger effort."

"I don't want to outstay my welcome."

"No, I think you'd always be welcome here."

"I don't think so. They can't wait for me to be gone."

"Believe what you want. Did you even ask to see if he would take you?" Eva pulled her clothes out of Doris's hands. "This is a bad idea."

"This is a perfect plan. I spoke to Josh before he left, and he said that he'd be willing to take us with him."

"I don't care. I'm not going to leave."

"Don't make me go alone."

"You don't have to go anywhere."

"I can't stay here. The Apostle Paul told the church that we must never tolerate sin. My sister..." Her voice broke. Taking a breath, she continued, "My sister and the others stubbornly rebel against God with their homosexuality and they refuse to repent. To save our own souls, we have no choice but to walk away and leave them to their rebellion."

"How can you say that? Don't you love them?"

"Love is speaking the truth, even if they hate you for it." Doris stepped toward the door. Looking back over her shoulder, she begged, "Please don't hate me."

Dropping her load, Eva threw herself into her mother's arms. "I could never hate you, Mom. I love you. Please don't leave me."

"I have to." She pushed Eva to arm's length. "Are you really going to make me go alone?"

"Make you go? I'm begging you to stay."

Doris sighed. "I've stayed as long as I could. This is the best thing."

"I don't believe it is best for anyone." Eva kicked the wall. "I can't believe you'd leave."

"I must. Please don't tell the others what I'm planning."

"I think they're going to figure it out when you walk out of here with all your stuff."

"Until then, though, I don't want to have them nagging at me, trying to change my mind."

"That should be the least of your concerns. You don't know anything about this Josh or where he's going."

"Obviously someplace with lots of traders, and that's all I need to know."

Eva sighed. "I think you're making a big mistake, but I'll keep quiet about your plans."

"I just can't live like this anymore."

"Like what? Free from fear or hunger? What is so terrible that you would even consider a life back in a nightmare like we left?"

"A life free of perversion."

"And that's more important than being around people who love and support you?" Eva started to cry. "More important than *me*?"

Doris pushed her daughter away. "I have to do this for my soul. It is death to tolerate sin."

"I don't care."

"If you don't want to come, Eva," Doris whispered, "that's your decision and one you'll have an eternity to regret." Without another word, she left the basement room and trudged up the stairs, every resolute step taking her farther from the sound of her child sobbing.

CHAPTER TWENTY

Martha sat at the foot of Susan's lounge chair and watched the youngsters play in the pond. While Carol and Cody were splashing each other and laughing, Eva just floated on the raft. Since her mom had left and her tears dried, she barely interacted with anyone.

"Should we be worried?"

"What?" Susan asked, looking up from her book.

"About Eva. She's as bad as Carol was after...uh, you know."

"It's only been a couple of weeks. Kids are remarkably resilient but, even they need time to grieve."

"Grieve?" Martha turned around to look at her partner. "Doris isn't dead."

"But she did abandon her child. That's a tremendous loss for Eva to bear. It also doesn't help that the rest of us are not so secretly happy that Doris is gone."

"I hadn't thought of it that way."

"That's because you aren't the most emotionally intelligent person on the planet."

"Why you!" Martha lunged at Susan and began to tickle her. Kicking and laughing, Susan yelled, "Stop, stop!"

"Take it back!"

"Never," she screamed between gales of laughter.

"Then I'm never stopping."

"I'm going to pee on you if you don't stop right now!"

Martha jumped off the chair. "Gross."

"I didn't say I was peeing; just that I would if you kept it up. I am housebroken, you know."

Piper climbed out of the hot tub. "More housebroken than your boy, at least."

"What do you mean?"

"I think he's gotten worse since he and I are no longer sharing the living room. I needed some cloth from under the daybed and his sheets are a crusty mess."

"I'll talk to him about washing them more regularly. And about using a towel."

"Cool." Piper tightened the robe around her body. "I'm going to head in and see if Jay needs any help with dinner. You two can go back to torturing each other."

"If I was going to torture her, we'd do it in the bedroom," Martha retorted.

Susan laughed. "As long as we're not scaring the wildlife, we can play like this anywhere. I mean, its not like we're having sex out here."

"You don't think that will freak out the kids?"

"Unlike my sister-in-law, I don't think showing affection to your partner is a bad thing. I think we need to model positive behaviors if our children will have any hope of forming healthy relationships of their own."

"And who are they going to find, out here in the middle of nowhere?"

"We aren't that isolated," Martha replied. "We've met some of her neighbors now and there are always bartering trips down the mountain a couple times a year."

Susan nodded. "Love will always find a way."

"You seriously think so?" Piper frowned. "I've given up on ever finding what you guys have."

"The hell you have," Martha scoffed. "Do you forget you kissed my sister? And, don't think I haven't seen you looking at Jay."

Piper looked abashed and busied her hands with retying the knot on the sash of her robe.

A smile playing about her lips, Susan said, "You dog!"

"I'm not a dog," Piper replied. "I know she's still hoping that Harmony will come back."

"But what if she doesn't?"

"If she never comes back and Jay never finds out what happened, I don't think she'll ever get over it." Piper sighed. "Unless she gets word, her heart won't be free." She rolled her eyes at the expressions on her friends' faces. "Don't act so surprised. I can be sensitive and shit."

"But what about your heart?"

"I've been alone since before things went to hell. Even then, I never really risked anything with the women I was with. I knew it wasn't love, so I never thought of any of them as relationships."

"I don't think you ever brought anyone over to our house for any of our get-togethers."

"The women I dated were temporary and they left once we got what we wanted from each other."

"Did you want more?" Susan asked.

"Doesn't everyone?" Shrugging, Piper added, "I know what love is like from what I've seen from you two."

"I hate to break it to you but we're not the perfect couple." Martha blew a kiss at Susan. "Sorry, sweetie, but it's true."

"I know that. I've seen that it isn't all wine and roses. There is a lot more that goes into keeping the love alive. I guess I've just been holding out until I found someone worthy of the work."

Susan got off the lounge chair and gave Piper a hug. "I believe you will."

"What are you going to do if Jay never sees in you what you see in her?" Martha asked. "I don't mean to be a downer, but you two are in way different places and I haven't seen any sparks between you."

"I think I felt the first spark when she was so ballsy down at the rest area. I mean, she faced us down and we can be pretty darn scary, if I do say myself." Smoothing her hands along the soft robe, she added, "I was so worried when she was recovering that I'd never get the chance to tell her what I felt and, then, once she did, I knew that I couldn't say a word. She didn't need the pressure of yet another person's expectations on her."

Susan gave her another hug, tighter this time. "It sounds like it could be love. I just hope you don't get your heart broken."

"It was due for a bruising." Piper wiggled out of Susan's grasp. "I really need to get dressed and help with dinner."

Letting her go, Susan walked over to Martha to get folded into her lover's arms. "Things are complicated, aren't they?"

"That's life, my love. That's life."

"I just don't want either of them hurt."

"We can't do anything about it but be there for them."

Susan sniffled a little and then smiled up at Martha. "Maybe you're not so dense about emotions after all."

Spinning her around, Martha smacked her butt. "You'll pay for that later tonight!"

"Big talker. We'll see if you can put your body where your mouth is." Susan looked through the window into the kitchen. "Looks like Jay needs us inside."

Hand in hand, they walked into the kitchen.

"What can we do to help?"

"Set the table and make a salad."

"I'll take the salad," Susan said. "Goodness knows what you two barbarians would consider salad fixings."

"Bacon?" Martha asked.

"Mmmm, bacon," Jay echoed.

"Plants, you goofs."

"No worries, Martha. We've got a different sort of venison stew for dinner."

"What's in the other pot."

"Grits."

"Grits? That's breakfast food."

"Not where I'm from. This meal is called Grillades and Grits. The meat is sliced thin and browned and set aside. I made a roux and then added peppers and onions and tomatoes to build up a rich dark sauce. I added a bit of heat when I put the meat back in."

"I don't like spicy foods."

"It isn't that spicy, but that is why it is served with grits. You just take a bite of grits with the grillades and it cuts the heat back a notch."

"It sure smells good."

"I think you'll find it quite tasty." Jay picked up a towel and wiped her face. "I can't wait until this weather breaks."

"Yeah, it's been a really warm fall."

Susan nodded. "Maybe that means a mild winter."

"I hope so. A tough winter is hard on everyone, especially when you've got loved ones out in it." Jay tossed the towel on the counter. "Eva will suffer as much from the not knowing as the cold."

"Like you do?"

She rubbed her eyes. "Yeah. Last winter was a nightmare."

"We're here for you."

"I'm a big girl now. You need to worry about Eva."

"We can be here for you both."

"I don't want her neglected."

"She won't be. Our love for her doesn't diminish in any way our love for you." Susan stepped closer but didn't hug her. "You've been alone with this for a long time. Let us help you."

"It's hard."

Piper came into the kitchen and hopped up on the cabinet near the sink. "Teddy Roosevelt was convinced that hardship was a good thing. He used to say, 'Nothing in the world is worth having or worth doing unless it takes effort, pain and difficulty.'"

"Just sometimes I'd like to do without the pain."

"Life is pain, princess. Anyone who tells you different is selling something."

"Excuse me?"

Piper grinned. "It's a line from the movie *Princess Bride*. Any of you ever seen it?"

"I love that film," Susan replied. "Gosh, I miss being able to pop in a DVD or click on a digital download whenever I want to see something."

"That's the one with the Dread Pirate Roberts?" Jay asked. At Piper's nod, she said, "I might have it somewhere and today was sunny enough for us to watch it tonight."

"That would be great!" Piper drummed her hells against the cabinet. "It is going to be so great to see it again."

"I think that is what I really miss. Being able to share culturally relevant stuff with the kids," Martha said. "Our kids are growing up not knowing many of our references."

"It was the same for our parents. They had no idea half the stuff we were talking about, especially when we used slang."

"Yeah," Susan agreed. "I think every generation has that experience."

"But what about them? They don't have the new music, new films or any of those other things we did."

"Then we'll just have to teach them. Maybe go back to working on that school idea."

"You're right," Martha said. "We'll start tonight with *Princess Bride*."

"As you wish," Piper intoned.

After the laughter died down, they hurried through the rest of the meal preparations, excited about their after-dinner plans.

CHAPTER TWENTY-ONE

"Jay! Jay!" Susan's shout shattered the midafternoon quiet.

The women in the garden looked at one another and then to the top of the cliff in almost fearful fascination.

"What now?" Piper muttered.

"Susan doesn't generally get too excitable. What do think she wants?"

"Do you think we should go up there?" Carol and Eva spoke at the same time.

"Hey, Jay!" Calling again, Susan appeared at the top of the stairs.

"She's not down here with us. I think she's in the dome," Martha called back. "What's up?"

"You've got to come see this." Susan waved excitedly and jumped up and down.

"What in blazes are you yelling about?"

"There's a guy up here and a whole bunch of goats." She glanced over her shoulder. "And when I say a whole bunch of goats, I mean more goats than I've ever seen in one place."

"Cool." Eva looked at her aunt. "Can we go see?"

"Sure. It's not like I'd get any more work out of you now that goats are involved."

"Like you're not dying of curiosity," Piper added.

"That's not the point."

Susan shouted, "What should I do?"

"Keep yelling. If Jay's in the county, she'll hear you." Martha led the group up the stairs. "Why don't you girls go up and check the dome?"

The cousins raced each other past the pond to find Jay trimming herbs in the biodome. They told her about the goats between panting for air.

Jay laughed. "That's Frankie."

"Who's Frankie?"

"Didn't I mention him? He and his family live on the next mountain over." Jay wiped her hands and began to walk toward the house.

"What's with the goats?"

"He brings his small herd over to cut our grass four times a year."

"Why?"

"There is always the danger of fire up here. That's why I've cleared the area around the house and stacked the wood so far away. The goats eat everything, and that includes enough of the scrub growth and ground litter to give us a sufficient firebreak. They also give us a good quality manure, and you can't discount the milk to make cheese."

"What does he get out of it?"

"Beside that nice warm feeling from helping his neighbors?" asked Jay sarcastically. "It's all barter. We need to find out what he wants and if we can supply it."

"It would be good to have some cheese."

"You only get cheese if you're willing to milk the suckers." Jay wiped her hands on her pants. "He usually gives some of the milk to the landowners, but we'll need to negotiate for what we want. Let's go do some business."

The other members of the household followed her down the driveway where they could watch the four-legged invasion. About twenty goats were milling about the yard, munching everything in their path.

Glancing over her shoulder, Jay yelled, "Shit. Cody, Eva, Carol. I need you three to go back down to the garden and bring up the roll of chicken wire."

"Sure but why?"

"The little buggers are eating my rosemary tree." Jay stomped over, waving her arms and scaring the goats away. She turned her glare on her housemates as they all fell over themselves laughing at her. "Fine. I hope you all pee on yourselves."

After the minor catastrophe was averted, everyone sat on the patio with the bandy-legged herder. Jay encouraged the others to discuss barter possibilities with him.

"While I'm here you can have all the milk." He spat on the ground. "Of course, you've got to do the milking."

"Can you show us how?"

Frankie nodded. "Sure. For dinner," he added, slyly.

"I would've fed you anyway." Jay glanced at Susan. "Any ideas? It's your night?"

"Fish?"

"Yeah, that'll be good."

"We're going to be inside. You can show them how to milk while we get dinner ready."

As Jay and Susan headed into the house, discussing different options for cooking the fish, Frankie led the others over to several of the slower-moving goats whose udders were hanging low. The lessons were smelly and hilarious, but in the end, they had two buckets of milk.

Cody and Carol carried the buckets into the kitchen and proudly set them down before Jay.

"Good job! That's a lot of milk."

"It was fun," Carol said. "I liked learning how."

"What are you talking about? It was gross!"

"Gross is how a lot of good things start. Take cheese, for instance."

"How do you make it?"

"It's pretty easy," said Jay. She put a cooking pot on the stove and then bent down to stir the embers to life. Walking over to the kitchen door she pulled out a couple of pieces of firewood off the stack and slid them into the firebox. She opened up the baffles, so there was a lot of air movement to help the fire build.

"Pour the milk into the pot," she directed. "We're going to heat the milk until it almost boils. This pasteurization will make sure that the finished cheese won't kill us." Handing over a wooden spoon, she told Carol to stir the liquid. "Keep stirring. Once it comes close to bubbles, we need to take it off the fire."

"Cody, there's a bottle of vinegar in the pantry. Please get it."

He walked in and then leaned back out of the door. "White or apple cider?"

"The white is fine."

"What do you need that for?"

"We need to curdle the milk. The chemical reaction will cause the milk to separate into curds and whey."

"Like the rhyme?"

"Exactly, though unlike Little Miss Muffet, we won't eat the whey. We'll pour everything into a strainer to drain it really well. Then we'll have to squeeze it to make sure all the liquid is gone."

"Then we can eat it?"

"Well, it needs to sit for a few days to age, but then, yes, it's cheese."

"What do you do with the liquid?"

"I pour the whey over the dogs' food. It's high in protein and good for them."

"I think the goats are cute," Eva announced. "Can we keep a couple?"

"It's not that easy." Jay took the spoon and stirred the mixture, being sure to scrape the bottom of the saucepan. "Right now, Frankie comes when we need him. If we had the goats, he'd be out of job. We'd also have to maintain them—they can forage, but we'd have to keep them away from all the herbs and plants we want to eat, milk them daily, care for them if they get injured…And you can't get attached. They wouldn't be pets, but sources of cheese and now and again our main dish."

Susan leaned against the counter. "I still think we should get some kind of domesticated animal."

"As long as I don't have to take care of them. I hate milking anything."

"Don't worry, Jay. We'll do the gross stuff."

"So what are our choices?" asked Piper.

"No room for cows, but chickens, pigs, goats…" Martha ticked them off on her fingers. "Any suggestions?"

"Didn't we discuss this before?" Jay sighed. "We should probably start easy—with chickens as they can eat bugs and stuff. You've got to remember that whatever we raise won't just feed us. We'll have to feed it too."

Jay turned the stirring back to Carol. "Consider what kind of roost or living arrangement you want to set up, and we can bring down a couple more trees. We could build what we needed after winter and then go down to the city at the next trade festival and see what we can find."

"Cool," the teenagers enthused.

"Yeah, you say that now," she grumbled.

"Jay, don't be such a stick in the mud." Susan said as she began to set up the kitchen for fixing dinner. "We already agreed that we'd take care of the extra work. Now, I need someone to go and get me some lemons."

Eva and Carol got the task, and they left Cody to watch over the pot of curdling milk. He was looking rather queasy from the smell by the time the mixture was ready for cooling.

The group gathered for dinner on the patio. Piper and Martha had constructed a long table and two benches from one of the trees they had brought down. Now, there was room for everyone and all the food. The cedar plank with the fish took the center place. There was a large bowl of rice and roasted carrots. For a change of pace, Jay had made corn bread. Conversation flowed with the light, white wine and mint tea.

Frankie shared stories of the other families on his route around the valley. It was good to hear that there were others who had been able to carve out a living in the post-apocalypse world.

The group also learned that there was a plan afoot to create a school for all the children in the several square miles that made up their area.

"I knew it was a great idea," Susan said. "Just think, kids, you'll be able to interact with people your own age."

"We're doing fine. The three of us are plenty."

"But you need more than what we can give you." Susan looked meaningfully at Martha. When her partner did not respond, she kicked her.

Grimacing, Martha agreed. "There is also stuff you need to learn that we can't teach you."

"Like what?" Cody challenged. "I bet you guys know everything."

"Flattering but no." Piper laid her hands flat on the table. "There are many subjects I'm not familiar with—biology, genetics, physics. Frankly, most of the sciences are beyond me. So many revolutionary discoveries have happened to increase our knowledge of the world we live within. To lose that knowledge would be a greatest loss the planet could endure."

Susan squeezed Piper's hand. "I agree. What would you feel comfortable teaching?"

"My knowledge is mainly practical, but I really loved history and social studies in school. I could probably dredge up enough about that to be worth sharing." She smiled. "I was in the band too, so I could also teach music appreciation."

"See, I never knew you were a band geek!" Susan laughed. "I, of course, know the law, and while a lot of tort and contract law is no longer applicable, the principles and theory are still good to know. I read everything, so maybe I could talk to people about literature."

"Literature?" Martha scoffed. "You call what you read literature?"

"Sure, I read a fair bit of escapist fiction but that doesn't mean I haven't read the classics and can't tell a good book when I read it." She raised her eyebrow. "What are you going to teach?"

"My life was spent in law enforcement in a major metropolitan area. I know police procedure, criminal investigations and how to write reports. I'm not sure any of that is useful."

Susan shook her head. "The job wasn't just that. You had to know psychology and forensics, urban studies and violence prevention. In fact, most of your work involved problem-solving and analytic skills, something people still need to know."

"I hadn't thought of it like that." Martha looked at Jay. "What about you?"

"I'm a jack of all trades and the master of none. I thought about it after we first talked about this and still don't know what I could offer other than math."

"You taught me about bees," Eva said.

"True." Leaning forward to catch her eye, Jay added, "Although, maybe that could be something you are now ready to teach someone else."

"Right! This isn't just for the adults. You all are closer to remembering your schoolwork anyway," Susan said enthusiastically. "We should each write down what we can offer." She looked at Frankie. "Would you be willing to take the list with you and give it to those organizing the school?"

"Not a problem. I'm glad to see that you guys are taking an interest outside of your mountain." He pointed at Jay. "I'm pleased to see you break your isolation."

"It has been hard, up here on my own."

"I understand. I'm glad you've got your friends around you now." He pushed back his plate. "That was a delicious meal. Thank you."

"You're welcome," Susan answered.

Martha asked, "What are you doing next?"

"Well, I'm going to finish this mountain. I'll be seeing your higher neighbors and should be ready to head back home very soon."

"Where do you live?" Eva asked.

"Just across the valley. From your mountaintop, you can sometimes see the evening campfires." He looked around at the cohesive unit and grimaced ruefully. "Seeing all your smiling faces lets me know that it is past time for me to see my wife again."

"Why doesn't she travel with you?"

"Because she and the rest of my family have to work to get ready for winter." He waved his hand around the grounds. "Firewood to be cut, food to set up for winter, everything that you've been doing."

"But aren't you lonely?"

"Not with my goats."

Jay laughed. "That's way more information than I wanted to know about you."

"Get your mind out of the gutter. Those wee beasties are my friends."

"Friends?"

"Yeah. They've got personalities."

"But they can't be good conversationalists."

"Well, maybe not. However, they lack the capacity to lie, and on that count alone I'd rather have them than most of the folks I've ever met."

Piper raised her glass. "Hear, hear."

"Present company excluded, of course."

Jay inclined her head in acknowledgment. "I'm sure that we take no offense. Now, did you want to clean up before heading to bed?"

Cody nodded enthusiastically. He knew that he would have to share the living room that evening with him. The herder smelled a bit too goaty for his comfort.

Laughing, Frankie agreed. "I'd be a fool not to take advantage of the hot water I know you have."

That night, Frankie unrolled his sleeping bag in the living room to sleep inside for the first time in a week. He usually ended up sleeping outside with his goats, but here he trusted Jay's dogs enough to set them to watch over the small herd.

His sleep left him in a good mood the next morning. Jay noticed and led to their negotiation for one of the goats that was too old to make the trek back across the valley or survive another winter. By parting with several quarts of honey, some dried fish and some of the nails that Josh had given them, they received in return a welcome change to their diet.

Frankie packed everything carefully in his cart and harnessed two of the goats to pull. He rang his bell to signal the herd that it was time to move along. "You need to tie that one up," he said, pointing, "or Sammy will find a way to follow." He dashed a tear from his eye. He hated when it was time to part with any member of his herd, but the barter was too good to pass up.

Cody tied their new goat to one of the trees. The old male bleated plaintively for several hours after all of his fellows left him behind. They endured two days of this before Piper announced that it was time to silence him forever. Martha agreed.

The teenagers and Susan were in tears at the thought of butchering the animal.

"I told you all not to make a pet of it."

"But he's so cute." Carol batted her eyes at her stepmother. "Please, can't we keep him?"

"No. We got him for food and food is what he'll be." Piper was adamant.

Jay glanced at Martha. "Look, raised voices and tempers aren't going to solve anything. It's past time we went foraging for mushrooms. How about we make a trek up the mountain today? Things might look better afterward." Making sure the children weren't watching, she winked at Piper.

Tapping a finger on the side of her nose, Piper agreed. "Why don't you all go? I've got some clothes to repair and I could use the break."

"If you're sure you'll be fine here alone?" said Martha, smiling at her and grabbing up a couple of wicker baskets before Piper could change her mind. "That's settled then. Shall we take off?"

"Don't we need to pack a snack or anything?" asked Susan.

"We just need a distraction. We won't be out that long," said Jay as she and Martha led the small group up the path to the best fungus-foraging area.

The outing was not as distracting as Jay had hoped. The young fungus hunters all screamed when they returned to see the corpse hanging from a tree. Stripped of its hide, it hung in an inverted Y from its hind legs.

Piper raised her arms in confusion in the face of the hysteria. "What? What did I do wrong?"

Neither Susan nor the children would speak to her as they walked past her into the house.

Martha clapped her sympathetically on the shoulder. "Sorry, buddy."

"You knew this was going to happen?"

"I was afraid that whoever did the deed would end up in the doghouse. I'm sorry I was right, but I'm not sorry that it's not me getting the silent treatment."

"Great." Piper crossed her arms. "So what do I do now?"

"Nothing. Just wait it out."

Jay agreed. "Yeah. They'll grow out of it eventually."

"This is perfect. I'm destined to be the group pariah."

"Probably only until we roast that baby and serve him. Satisfied stomachs will go a long way toward attaining forgiveness." Martha grinned at Jay and walked into the house with her, leaving Piper to sulk alone in the yard with her kill.

CHAPTER TWENTY-TWO

Almost three weeks from the day he left, Josh returned. Eva looked down the driveway to see if her mother had changed her mind and returned with him. When instead he handed her a small box, she burst into tears and dashed inside.

The rest of the group gathered around the cartload of supplies Josh had brought back and helped to unload. Near the bottom was a large, brown paper-wrapped package with Jay's name and Trinity Mountain written on it. While the rest of the household acted like children on Christmas morning, Jay walked away to open her mail in private.

She turned the envelope over in her hands. Almost reluctantly, she opened it to find a notebook and two letters. She recognized the handwriting immediately. Sitting in a patch of sunlight, she read what Harmony had written. It was dated eight months earlier.

Sweetheart,

You won't believe it but I made it. The trip was even worse than we'd feared. It took me forever to get down here—the Bay Area is bad, but the whole area from San Jose to Santa Barbara is a wasteland. They've never recovered from the fires. I had a bit of trouble when I passed through Bakersfield, but it turned out for the best—some guys who came to my aid told me about a whole bunch of UCLA folk that have set up a campus in Ventura. They've basically taken over the city, and it's the first place I've been that has any real community feeling. It is a brave new world—sort of a mix of Plato's Republic *and* Walden 2. *Take heart, my darling, the commune is alive and well in southern Cali. When I get back, I'd like to discuss starting our own.*

I've been here a month and finally found friends that knew Tim. Last they knew he was heading south to San Diego to try to cross over to Mexico. Rumors are rife down here that Mexico is reopening the border for Californians. I'm going to follow this trail. I know I've been gone a while now, but I'm so close. I can't stop now.

I see you in my dreams and can't wait until I can hold you again in my arms.

Your loving wife,
Harmony

Jay finished reading the letter and held it to her nose but couldn't smell anything on it. Folding it carefully and setting it down, she removed the second letter from the package, this one dated four months ago:

Jay,
You don't know me and I don't know what to say. I found this letter and diary in Harmony's stuff. She

left it here when she went on to find Tim. I'm giving it to a friend who's heading for Canada. I hope it reaches you.

I heard from a reliable source that she never made it through Los Angeles. We told her about the gangs, but this is a bad time to try and make it the long way round. With no rain since January, there isn't any water. She didn't suffer, if that's what you're thinking. She went in a convoy that was hit by the Bloods. A stinger took out the bus near Compton. There were no survivors.

She spoke of you often and of how much she missed the mountain. I'm sending you the notebook; it seems to have been written for you. I hope you don't mind, but I'm leaving the rest of her stuff in case Tim ever comes back. I figure her brother should inherit something.

Mark

Her eyes burned as she finished. Gripping the package so tightly that her fingers ached, she tried to remember how to breathe. In a despair so deep she could hardly see, she stumbled back to the house.

She made her way to the spiral staircase without running into anything. Suddenly dizzy, she gripped the railing tightly with both hands and doubled over.

"You okay?"

She turned toward Piper's voice, her eyes passed unseeing over the other woman. Unable to speak, she hung on, just staring blankly.

Piper and Eva looked at her and at one another. "Any ideas?" she asked the teenager. At the full body shrug, Piper moved closer to Jay. "What's happening?"

Standing like a statue, Jay did not react even when Piper took a hold of her upper arm.

"What's wrong?" Piper asked. The bicep under her fingers was thrumming with tension. "Can you answer me? You're starting to scare us."

Jay started to shiver. She looked around, seemingly unable to recognize anything. When Piper waved a hand in front of her face, she flinched.

"Okay, this is not good." Glancing at Eva, Piper asked, "Should I leave her alone or what?"

"Maybe she needs to rest?"

"I'll try." She took a hold of Jay's arm. "Why don't you lie down for a bit?" Piper asked as she pulled her toward the couches. She hardly had time to react when instead Jay dropped bonelessly at her feet. "Fuck me," she exclaimed.

Bending down, she was able to slide her arms under Jay's knees and neck. Piper lifted her up and carried her into the bedroom she had taken over when Doris left. Laying her on the bed, Piper loosened her pants and unbuttoned her shirt. Attempting to pull the shirt off, she was stopped by the grip that Jay still had on the package.

She could see only that the wrapping had Jay's name and the notation to deliver it to the mountain. Unable to pry it out of her hand, she gave up and pulled a blanket over the still form. On impulse, she leaned over and touched her lips to Jay's cool forehead. Not feeling any sign of fever, she felt a little less panicked. Deciding there was nothing else for her to do, she rejoined Eva in the living room.

Eva tried to glance over her shoulder into the room. "What do you suppose happened?"

"I don't know. There isn't a mark on her, just a package she didn't have before Josh came back."

Coming in noisily from their unloading, Susan and Martha were shushed by everyone. "What's wrong?" Martha asked.

"Jay's having a meltdown."

"What do you mean?"

"She freaked us out."

"Where is she now?"

"She's in my bedroom."

"Didn't take you long to try to get her into your bed."

"Not funny, Martha. I'm really worried about her."

"How long has she been in there?"

"Not long. Did anyone see what he gave her?"

"Just a package. It looked harmless."

"Okay. We'll just see how she is when she wakes up."

"That's it? That's all you're going to do?"

"I don't know what is wrong. I don't know what else to do."

Martha chewed on her lip for a moment. "Eva, why don't you go help Cody and Carol organize the rest of the stuff Josh dropped off in the basement while we talk to Jay."

"Is she going to be okay?"

"I hope so, honey."

Jay was sitting up when Piper and Martha stepped inside the bedroom. She had been staring down at the notebook in her hands but looked up when Piper spoke.

"You're going to get dehydrated." At Jay's confused look, she pointed at her face. "The waterworks."

"Huh?"

"Do you even know that you're crying?"

Jay reached up and touched her cheeks. She glanced down at the wetness on her fingertips before she furiously scrubbed her face with the heels of her hands.

"Anything you want to talk about?" asked Piper. She wasn't expecting the deeply searching gaze that was turned on her. She met Jay's eyes guilelessly. "Tell me."

Instead of answering, Jay handed her two sheets of paper. After Piper took them, she started turning the notebook around in her lap.

Piper read both letters twice before handing them to Martha. When Martha looked up, Jay was crying again. "Jesus, Jay. I'm so sorry."

The bowed head nodded. Jay's knuckles whitened as she gripped the book.

"What's that?"

"Her diary."

"Oh." Piper touched Jay's knee. "Are you going to read it?"

"Not right now. I can't." Holding the book to her chest, Jay closed her eyes and started rocking. "I just can't."

"It's okay. Don't worry about that now." Martha stepped out of the room to fetch Susan. She hoped that her partner might have a suggestion on how to deal with the emotional maelstrom that Jay was feeling.

Susan sat with Jay for a while before her presence was noticed.

Jay asked, "What happened to Cheryl?"

Startled, Susan had to take a deep breath before she could reply. "There was no running water after the bombing. Each day, a water wagon would come by the neighborhood. We never knew when they would come. That day Cheryl was alone in the house, and she went down to get the water by herself. On the way back up, she was mugged by some lazy bastards who wanted what she had."

"She didn't give it to them?"

"I don't know whether she fought or they were just trigger happy." Susan sighed. "We found her body in some weeds by the side of the road."

"How did you go on? Afterward, I mean."

"You just do. Other people were counting on me. I don't think I'll ever be over it."

"You don't talk about it."

"No, even after all this time, it's still too hard."

"Harmony was gone too long. I guess I sort of knew something had happened."

"I'm sorry, sweetie. Is there anything I can do?"

"I want to be alone for a while. Is that all right?"

"It's fine. I'll go and tell the others." Susan stood and headed for the door. Once there, she looked back over her shoulder. "You know I'm here for you, right?"

"Yeah. I know."

"Good." Susan went into the dining room and sat down with Martha and Piper. "We need to give her plenty of space. She needs to come to terms with this in her own time."

"That doesn't sound very helpful."

"Piper, your being snippy isn't helpful either." Susan raked her fingers through her hair. "Look, we all had a sneaking suspicion that this news was coming. Jay's not naive. I know that she at least considered the thought a time or two. If we give her the room to grieve, she'll realize that she'd already moved to the acceptance stage long ago."

Martha sighed. "That makes sense."

"I just feel so helpless." Piper cracked her knuckles.

"Well, if you need something to do, we've got to find places to put all the stuff Josh brought back. Without Jay's guidance, we'll have to figure it out on our own."

"All right. I'll work with you."

"Good." Susan impulsively hugged Piper. "I know that it will be hard for you to watch her hurting. Just be available for when she comes around."

"I'll be here," vowed Piper.

"Great. Now, where do you think we should put the dried fruit?"

The women made their way to the basement, never knowing that Jay had been standing beside the door and had heard every word. She whispered a heartfelt "thank you" into the empty room. She hurt, but she was grateful to have such understanding friends.

CHAPTER TWENTY-THREE

Jay came downstairs a few days later, tucking her shirt into her pants. It felt good to get out of bed, take a shower and get into clean clothes. Buckling on her fanny pack, she picked up a basket and stepped outside. It took a moment for her eyes to adjust to the bright sun.

About to whistle for the dogs, she spied them all by the dock. As she walked closer, she saw they were getting belly scratches from Eva.

"Good morning."

Eva looked up, her eyes puffy and rimmed in red. "Hey."

"Can't sleep?"

The teenager wiped her nose on her sleeve. "Not so much."

"You want to take a walk with me?"

Eva blinked at her. "You never take anyone on your walks."

"Not never. Just rarely."

"Are you asking me because you pity the poor orphan girl?"

Jay shook her head. "Nope. I asked because you're the only one up and about."

After giving final ear scratches, Eva stood up. "Okay. I'll go."

Pointing at the dogs, Jay ordered them to stay and guard the house. "We'll head to the far side of my property and then swing up and back."

Eva trailed along behind her as a silent shadow. They came across a couple deadfall trees before Jay sat down on a stump. They had covered a couple of miles, mainly uphill, and both were grateful for the rest.

"Do you think your mom is dead?"

"Huh?"

"You said you were an orphan. Do you think she's dead?"

"No. That old guy said she found a job at the mail station, so I figure she's still there." Eva picked up some rocks and began to throw them at a small stand of wildflowers. "I just feel like an orphan. I mean, my dad died, and now my mom has left me."

"She left you where you could be safe and grow up happy."

"I know. I just wonder why I wasn't good enough for her to stay."

"It didn't have anything to do with you. Your mom needed to leave for her own reasons."

"Because she was a bigot."

Jay scratched her chin. "I'm not going to say I agreed with your mom on much of anything, but I know she loved you. I'm sure she had reasons for her beliefs."

"Reasons? You think that after all she said to you?"

"I think she was afraid a lot, and I think she had a habit of hate."

"Why do you think she was like that?"

"I don't really know. I know a lot of people ignore that whole part in the Bible about loving your neighbors and not judging because they can't get beyond thinking that everyone is either with you or against you. It is how a group that calls themselves the Confederacy of Christ could justify killing so many people and destroying our country."

"I don't want to be like that."

"I don't think you have to worry." Jay smiled at her. "Did you ever consider going with her?"

"No." Eva stood and picked up more rocks. Once she sat back down, she said, "At first I was just really angry that she didn't even ask if I wanted to leave. I remembered all the other times we left places because she couldn't get along with anyone."

"It is hard to have wandering feet when you've got a closed heart and an intolerant mind."

"I guess." Eva threw a few more stones. "Did you ever think about going after Harmony?"

Jay clenched her fists before exhaling out a gust of air. "Yes and no." She looked up at the sky. "We argued so much before she left. It really pissed me off that she'd take the word of someone she'd never met and leave me to go off on a wild-goose chase for a brother she hadn't had much contact with before the troubles began. I know he was family, but so was I." Turning her head, Jay looked at Eva. "There were times when she first left that I wanted to chase after her because I wanted to keep her safe. Then I wanted to follow so I could swoop down and rescue her. But even then I kept remembering our arguments."

"I hated being mad at my mom. I really didn't like fighting with her."

"Yeah, me too. It is hard when you love someone to let them go. We get angry for our own protection. If we're angry, then we're not feeling the pain of their leaving."

"I feel so alone."

"You're not, Eva. You've got a strong and loving family surrounding you. We're all here to help you become the best person you can be."

"Thanks."

"No need to thank me for telling the truth."

Hearing a strange noise, they fell silent and turned toward it. Something was crashing through the thick forest nearby. As it got closer, they could hear it panting and grunting.

"Oh, no!" Jay shouted. She looked around and saw a sturdy tree. Grabbing Eva's arm, she pulled her over to the tree. "Get up. Quickly now!"

"What's wrong?"

"We need to get off the ground." Jay laced her fingers together. "Give me your foot."

Eva obeyed and was boosted up high enough for her to grab the lowest branch and pull herself onto it. "Now what?"

"Move a little so I can get..." Jay started to say, but then the underbrush behind her parted and a large, feral pig barreled into the clearing.

Upon seeing them, it squealed loudly and lunged forward. Jay barely managed to jump up and get her legs out of the way as the pig crashed into the base of the tree. She fell back on the dazed animal before leaping to her feet and sprinting to a nearby pile of rocks.

The pig recovered quickly and took off after her, only to be thwarted by the boulder's height. Its beady eyes glared at her as it tried to scrabble up the rocks to get at her. With shaking hands, Jay pulled out her pistol and fired three times into the animal's head, silencing the horrible squealing.

"Jesus Christ!" Jay exclaimed, collapsing back on the rocks. After a moment to regain her breath she looked up into the tree. "Sorry about that."

"No problem. That Lord's-name-in-vain-thing was more my mom's issue than mine." Eva peered down from her perch in the tree. "I thought pigs were gentle."

"You read too much *Charlotte's Web* as a child, I'd guess." Jay put the safety on her weapon and slid it back into her pack. "Feral pigs are a whole different breed. They are hugely territorial."

"Is it safe to come down?"

Jay leaned over the edge and stared at the bristly black animal. Not seeing any signs of movement, she slid off the rock and poked it with a stick. "It seems dead. Can you hop down or do you need help?"

"I think I can make it." Eva tumbled from the tree. Brushing herself off, she stared down at the pig. "It is really ugly."

"And scary as shit. I think it took ten years off my life!"

"You're telling me." She nudged it with her foot. "What now?"

Jay fumbled with her fanny pack and finally pulled out a bundle of parachute cord. "He's too heavy for us to lift. If we tie his back legs together, we could drag him down to the road and then go get help to bring him the rest of the way home."

The two of them wrestled the deadweight of the pig over numerous obstacles, ending up almost as bruised and bloody as he was by the time they reached the road.

Eva dropped her end of the cord and sank onto the ground. "I'm pooped."

"Me too." Jay sank down beside her. "Once we catch our breath, we can go get help." Lying back, she added, "I think we should make them do all the work of butchering."

"Good." Taking a stick, Eva poked the beast. "I'm sure going appreciate bacon a lot more after this."

Jay laughed with her and relaxed, the sun's warmth baking some of the ache from her sore muscles.

CHAPTER TWENTY-FOUR

"How do you think Eva is handling everything?" Piper asked, joining Jay in a walk around the base of the mountain.

"She's a good kid. Well balanced. I think she's still upset, but she knows she's better off here with us."

"She seemed calmer after your talk with her. She hasn't really talked to anyone except Carol since her mom took off."

Jay shrugged. "She knows that her mom wasn't too popular around here."

"With very good reason."

"I should have made more of an effort to get along with her."

"You did plenty. Doris didn't make it easy on any of us." Piper shook her head ruefully. "I've never made a pretense of caring for Martha's sister, even in the good old days."

"That why you kissed her?"

"God damn. If only I could answer that question."

"Try."

"I don't know what possessed me."

"No," Jay responded immediately. "That's way too easy. Put a little thought into your response."

Piper blew a raspberry. "It's true that she infuriated me from almost the first day we met. I really can't begin to explain what came over me. Maybe it was the challenge to my dykehood."

"Challenge? She was a 'phobe."

"I know. I guess I figured that she shouldn't knock it until she tried it."

"Getting laid is not the answer for everything."

"Maybe. It always worked for me in the past."

"The times, they are a'changing."

"I wish that there was some deep, dark reason behind my actions." Piper kicked at a loose stone. "I think back on that afternoon with almost horrified fascination."

"I would think the horror would have been enough to stop you."

"Unfortunately not."

"Did you think she would be receptive to your advances?"

"She had been married, right? And had a kid, so some sort of intimacy must have taken place at some point. I don't know, maybe I wanted to see if there were any hidden layers that we just hadn't seen yet."

"Still waters run deep, but stagnant ponds just stink."

Piper grinned at her. "You're biased."

"I freely admit that I don't like her."

The two women walked in silence for a while. Finally, Jay cleared her throat. "So, was she a good kisser?"

Piper looked over at her in astonishment. "Why would you ask that?"

"No reason."

"Now it's your turn to have to think a little harder on your answer."

They walked for about a mile before Jay spoke. Piper had almost forgotten the topic when Jay cleared her throat.

"Sometimes, mainly at night, I've thought about kissing someone. As the time passes, I find it harder and harder to remember exactly what Harmony looked like. Or felt like." She sighed. "It's been so long."

"Oh." Piper watched her feet walking down the road. "She wasn't good. Doris, I mean." Laughing bitterly, she said, "While some of that might have been from surprise, I think she was pretty generally a cold fish."

"That's a sad epitaph."

"I'm sorry."

"Don't be." Jay glanced over at her. "Have you ever thought about kissing me?"

Piper walked silently, chewing on her bottom lip. Finally, gusting out a breath, she nodded. "Yeah. I've thought about it."

"And?"

Turning toward the smaller woman, Piper took her by the upper arms and proceeded to kiss her senseless.

"What are you doing to me?" Jay eventually gasped.

"If you have to ask, I must not be doing it right."

The two women leaned against one another in a loose embrace. Slowly, the frantic beat of their hearts found a more normal rhythm.

When she could trust her voice again, Jay whispered, "I don't think that I'm ready for this." Jay rested her forehead on Piper's shoulder.

"I'm sorry."

"Don't be. It's my own fault."

"What is?"

"I wanted to see what kissing you would be like."

"And?" Piper asked.

"You taste good." Reaching up, Jay drew her finger along Piper's jaw. "Doris was an idiot."

"Thanks, I think."

"I'll be more plain. You're a good kisser."

"I'm glad all that practice has finally paid off."

"Brat." Jay swatted her shoulder. "You don't take compliments well."

Piper lowered her head and lightly kissed the slightly swollen lips. "I haven't had much practice."

"I find that hard to believe."

With her tongue and lips, Piper encouraged Jay to open up to her. When she broke the kiss, they were panting. "Believe it."

Jay pulled back. "What were we talking about?"

"I can't remember."

"Oh, right, practice." Jay cocked her head. "You're no virgin."

"No, but I'm not a slut either."

"Those are our only choices? Neither am I, then." Jay shrugged. "I've had three long-term relationships and a few more girlfriends."

"I've never had a wife or a partner. I'd have the occasional girlfriend, and if it wasn't immediately love, I moved on."

"That's a bit cold. How did you know it wasn't love?"

"No fireworks when we kissed."

Jay tugged on her ear. "You heard explosions just now?"

"And saw flashing lights."

"Are you sure you're not feverish? Or just horny?"

"Not either. Well, not just horny anyway. I've been drawn to you since you turned your back to us when we drew on you."

"I didn't really have a choice there. My bow was no match for your shotguns."

"But that's the point." Piper tugged Jay over to a fallen log and pulled her down beside her. "Even when you face impossible odds, you've got this *presence*. We were close to panicking and killing you out of hand. You walked over to the table like you were bulletproof, and we stopped and listened to you."

"You didn't want to kill me."

"But we were scared and anything could have happened." She squeezed the hands she clutched in her own. "You're like a breath of fresh air. Your very being brings order to chaos."

"You'll turn my head with that talk."

"I can only hope."

Jay shook her head. "I meant what I said before. I don't think I'm ready. Losing Harmony is a fresh wound."

"I wouldn't want you to be less than the person who she loved and who loved her back."

"Thank you." Jay jumped up and started walking again.

Once Piper had caught up with her, she reached out and clutched Piper's hand tightly in her own. Without a word, they continued to walk.

After a while, Jay cleared her throat and asked, "Will you wait for me?"

"As long as you'll let me. My life makes sense with you in it."

The two walked companionably down the road. Piper could not help the smile on her face. She glanced up to see the position of the sun and asked, "Are we heading anywhere in particular?"

"Yeah. There's just something I need to do. Well, not really need. I want to do it and I don't think you will mind doing it either. I mean, I…"

"Take a breath, Jay." Piper looked curiously at the other woman. "I've never seen you go into babble mode before."

"Sorry."

"Don't be. It's kind of cute."

Jay blushed. She began walking faster, as if she could outrun the rush of blood to her face.

"So where are we going?"

"Over this hill. It used to be the site of a meditation center." Jay led her around the skeletal remains of the building.

"Creepy," whispered Piper as she looked up at the twin chimneys standing by themselves on either side of the burned-out building. "Tell me more about this place," she demanded.

"I don't really know that much about it. I only came out here a couple of times when it was open." Jay led the way down a small rise. She smiled when she saw the design of paving stones nestling in the hollow. The grass had grown tall around it, but the path was still clear.

"What is that?"

"It's a labyrinth."

"That doesn't really mean anything to me."

"A labyrinth is an ancient way to find peace."

"It looks like a maze."

"They share some similarities. A maze has twists and turns and is a puzzle to be figured out. You must search to find the center and then to escape again. A labyrinth has only one path. The way in is the way out."

"So why are we here?"

"I want to walk it."

"And the point would be?"

"To get some closure."

"Why?"

"As you walk, let your mind drift on all the things that are affecting you. When you reach the center, give yourself permission to be free of those worries. As you retrace your steps, you let them go."

"Very hippy-dippy."

"True, but walking these has helped me out of some pretty daunting situations. It's how I broke out of the downward spiral when my folks died." Jay took a deep breath and, with her eyes on the ground, began to follow the turns of the trail. When she reached the center area, she opened her arms wide and leaned back. She smiled when Piper joined her.

"Am I doing this right?"

"There are no wrong turns." The smile came easier to her face. Jay took another series of deep breaths and made her way back out of the labyrinth. She waited for Piper to join her before heading back in the direction of the house.

"That's it?"

"Yep. If you want angels and trumpets, you'll have to go somewhere else."

"It just doesn't seem like much."

"It was enough for me. I could feel the tension letting go as I retraced my steps." She rotated her shoulders. "For a long time, I've been really angry at Harmony for leaving me. I didn't want her to go." Jay kicked at a pinecone.

"That's entirely normal."

Whispering, Jay confessed. "I almost felt that she got what she deserved."

"I can understand that. Going to LA was a dangerously stupid thing to do." Piper raised her hands. "I don't know her, but I don't think she was thinking rationally when she left."

"We both knew that she was risking everything."

"It's amazing that she ran into somebody who knew of her brother."

"You're telling me. It's a small world, sometimes."

"Made smaller by the fanatics that tried to bring on the Second Coming."

"And those that prey on the survivors." Shrugging, Jay dismissed all of them. "I accept that Harmony is gone. She left me long before she died. I've just stayed in limbo for so long because I didn't want to be alone."

"You're not alone anymore."

"No, I'm not. I've got a house full."

"I hope that one day you can find a place for me in your heart." When Jay would have spoken, Piper shook her head. "You don't have to decide anything now. I'm not going to be going anywhere anytime soon."

"What if I'm never ready?"

"We'll still be family. That won't change."

"And friends?"

"Of course." Piper walked a few steps. "You know what they say?"

"What?"

"Love is just friendship set on fire."

The smile that Jay bestowed on her rivaled the sun. Joining hands, the friends walked back toward home, helping each other over the rough patches on the road.